**Praise for the Novels
of Jo Davis**

Under Fire

"Four stars! A totally entertaining experience."
—*Romantic Times*

"Scorching hot kisses, smoldering sex, and explosive passion make *Under Fire* a must read! Experience the flames of *Under Fire*!" —Joyfully Reviewed

"Exhilarating [with] a 200-proof heat duet . . . a strong entry [and] a terrific, action-packed thriller."
—*Midwest Book Review*

Trial by Fire

"A five-alarm read . . . riveting, sensual."
—*Publishers Weekly* Beyond Her Book Blog

"Jo Davis turns up the heat full blast with *Trial by Fire*. Romantic suspense that has it all: a sizzling firefighter hero, a heroine you'll love, and a story that crackles and pops with sensuality and action. All I can say is keep the fire extinguisher handy or risk spontaneous combustion!"
—Linda Castillo, national bestselling author of
Sworn to Silence

continued . . .

ALSO BY JO DAVIS

The Firefighters of Station Five Novels

Hidden Fire
Under Fire
Trial by Fire

I Spy a Wicked Sin
I Spy a Naughty Game

LINE OF FIRE

THE FIREFIGHTERS OF STATION FIVE

JO DAVIS

A SIGNET ECLIPSE BOOK

SIGNET ECLIPSE
Published by New American Library, a division of
Penguin Group (USA) Inc., 375 Hudson Street,
New York, New York 10014, USA
Penguin Group (Canada), 90 Eglinton Avenue East, Suite 700, Toronto,
Ontario M4P 2Y3, Canada (a division of Pearson Penguin Canada Inc.)
Penguin Books Ltd., 80 Strand, London WC2R 0RL, England
Penguin Ireland, 25 St. Stephen's Green, Dublin 2,
Ireland (a division of Penguin Books Ltd.)
Penguin Group (Australia), 250 Camberwell Road, Camberwell, Victoria 3124,
Australia (a division of Pearson Australia Group Pty. Ltd.)
Penguin Books India Pvt. Ltd., 11 Community Centre, Panchsheel Park,
New Delhi - 110 017, India
Penguin Group (NZ), 67 Apollo Drive, Rosedale, North Shore 0632,
New Zealand (a division of Pearson New Zealand Ltd.)
Penguin Books (South Africa) (Pty.) Ltd., 24 Sturdee Avenue,
Rosebank, Johannesburg 2196, South Africa

Penguin Books Ltd., Registered Offices:
80 Strand, London WC2R 0RL, England

First published by Signet Eclipse, an imprint of New American Library,
a division of Penguin Group (USA) Inc.

First Printing, May 2010
10 9 8 7 6 5 4 3 2 1

To my in-laws, Richard and Mary Dittman,
for your love and unfailing support. After fifty years of
marriage, I'd say you two know more than a little about
romance and keeping the spark alive through life's triumphs
and challenges. We should all be so blessed.

Tommy's story is for you.

Acknowledgments

My heartfelt thanks to:

My husband and children for putting up with my insanity during deadline . . . and all the other times when I don't really have an excuse.

The Foxes: Tracy, Suz, Addison, Jane, Sandy, Lorraine, Alice, Julie, and Kay. I couldn't survive without you all serving the buttery nipples.

And to *you*, dear readers, for being my cheering section and for loving my heroes. You keep me motivated with your smiles and e-mails. I hope you enjoy Tommy's story.

1

"Go wide! Go wide!"

"Come on, Skyler! Pass the ball!"

Tommy Skyler pedaled backward, fingers gripping leather, muscles tense. A good quarterback never rushed.

A *star* quarterback locked on his receiver, fired, and planted the pigskin dead in his chest. Every single time.

For a couple of seconds, Tommy was back at Bryant-Denny Stadium. A crowd of over ninety thousand. Half of them on their feet, screaming his name.

Better than being a rock star. Almost better than sex.

He'd go down in fucking history.

Zeroing in on his target, he pumped his arm and let the football fly. It left his fingertips, spiraling in a perfect arc toward his receiver.

He had a split second to see Eve Marshall catch the pass with a muffled *umph* before his lieutenant at Fire Station Five, Howard "Six-Pack" Paxton, broke Julian Salvatore's block, barreled into Tommy like a two-ton freight train, and put him on his back, the wind temporarily knocked out of his lungs.

Tommy heaved a breath, then barked a laugh as Six-Pack rolled off him. "Jesus. You missed your calling, man. You should've played in the pros."

"Nah. I was completely disillusioned when I found out

the players couldn't date the cheerleaders. Ruined it for me."
The lieutenant pushed to his feet, brushed the grass off his
regulation navy blue pants, and offered Tommy a hand.

Tommy took it, letting the big man yank him up. "I hear
you. One of the dumbest rules on the planet if you ask me."

"Maybe that's changed by now?"

"Got no clue."

He suppressed the twinge in his chest. Once upon a time,
he knew practically everything there was to know about the
world of pro football. A world that had been his for the taking. And he'd been out of the loop for only two years.

Fuck, it felt like a lifetime. Might as well be.

"Great pass," Eve said breathlessly, jogging over. She
tossed the football back to Tommy, who caught it, grinning.

"Nice catch."

Eve propped her fists on her slim hips. "Maybe *you*
should've gone pro. Ever consider it?"

Eyeing their pretty teammate, the only female firefighter
at Station Five, he was distracted from answering right away.
The woman had some serious mojo goin' on, if a man didn't
mind them a little tough—both mentally and physically.

And Tommy *so* did not mind. From the top of her dark
head, to her lean, muscular body, to her long legs, the woman
was strong as hell. The curve of her angular jaw hinted at
more than a thin streak of stubbornness—more like a will of
iron. He should know. He'd flirted with her, half-seriously,
over the past couple of years, only to be firmly shut down.

Oh, she didn't mind his teasing, even seemed to get a
kick out of it, but never failed to get across that their byplay
would not evolve into something else. Ever.

Should his ribbing cross the line, she'd tear off his balls
and feed them to him for lunch.

If their captain, Sean Tanner, didn't do the deed first.

Not that Eve was his type anyway, since he'd met—

"Skyler? Yoo-hoo!"

He blinked at her. "What?"

"Focus, kid. I asked if you'd thought of going pro?"

"Not a kid, Eve," he said, suppressing a sigh of annoyance. *Now where have I heard that song and dance before?* "And yeah, I thought about it. Didn't work out."

She frowned at his clipped tone, the absence of his usual comeback filled with innuendo. Something she wasn't used to from him, he figured. "Why not?"

He barked a short laugh, surprised at the bitter sound. "I decided being rich and famous didn't appeal."

Tommy barely caught her scowl as he spun and strode for the bay. Behind him, he heard Julian caution quietly, "Leave it alone, Evie."

"What? What'd I say?" Her voice rose. "Skyler—"

Three loud tones over the station's intercom system ended her protest, and Tommy broke into a jog as the computerized female voice began to relay their call. Saved by the bell.

Or not. Crap. Had he heard correctly?

Zack Knight, their FAO—fire apparatus operator—stuck his head out of the bay and yelled, "Come on, slackers! Haul your asses!"

Tommy rushed into the bay and skidded to a halt next to the big quint, shoved his feet into his boots, and yanked up his heavy fire-retardant pants. The others followed suit as Tanner joined them.

Tommy glanced at Zack. "Did she say—"

"Scaffold collapsed downtown," Sean interrupted, jerking on his own gear. "Two construction workers dead, one clinging to what's left of the scaffold. Forty-four stories up."

"Shit," Tommy breathed. Quickly, he donned his coat and reached for his hat. "Aerial ladder on the quint's not gonna reach."

"One of you will have to rappel down to him, get him into

a safety harness." Ready, the captain yanked open the passenger door of the quint, braced a boot on the running board, and hauled himself up. "Let's go!"

Tommy climbed into the backseat of the cab, Julian right behind him. Zack slid behind the wheel and Sean took the place of the commanding officer in the passenger's seat. Since the two commanding officers never rode in the same vehicle, the lieutenant took the ambulance, Eve joining him.

Tommy glanced at Julian, musing that just a couple of months ago, their resident bad boy had been practically shackled to the lieutenant's side out of sheer necessity. The man had needed a keeper, for damned sure. But exorcising one's demons, not to mention finding true love, had a tendency to change a man for the better.

I don't need to change, but I wouldn't turn down the lovin'.

As if. Settling back in his seat, he frowned, attempting to force his mind away from a certain cute-as-a-button nurse with shoulder-length curly brown hair and liquid brown eyes. Freckles across her pert nose. Smart as a whip.

And harboring an apparent aversion to getting too close to him, no matter how hard he tried.

"I can hear your brain grinding, *amigo*. What gives?"

Tommy studied Julian, surprised, not for the first time lately, by the genuine concern on his friend's face. "Dude, am I that obvious?"

"To me, sure." Julian shot a pointed glance to their companions in the front.

Tommy gave him a small smile, grateful the man had his back yet again. Jules wasn't the type to flap his lips in front of the others, especially about two very painful subjects— the elusive Shea Ford for one. Second, how Tommy's own dreams had died along with his older brother.

On the topic of Shea, at least, he could let his friend off

the hook. Besides, Zack and the captain weren't paying attention anyway.

"Same girl problem, different day," he replied simply. Julian nodded in understanding, giving him a grin.

"Hmm. Shea still thinks you're too young? Didn't I tell you the first thing you need to do is give your vocabulary a dude-ectomy? A woman doesn't mind her guy having the *stamina* of an eighteen-year-old. Just don't sound like one."

He laughed in spite of himself. "Girl advice, coming from the man who used to change women more often than his boxers. That's scary, Jules." Though the man did have a point.

The other man arched a black brow, his teeth white against his bronzed face. "Caught one, didn't I?"

"Touché. How is Grace, by the way?"

"Uh-uh, no changing the subject. What seems to be the problem with you and your lady? I mean, you said you've been out together, right?"

"For a quick burger, and then once to a movie." Tommy shrugged, not letting on how much her rejection of him as a man truly hurt. "We had a good time, got along fine. But I might as well have been her brother, considering the distance she kept between us. When I dropped her off after the movie, she shook my freakin' hand, man."

Julian grimaced. "Ouch. Even a brother would get a hug."

"No shit."

"I hate to say this, but . . . maybe there's just no spark."

"No, that's one thing I'm sure of," Tommy said firmly. "I said she kept it on the down-low, not that there wasn't a current flowing. Seriously, you could power Sugarland for a week with the electricity we got goin' on when we're together. She just won't let me close."

"Well, there might be your answer." Julian waved a hand at his friend. "The problem isn't you at all, but something going on with *her*. Ever think of that?"

Tommy blinked at him, the light dawning. "I'm such an idiot. Why didn't I think of it first?"

"Because you're a *guy*. And in typical guy fashion, you've thought of nothing but your wants and needs right from the start. What about what *she* wants and needs? I grew up with four older sisters. Believe me, I know what I'm talking about."

Tommy felt his cheeks grow hot. Dammit. "Aw, crap. I've really screwed up everything."

"Not necessarily. Give her time, be there for her. Listen to what she has to say. It's not a race, so don't push her away by moving at warp speed."

"I never thought of it that way before," he muttered. "Thanks, du—Julian."

The other man snickered at his self-correction. "There's hope for you yet, kid."

"Not a kid." He sighed, mulling over Julian's advice. Had he been so self-absorbed he'd missed some serious signals from Shea? Ignored her needs? If so, that was about to change. Maybe there *was* hope for them after all.

They fell silent and he focused on the problems they faced as they neared their destination. When the building came into view, the collapsed scaffold crumpled against the unfinished side like a child's pile of pickup sticks, Tommy gave a low whistle.

"We've got a worker stuck up there? Fuckin' A, this is gonna suck."

The others muttered in agreement, and the tension in the cab became palpable. Zack pulled the quint past the construction fence, well away from danger should the rest of the structure come down. The second he stopped, they jumped from their vehicles, gazes automatically fixed on the wreckage before them. The captain began barking orders.

"Howard, I want you, Salvatore, and Skyler on the roof.

Take the ropes and harnesses, and decide who gets to play Spider-Man."

"I'll do it," Tommy volunteered.

Julian looked relieved and Howard said, "You're in."

"Marshall, you'll work the ground with me," Sean continued, ignoring Eve's scowl. "There's no telling what damage, if any, has been done to the framework of the building or whether it'll shift, so let's move it!"

Eve stepped forward, voice hard. "I'm just as capable of—"

"Not now, goddammit," the captain snapped. Then he turned his back on her and keyed his radio, calling the battalion chief to find out his ETA.

Tommy didn't blame Eve for being pissed. Wasn't the first time Sean had passed her over for the more strenuous or exciting task. But nobody had time to debate the matter. Tommy helped the lieutenant and Julian with the gear, then followed on their heels. On the way, his gaze fell on two man-sized lumps covered by a black tarp, at least a half-dozen workers standing by, looking on mournfully.

Jesus Christ. How awful to start a workday as normally as any other and have it end in tragedy. He averted his eyes and took in the distance from the roof to the scaffold, concentrated on the job ahead.

This wasn't going to be easy. Even from here, the piteous cries of the worker drifted to them, raising the hair on the back of his neck. The only thing worse than hearing the man's panic would be if it abruptly ended, in a bad way.

They rode the construction lift to the roof and set about securing the rope and pulley system to nearby support beams. Tommy quickly shed his heavy fire coat, which did nothing to relieve the stifling July heat, but at least his movements wouldn't be so restricted. The pants and boots, he left on in the interest of time.

He yanked on a pair of gloves, then let Julian help him with one harness; the other, connected to his own, he'd put on the worker as an extra safety measure before they were both lowered to the ground. Ready to go, he sat on the ledge of the roof, bracing himself until the rope was drawn taut.

Julian tried an encouraging smile, but it came out more of a grimace. "Be careful, man. Better you than me."

"I'm so touched, thanks."

"All right," Howard said. "When you're ready."

Tommy nodded. "Go."

As he eased himself over the side, the line remained tight, giving him a sense of relative security. He wasn't afraid of heights—just the fall and the sudden stop at the end. As long as the equipment did the job, he was good.

He held on to the rope, using his feet to "walk" down the side of the building. Technically, he wasn't really rappelling since he was being lowered by his teammates, but he figured that was semantics. His ass was dangling more than forty stories above the ground, so what the hell difference did it make what it was called?

Foot by foot, he crept downward. Two stories. Three. Sweat rolled down his spine, into his eyes. Glancing below, he finally caught sight of the worker clinging to a metal pole a few feet from the side of the building. His hard hat was missing, revealing a balding head. Beefy shoulders, gut riding over his belt. Big sonofabitch, probably outweighed him by fifty pounds or more.

Fantastic.

"Hurry!" the man bellowed, panic cracking his voice. "I can't hang on much longer!"

"Don't move!" Which, of course, the man did, becoming more agitated the closer Tommy got.

"I—I can't help it! I'm slipping!"

"I'm almost there," he called, hoping he sounded reassuring. "Just a few more seconds, okay? What's your name?"

"R-Russell."

"I'm Tommy. Hold tight, Russell. I'm comin' your way."

"Oh, God, I'm gonna fall!"

Dread settled in the pit of his stomach. This situation had clusterfuck written all over it. "No, you're not. Look at me, all right? Focus on *me*."

At last, Tommy became level with Russell, quickly assessing his only option. Carefully, he pushed away from the wall with one foot and used the other to test the sturdiness of a cross-pole. Gradually, he put all his weight on it, relieved when it held. He needed only one minute more. Maybe luck was on their side.

Bracing one hand on another pole to steady himself, he began to inch toward Russell, talking calmly, crossing the few feet separating them. "Easy does it. I've got a harness here with your name on it, connected to mine. Soon as I get you strapped in, we'll—"

The structure shifted, shuddering under Tommy's boots. For Russell, that was all she wrote.

He yelled, eyes rolling, terrified, as he scrambled toward Tommy.

"No! Stay right—"

Tommy barely had a split second to react. Russell launched himself across the remaining distance, forcing Tommy to catch him in an awkward bear hug.

Just as the rest of the scaffold collapsed.

Tommy's boots slipped and he swung free, toward the side of the building, with two hundred fifty pounds of deadweight in his arms. Metal groaned, rained down on them. One rod struck Tommy's fire hat, sending it flying.

Along for the ride, struggling to retain his hold on his

heavy burden, he braced himself for the impact with the side of the building.

Tommy hit the bricks on his right side, pain exploding in his head and shoulder. The world spun crazily, but he held on to Russell. Who clung to him for dear life, screaming like a little girl.

Shut up, jackass! This predicament is partially your fault.

That was what he wanted to yell at Russell, who was too far gone to care. *Just focus on getting him to the ground.*

From above them, Howard yelled, "Hang on! We're sending you down!"

They were moving, Tommy realized through the buzzing between his ears. Lower and lower. Peering over Russell's shoulder, he saw another engine company had arrived, bringing more firefighters from another station as backup. Yellow coats and pants everywhere, rushing toward him.

The ground came up to meet him, and Tommy stood on rubbery knees, releasing his hold on the worker. Several pairs of hands grabbed Russell and led him away. More hands worked at Tommy's harness, getting him free.

". . . okay?"

Tommy blinked, trying to find the speaker. "What?"

A hand gripped his shoulder. "I asked, are you okay?"

Eve's worried face swam in front of him, and he waved her off. "I'm fine. Ready to run laps."

His grin felt wrong, like his muscles wouldn't work. He shook off another pair of hands and took a couple of steps so they could see he was perfectly all right.

Tommy's knees buckled.

The last thing he saw was the captain lunging to catch him.

2

Shea Ford glared at her twin brother, Shane, across the table in the nurses' lounge. Resting her elbows on the slick surface, she captured her straw and sipped her Diet Coke, taking a couple of seconds to form a calm response to his nosy probing.

Shane crumpled the wrapper from his burger into a ball, tossed it into the takeout sack, and relaxed in his chair like a lazy cat, one ankle crossed over the opposite knee. He returned her gaze steadily, unruffled, sable hair falling into eyes so like her own it was uncanny, except that his were gray.

He was so confident, exuded such unconscious power, most people believed him to be older, in his early to midthirties instead of twenty-eight.

"Come on, Sis, toss me a bone. Tell me why you want to go out with a tightwad like Forrest."

Because he's boring and safe. No spark whatsoever.

"Gee, let me think. He's attractive, cultured—"

"With a stick so far up his ass, his spine won't bend."

She rolled her eyes. "You're the one who introduced us at the police charity thing, remember?"

"Under duress," he pointed out. "Forrest insisted on meeting you, and I had to be civil."

"Hope you didn't hurt yourself."

"Very funny. Did you know he's influenced the city council to strike down the department's last two requests for new radios and Tasers?"

"No, I didn't. But times are tough, Bro. Budget cuts are the norm everywhere, even here at Sterling. I mean, nobody planned on the economy going down the toilet right after the hospital opened. So to be fair, you can hardly blame Forrest for being cautious with the city's money."

Shane's mouth thinned. "I'm not. It's just that when lives are dependent on your equipment working properly, the budget should be cut somewhere else. Like the stupid flowers and trees the city planted in the medians and around the courthouse downtown."

Oh, boy. She knew that look and tone. Like a snapping turtle on a fishing line, he wouldn't let go until it thundered.

"Point taken. Maybe I should talk to Forrest about it."

"Dammit, Shea—"

"Don't curse at me," she said evenly. "I'm not one of your detectives."

"I'm sorry, Sis. But you're totally *missing* my point."

"You think he's all wrong for me. I'm not dense."

"Then don't *act* dense," he snapped.

Shea stood, chair scraping loudly on the tiled floor, but her brother's fingers captured her wrist before she could make a dramatic exit.

"Sit down, please?" He gave a tired sigh. "Do you have any idea how hard it is playing Mom and Dad?"

Oh, that was dirty pool. But looking down into his handsome, worried face, she knew he didn't mean it as a guilt trip. Shane had been a mountain of strength, love, and support in the years following their parents' accident. And that they were killed in the midst of a horrible family crisis . . . Looking back, Shea couldn't imagine how Shane had pulled them both through those dark days without losing his mind.

Shea sat and covered her brother's rough hand with hers, anger dissipating, love welling in her throat. "You don't have to do that anymore. I take care of myself, and I can make my own mistakes without breaking."

Unlike the sad, broken girl of ten years ago.

He gazed at her and nodded, his smile wistful. "Old habits. I'll stop worrying when they put me in the ground."

"God, don't say that!" She slapped his arm playfully, hoping she hid the chill his words sent through her.

He only laughed, then studied her, expression full of mischief, mood lightened. "Speaking of dates, whatever happened with the firefighter Cori introduced you to? When I spoke with him at the scene of that arson murder last year, he seemed like a cool guy—"

"Whoops, break's over," she announced with a cheerful smile. She was *not* discussing Tommy Skyler with brother dearest. "Gotta run. Thanks for the fat and carbs."

He rose to tower over her, shaking his head. "You're welcome, but don't think you're getting off the hook easy."

"When it comes to my nosy homicide detective brother, I don't doubt that."

Chuckling, he wrapped her in a fierce hug and planted a quick kiss on top of her head. "Don't work too hard, short stuff."

"I'll make a note, and same goes."

Shea walked him to the double doors leading to the emergency room's waiting area. "Bye."

"Call you later."

She smiled as his lean-hipped, long-legged stride carried him across the waiting room, turning more than one head. Even Mrs. McCarty, wrinkled and eightysomething like her hubby, who was being seen in one of the exam rooms, peered at his retreating ass over the top of her newspaper.

"Gawd a-mighty, that's the finest man I ever laid eyes on!"

Shea turned to grin at her friend Dora, who stood smacking her gum and watching until Shane left the premises. The older nurse pushed a stray lock of scraggly dishwater-blond hair from her thin face and gave an exaggerated sigh of appreciation.

"You say that about every man who walks through here," she teased, heading back to the nurses' station.

Dora fell in step beside her. "Do not! Well, okay, maybe I do. But can you blame a gal with no man and three kids under the age of ten?"

"True. Hey, be patient and you'll find your prince."

"Honey, I'd settle for someone fat and bald who'd mow the yard and fix the plumbing." Dora laughed heartily at her own joke.

Behind the counter, Shea lifted a chart, amazed at the woman's fortitude. Dora might run on exhaustion more often than not, but nothing ever got her down.

"The boy in room three is going home?" Shea asked, getting back to work.

Dora came around to stand next to her, resting her hip on the edge of the desk. "Yep. Got the broken arm in a cast and his parents are itching to make tracks."

"Mr. McCarty?"

"Gallbladder. Dr. Brown's going to admit him, I think."

"Okay. What else?"

"That's it," Dora said. "No new patients came in while you were at lunch. It's so damned quiet it's making me all prickly."

One of the other nurses passing by groaned. "Great, now you've jinxed us."

Shea suppressed a shiver, and nodded in agreement. Any experienced nurse knew better than to dismiss the lull-before-the-storm feeling. They didn't like to use the word "quiet"—except for Dora, who didn't have much of a filter.

"You'd better go eat, then, before—"

A crackle on the desktop radio unit interrupted, and as Dora snatched it, Shea braced herself. The paramedics always radioed ahead when they had a bad situation and were bringing in a trauma case. The lull certainly hadn't lasted long.

"Sterling ER, charge nurse Carlisle speaking." Dora scrabbled for her pad and pen.

Shea waited, dread building while Dora took down the pertinent information on their incoming patients.

"All right. We'll be ready." Replacing the handset, Dora cleared her throat, humor set aside for now. "That was one of our fire captains. We've got four men coming in from a scaffold collapse on a construction site. Three are workers with relatively minor injuries—cuts and bruises, a sprained ankle, and a cracked rib. The fourth man is a firefighter. Got his head busted open rescuing one of the workers, but he's stable."

Her stomach gave an unpleasant lurch and she peered at Dora's spidery handwriting. At this point no names were taken, so she scanned, trying to locate the age of the firefighter. But the woman scooped up the pad, already in action. "Is he—"

"We need four rooms ready. Round up the others while I drag Brown's ass from the doctor's lounge. Get movin', girl!"

Dora's most amusing quality was her rough, no-bullshit personality. It was also her most formidable. Shea hurried to prepare for their arrivals, squelching the unease skittering along her nerves. There were plenty of firemen in Sugarland, and the one coming in was stable.

The man was most likely nobody she knew.

Three other nurses helped her make sure the rooms were

prepared, the necessary forms and charts on hand. Dr. Brown arrived with the young resident, Dr. Freeman, and none too soon.

The first wave began, two men wheeled in on stretchers by a team of firefighters, one after the other. Anxious, Shea studied each of the firefighters, and finally let out a relieved breath. These guys weren't from Station Five.

Thank God.

Dora and one of the other nurses assisted Brown and Freeman with the two workers, taking their vitals and checking their complaints. On the counter near Dora sat the notepad with the victims' information. Might as well look, put her fears to rest.

Shea took a step toward it, but her attention was diverted by a big construction worker shuffling through the doors, one arm slung over the shoulders of a companion, his fleshy face scrunched in pain.

"Let's go in to room nine," she said in a calm, soothing tone, gesturing to the next cubicle. "You weren't transported by ambulance?"

"They were occupied. My friend decided to drive me here instead of waitin' on the next one."

"What's your name?"

"R-Russell Levy. Christ, I think that guy broke one of my ribs." He panted as his friend led him to the bed, where he sat with a groan.

"I need you to unbutton your shirt so we can have a look." He struggled with the buttons and his friend pushed his hands aside, finishing for him.

"All right, lie back for me. This side?" She helped him as he nodded, noting the bruise forming around his torso. He winced as she gently probed the area in question. "Is this where it hurts?"

"Damn!"

She took that as a yes. The rib was likely cracked, but she wasn't allowed to say so; only the doctor could give a diagnosis. "How did this happen?"

"Firefighter grabbed me when the rest of the scaffold fell and squeezed me like a fuckin' boa constrictor. Kept me from plunging over forty stories." His eyes widened as he recalled the terrifying experience. "Sweet Jesus, I coulda died! How is the kid, anyways?"

Shea froze. "You mean the firefighter?"

"Yeah. He got the livin' shit knocked out of him when we hit the side of the building."

"I don't know. He hasn't been brought in yet." Taking Levy's wrist to get his pulse, she asked casually, "Can you describe him?"

"Nah. We weren't exactly trading phone numbers, ya know? He told me his name, but I was so freakin' scared, I don't remember what it was. Strong sonofabitch, though."

Schooling her expression to remain neutral, she eyed the man's substantial girth. No way could Tommy have held on to this giant. She forced herself to concentrate on caring for the patient, jotting down his vitals, which were fine. Next, she handed his friend a sheaf of forms.

"The doctor will be in soon to take a look, and I'm sure he'll want a couple of X-rays. You might have to help Mr. Levy fill these out—" A commotion outside broke into her instructions. "Excuse me for a moment."

Shea stepped into the hallway just in time to see a gurney burst through the double doors, being pushed fast by two firefighters, one holding up an IV bag, and trailed by three more. These men she recognized because she'd met them all before. Among those bringing up the rear was Zack Knight, her best friend's fiancé. Under different circumstances, she'd smile and say hello.

But her gaze was fixed on the blond-haired man on the

gurney, his eyes closed. Eyes she knew were as pale blue as the summer sky. The gauze pad and the hair on the right side of his head were soaked with blood, with more smeared down the side of his face.

Her knees turned to water and she leaned against the desk for support, the breath sucked from her lungs. Captain Sean Tanner's voice competed with the roaring in her ears.

"Open head wound," he barked to Dr. Brown, who'd emerged from one of the rooms. "He's unconscious, but his vitals are stable. He took a blow to the right side of his body, but he sustained no broken bones and there's no evidence of internal bleeding."

Shea closed her eyes, and her hands began to shake. *Oh, God. Tommy.*

"Shea! Need you in here."

Dr. Brown's firm order got her moving. Part of her fought the wild urge to run out the door, jump in her car, and hightail it home to hide. She didn't want to see Tommy like this. Tommy was strong, sunny, gregarious. Sexy.

The pale man on the bed appeared heartbreakingly young. Vulnerable. Despite the well-defined muscles roping his bare chest and torso, to see him now, nobody would believe he'd used nothing but his upper-body strength to keep a man almost twice his size from plummeting to his death.

Which was precisely what Tommy had done. At great risk to himself.

Working like a well-oiled machine, two of the firefighters, Dr. Brown, Shea, and a tech surrounded Tommy and prepared to move him from the gurney to the hospital stretcher.

"On three," Dr. Brown said. The move went smoothly, and the doctor glanced at the anxious group of firefighters. "The captain can stay in case I have questions; everyone else, out. Give us some room, please."

Sometimes Brown stretched the rules when it came to injured men in uniform. Nobody protested.

Zack gave her a tremulous smile and nod, which she returned, before filing out with the rest. Moving to Tommy's side, Shea worked with quick efficiency, hooking him up to a blood pressure cuff, pulse oximeter, EKG monitor. Dr. Brown pried open one of his lids, then the other, shining a penlight into his eyes.

"How long has he been out?"

The captain straightened, rubbing his stomach as though to soothe an ache. "Not long, maybe fifteen minutes. We got him here pretty fast."

Brown nodded. "Pupils are a bit dilated but equally reactive to light. I imagine he'll come around soon," he announced. He pocketed the light and bent over his patient, prying the gauze from the side of his head. Peering intently, probing, he made a humming noise in his throat. "Can't stitch that. The wound is too shallow and abraded, skinned more than punctured."

"He'll have a mild concussion," she said. *Please let that be all.*

Brown grunted in agreement. "Most likely. I'll feel better once he's cleared by neurology, and is awake and talking. Get these wounds cleaned and dressed while I order a CAT scan."

"Will do."

After donning latex gloves, Shea parted the hair above Tommy's temple and began to clean the area with antiseptic. He moaned and stirred some, starting to come around, which made her dizzy with relief. The noise also brought the captain immediately to his side.

"Skyler? Can you hear me?" Sean leaned over, rugged features lined with concern.

Tommy turned his head toward the man's voice and groaned something unintelligible.

"Don't move," Shea said, carefully turning his head toward her again. He sucked in a sharp breath in response to her ministrations, but held still.

"He's already coming awake. That's good."

"Yes, it is." She set the bloodied cloth on a tray and grabbed a fresh one. "Okay, it's clean. Since the bleeding has stopped, I'm not going to try to tape a bandage over it—with the hair in the way it wouldn't stick without shaving his scalp."

"Like my hair where it is, thanks," Tommy mumbled.

Shea's heart leaped and she looked into his face. Slowly, his lashes fluttered open and she found herself staring into unfocused crystal blue eyes. She'd never seen anything more beautiful.

"You're lucky your brains are still inside your skull, kid," Sean said, relief stamped on his face.

"Brains. Yeah, brains are good."

The captain's lips curved into a smile. "Time for a little test. What's your full name, son?"

He hesitated for a couple of seconds. "Thomas Wayne Skyler."

Shea began to clean the scratches on his right arm, hiding her surprise. Why hadn't she known that before? Hearing his full name made him more . . . real, somehow.

Sean continued. "How old are you?"

"Twenty-three."

"Who am I?"

Those pale eyes, a tad clearer now, danced with humor. "My asshole of a captain. Sir."

Sean laughed, the sound rusty, unused. "Since it appears you're going to survive, I'll let you get away with that. Just this once."

"Thanks, Cap."

He really hasn't noticed me yet. How will he react when he sees me? Will he be glad? Angry? Distant? God, anything but the last.

Shea quelled her trepidation and took the plunge. "What about me? Do you know my name?"

He turned his head and blinked up at her for a few seconds. Then his face broke into a wide, happy smile. A smile that stole the oxygen from the room. Made her light-headed. "Shea. How'd you get here?"

"I work here, hotshot. Remember?" Finished cleaning his arm, she tossed the cloth and peeled off her gloves, then discarded those as well.

His happiness dimmed some. "Oh. Right."

Had he thought she'd come especially to see him?

She crossed her arms over her chest, confused as to why his disappointment would hurt. "Quite a heroic feat you performed saving that worker. Do you recall what happened?"

He snorted. "Told him not to move, but he panicked. Jumped on me. Almost turned me into a human wrecking ball."

"You did good, kid," Sean praised.

His cheeks colored, but he gave a slight nod. "Thanks."

The captain rose, clasped Tommy's good shoulder. "They're going to do a CAT scan as a precaution, but I believe you'll be out of here in a few hours. When they spring you, go home. Get some rest, and we'll see you in forty-eight."

"I appreciate it, Cap."

"Need a ride to your apartment? Or you want me to call your folks?"

"Ugh. Mom's gonna freak." Tommy swiped a hand down his face, then let out a resigned sigh. "Go ahead and call them, I guess. They'll hear about it sooner or later anyway."

"I'll make sure to emphasize that you're okay."

Tommy frowned. "Tell the others I'm sorry about pulling out for today. Hope you don't get any more big calls."

"Oh, I'm sure they'll cut you some slack, considering." Sean headed for the door and lifted a hand. "Take it easy. Good to see you again, Shea. Maybe next time it'll be under better circumstances."

"Let's hope so. Bye, Sean." Watching him go, she was impressed he remembered her, considering how drunk he'd been when they met. And unless she was miles off base in her observations as a nurse, his bloodshot green eyes, sour stomach, and trembling hands could very well be a product of withdrawal.

"How have you been, Shea?"

Shifting her attention back to Tommy, she found him watching her, gaze intense. Hot. Not a trace of his ordeal in evidence, save for the obvious scrapes on his face and the ugly bruise forming on his right arm and shoulder.

In fact, with his blond hair tousled and framing his angular face, bronzed male nipples tightening from the chilly temperature in the room . . . he looked good enough to eat with chocolate syrup and a cherry.

Down that path awaited disaster.

"Just fine," she said, hating how her voice squeaked. "You?"

His reply was a soft caress. "Lonely."

One word. One glorious word conveying a wealth of meaning, and her blood sang.

"You mean . . ."

"There's been no one else."

"Oh." *He hasn't been with anyone else since we met! What does that mean? He's waiting for me? Breathe.*

Lacing his fingers together over his chest, he tilted his head, lips quirking. "Yeah. *Oh.* You really don't know how much power you hold, do you?"

She blinked at him. Power? She'd never imagined herself as a powerful person, particularly when it came to the opposite sex. Able to deal? Sure. Mostly. But she couldn't tell Tommy any of that without getting into gory details.

She laughed, making a joke instead. "Right. I have an apartment, a cat, and a half-dead houseplant. I'm ready to rule the frickin' world."

"I meant power over *me*, and you know it."

"Do I? We've only been out a couple of times, haven't seen each other in weeks, so I don't see—"

"That can be remedied." Suddenly, he sat up on the bed, swaying a little. "Whoa."

She grabbed his arm to steady him. "What are you doing? Lie back down before you fall over."

"No. I can't ask you this while flat on my back." He removed her hand from his arm and curled his fingers around hers.

Oh, no. "Ask me what?"

"Will you go with me to Zack and Cori's wedding this Saturday? Be my date?"

Her throat shrank to the size of a pinhole. Why was it so hard to tell him? "I can't."

His smile blasted her full force. "Sure, you can. Just say yes, sugar. We'll dance, make merry. It'll be fun, and afterward I'll take you into Nashville for dinner. Someplace nice, anywhere you—"

"I can't. I already have a date."

His smile wilted like a balloon leaking air. "Oh." And the genuine hurt in his blue eyes was something she hoped never to see again.

Slowly, he let go of her hand and she felt the loss of his warmth like a physical blow. "I see."

"I'm sorry, Tommy. Really. But . . . save me a dance, okay?"

What a stupid thing to say. She had to get away from the pain etched on his face.

"I—I'm going to get another nurse to stay with you."

Shea turned and fled the exam room without looking back.

Fleeing the pain in her heart wasn't quite so simple.

3

William Hensley hid in plain sight, staring at the wreckage from across the street, right along with the other gawkers. Folks like himself, suddenly and cruelly reminded that your next breath often depended on luck.

Or on the stranger standing next to you.

When the first of the meat wagons arrived to collect the bodies, his stomach threatened to evict his lunch.

He'd done this, no way around it. Had made a terrible error, and men had died. It wasn't supposed to turn out this way, such a straightforward task, though his horror changed nothing.

Christ, I didn't have a choice!

Not if he wanted to keep his balls intact. A gay country boy in Homophobe, Tennessee—especially an HIV-positive one—had about a five-minute life expectancy. He needed every advantage he could get.

Great strides had been made in defeating HIV, and he needed those drugs. But to keep up with his medication, he had to have the cash, thanks to his worthless fucking HMO plan. Was as desperate for it as he was to keep his secret.

But this?

The first wagon left the construction yard at a sedate crawl, and William lowered his head to hide his tears. Turned and walked away.

He'd crossed the line. Whether intentionally or not, he'd killed two people. A couple of decent lives for his own sorry one. Hardly worth the trade-off.

Too bad he'd realized that much too late.

Sprawled in the backseat of his parents' car, Tommy grimaced as his dad hit every bump in Cheatham County, and tried like hell to hold in the stream of curses threatening to erupt. Wasn't their fault his head was pounding, he was pissed as shit, and ready to shoot somebody.

Namely the fucker who'd snatched the opportunity to enjoy Shea's company on Saturday clean away from him.

How well did she know this dude? How long had they been going out? Had they . . .

His mom's worried voice cut into his bleak thoughts. "You okay back there, sweetheart?"

Had he groaned aloud? "Fine, Mom." For the life of him, he couldn't manage to sound cheerful. Thankfully, his folks wouldn't expect him to be Mr. Sunshine after what happened at the construction site. They'd be wrong about the reason for his sullen mood, though.

Bethany Skyler half turned in the front passenger seat to frown at him, and tucked a strand of blond hair behind her ear. "I still wish they'd kept you overnight. Damned insurance jackals, shoving people out the door before they can even see straight."

Any other day, his mom's feisty protective streak would've made him smile and crack a joke. But he knew how shaken she was and couldn't bring himself to make light of that. "Insurance had nothing to do with it," he said, attempting to soothe her lingering fear. "The CAT scan was fine. I'm just banged up some, so there was no reason for me to take up a bed someone else needs."

"Still." With a disgusted *humph*, she faced front again.

"Are you sure you won't let us take you home? Just overnight?" This from his dad, Donald Sr., who glanced at him in the rearview mirror.

Home to his parents' would always be the house where they'd raised him and Donny. Not the cramped little apartment Tommy had insisted on moving into last year. In a way, he still felt guilty, as though he'd abandoned them when they desperately needed to cling to their remaining son. But his brother had been gone for two years by then, and Tommy knew it was time to cut the apron strings—for the second time.

No matter how much he loved them, he needed to be his own man, not a ghost of a little boy haunting his parents' home.

And yet . . .

"Sure," he heard himself say. "That would be great."

His dad blew out a breath and cracked a small smile. "Super. We'll get you all settled in, and you can rest."

He didn't know what had made him relent. Maybe it was to see the deep lines of stress disappear from his dad's brow. To watch the tension drain from his mother's slim shoulders.

Or maybe he just needed to be fed chicken soup and fussed over by the two people who would always love him. Unconditionally. Or they were supposed to, anyway.

His folks exchanged a quick glance—the one all parents master that's filled with indecipherable meaning—and fell silent. It made him feel very much like the kid most of his buddies referred to him as, and for once, he didn't mind.

He just felt safe.

Especially when his dad pulled into the drive and the warmth of their nice, older neighborhood embraced him like an old friend. He pictured Donny stepping onto the front porch to greet him, pull him into a brotherly hug. Peer at his face, tease him about getting into a fight with a Weed Eater or some other wise-assed comment—

"You getting out of the car, son?"

"Yes, sir." He hadn't even noticed they'd parked. His dad stood on the drive with Tommy's door open, dark brows furrowed, waiting to see if he required a hand.

Unfolding himself from the sedan proved to be more difficult than he'd anticipated. His body groaned in protest, already stiff and sore. But he made it without help and trailed his parents into the house. Once he was up and moving, it wasn't so bad.

Not compared to the ache deep in his chest. One that had nothing to do with cuts and bruises.

"Want to go lie down for a while?" his mom suggested.

How did moms do that? Make a question sound like a mandate?

"No, thanks. I think I'll park on the couch and watch the news or something."

"Well, if you're sure." She frowned, obviously searching for some way to make him more comfortable. "Hungry?"

Starving. "I can wait until you and Dad are ready for dinner." With that, his stomach protested loudly, making a big liar out of him.

His mom smiled. "How about I start early, then?"

He laughed, then lowered himself carefully onto the couch. "Sounds good, Mom."

Apparently happy to have someone extra to spoil, his mother disappeared into the kitchen. His dad flopped into his favorite recliner, grabbed the remote, and turned on the television. The drone of a CNN newscaster filled the living room, punctuated now and then by the banging of a pot or pan from the kitchen.

Tommy toed off his shoes and stretched out, comfortable in loose shorts and a T-shirt. "Thanks for coming to fetch me, and for the change of clothes."

His only answer was a grunt as his dad gave his attention to the Dow Jones. Tommy closed his eyes and had just started to drift off, thanks in part to the painkiller he'd been given before they left, when the older man's voice broke into the pleasant fog.

"What's going on with you and that cute little curly-headed gal who works in the ER?"

Tommy cracked an eye open to peer at his dad. "Not a thing."

"Sounds like a problem, the way you say it."

"You think? She doesn't know I'm alive."

He chuckled, eyes twinkling. "Oh, I wouldn't say that."

Tommy sat up some, wincing. "Why not?"

"Because she made about a dozen trips past your cubicle."

"She was busy, Dad."

"I know when someone is hovering," he said. "Besides, she even showed up when you were getting your noggin scanned. Checked on you, told me and your mother she was sure you'd be fine, and left."

His heart sped up. But her actions still didn't necessarily mean anything. "She's a professional, just doing her job. She helped treat me, and she probably wanted to reassure you both."

"If you say so."

"She's going out with someone else," he said, unable to mask his jealousy. "On Saturday. She's bringing some loser to Zack's wedding."

"Really? So what. Fight fire with fire, no pun intended."

"What?"

"Show up with your own date. Give her something to think about."

He blinked at his dad. "I—I can't do that."

"Why the hell not?"

"Because I don't want anyone else! I might blow any chance I've got with her."

"So you're just going to let this girl walk all over you?" He snorted. "What happened to the boy who used to think it was his God-given duty in life to test-drive every woman under the age of forty?"

"Dad," he hissed, shooting a glance toward the kitchen doorway. A flush warmed his cheeks. "That's not exactly the image I want to cultivate with Shea."

"Doesn't mean you have to roll over, either. Given the way she was acting earlier, my guess is she cares for you a lot. I think you'd make your point. Give it some thought, anyway."

As his dad turned back to the news, Tommy tried to doze again. But the seed the older man had planted took root. And grew to the size of a football.

His dad's advice made a lot of sense. Why should he play the doormat? She'd known Tommy would be at the wedding; he was one of the groomsmen, for God's sake! Obviously, she hadn't spared a thought for his feelings. Or maybe she'd believed he'd given up the chase and she simply didn't want to attend the wedding alone. Jesus, who knows *what* she thought!

His pride would not, however, allow him to believe for one second that she preferred this other dude over himself.

And he'd prove it.

Pushing himself off the couch with a pained moan, he shuffled into his dad's small study and closed the door. After walking over to the desk, he sat down and reached for the phone.

Fight fire with fire? He could manage a surprise for sweet Shea, all right.

And he knew just the girl to start the blaze.

Who knew weddings were so fucking much fun? Not.

Especially wearing a heavy suit when it was hotter than the center of the sun—inside as well as out, thanks to a blown air-conditioning unit in the little church in Cheap Hill.

Tommy's gut did a barrel roll, taunting him with the reminder that the last three rounds of ole Jackie D. at Zack's bachelor party last night hadn't been a fantastic idea. At two in the morning, he hadn't counted on being slow roasted like a chicken on a spit come this afternoon.

Or on spotting Shea with her *date* the moment he arrived.

Neither of which performed miracles on his headache. Or his sudden urge to commit homicide.

"Can't someone open a goddamned window?"

"Jesus, was that a snarl? I think the kid has rabies," Six-Pack announced with a grin. The only guy in the dressing room who didn't snicker was Zack, who was too freaked out about getting hitched to do much but offer a sickly smile.

Tommy shot the big man a withering glare. "Stuff it, Howie."

The snickers became snorts of laughter from everyone except Cori's brothers, Joaquin and Manny, who looked on in puzzled amusement. Six-Pack *hated* that nickname. Tommy pretended to adjust his tie in the mirror while the other bozos waited to see how the man would react.

"Nah, I've had better offers from prettier people," Six-Pack drawled. The others lost it, loud whoops and ribald comments echoing in the small room. And in his brain.

"Shitheads," he muttered, scowling at himself. "And they call *me* a kid."

"Damn, *amigo*." Julian appeared behind him and clapped

him on the shoulder. "Someone needs to shove a rainbow up your ass."

Get a grip, man. He didn't want to ruin Zack's big day.

Giving up on the tie, Tommy faced him and quirked a smile. "Think you're man enough to do the job?"

Julian waggled his brows. "If I swung that way, sure."

More laughter. "God, you guys are sick fuckers."

Six-Pack crossed his arms over his chest. "This little snit of yours wouldn't have anything to do with the slick-looking fellow on Shea's arm, would it?"

"Got any idea who he is?" There. He could be civil about this.

The lieutenant shrugged. "Seems vaguely familiar, but I didn't get a real close look. I can try and find out, though."

"I'd appreciate it." *Then I can rip his lungs out with a spoon.*

"In any case, you're not going to score any brownie points with Shea by killing her date," Zack said, ambling over to join them.

"Aw, come on. Just a little slow torture, then? Can't I make him scream like a girl, just once?"

"I can make the worm disappear for you," Joaquin offered with a dangerous smile. "Permanently."

Zack rolled his eyes. "Ignore Al Capone. Murdering the competition is never a good plan."

"Neither is flaunting another woman in her face," Julian said, shaking his head at Tommy's stupidity. "Who's the hot number you brought along?"

"An old friend from high school." Tommy sighed. "That was my dad's idea, to make Shea realize I'm not a pushover."

"Could backfire, big-time." The others made noises of agreement. Even Sean, who'd been sort of holding himself apart from the group.

Tommy gave his friends a grin he didn't feel, and elbowed Zack in the ribs. "Easy for you to dole out advice, lucky bastards. You've already got the girl."

"And most of us had to wait a lot longer than you," Six-Pack pointed out. "What's your hurry anyways? Don't get me wrong, Shea's a sweet girl, but what's so special about her that's got you in knots?"

He tried not to bristle. "I'm plenty old enough to know the woman for me when I meet her. She's fun, sexy, smart, and sometimes, when she looks at me . . . it's like the world ceases to exist around us. Like she can see into my soul and—"

"Holy love sonnet, Batman. My ears are bleeding." Julian's wisecrack was met with the sounds of gagging and someone humming like a violin.

"Real mature," Tommy muttered. "I give up on you bone-heads." Well, except for Zack, who was busy glancing at his watch and shifting his feet, nerves once again getting the better of him.

A man Tommy didn't recognize stuck his head in the door and announced it was time to take their places. The guys gave the white-faced groom last-minute backslaps, congrats, and advice to take it easy and not lock his knees during the ceremony. There was a tense moment when Joaquin offered his hand and Zack stared at him for a few heartbeats before accepting it. Then Cori's older brother left to take his place giving away the bride.

After waiting his turn, Tommy stuck out his hand. "I'm really happy for you, man. Relax, you'll be fine."

"Thanks." Zack clasped his palm and blew out a breath. "Well, here's to massive credit card debt and honey-do lists."

"And in a few more months, baby toys all over the house. Don't forget those."

"Oh, God."

Tommy laughed as a dazed Zack led the procession out the door. Maybe this falling in love crap wasn't all it was cracked up to be. Yeah, remaining in lust sounded like a whole lot less trouble.

Or he thought so, until they arrived in the church's foyer and he saw her.

Shea, at the head of the line, in her place as maid of honor. Curly sable hair piled on top of her head, little diamond studs glittering in her ears. Her sweet elfin face bright with happiness, caught up in the joy of the occasion.

His gaze caressed the graceful column of her throat to the swell of her breasts hugged by peach silk. The fabric of the dress nipped at her small waist, flared a bit at her gently rounded hips, and flowed to her dainty toes. God, he wished he could see her toned, pretty legs.

He stared, drinking in the sight of her. Letting her fill his soul. She was elegance personified. She was beautiful.

She's mine. And I'm hers.

Somehow, he had to convince her of that before he lost his mind.

Shea took Six-Pack's arm, wrapping her slender fingers around his biceps, and together they strode into the chapel at a sedate pace. Tommy squashed a nasty surge of jealousy, watching Zack's best man escort her to the front. To hell with the fact that Six-Pack and his wife, Kat, were deliriously happy. Tommy didn't breathe right again until they broke apart and took their places on either side of the altar.

How he'd get through the reception without killing her date, he didn't know.

"Psst!"

Startled, he blinked at Kat, whom he'd been paired with since her hubby was the best man. Crap, it was their turn and he was holding up the procession. Julian and his fiancée, Grace, had already gone, followed by Sean and Eve, who regarded each other, wide-eyed, as though they'd never met before. Weird.

Tommy offered his arm to Kat and they started off, leaving Manny and his bridesmaid, one of the nurses Cori worked with, to go last. This thing couldn't be over with soon enough.

Because having to stand there and look at Shea from across the short distance separating them, and not be able to touch her, knowing she'd accepted another man's company over his, was the purest form of agony.

Thankfully, the music swelled and Cori's arrival distracted him from his misery. She wore a high-waisted cream gown that accommodated her growing pregnancy. Honey brown hair tumbled about her bare shoulders because Zack preferred it down, and Tommy couldn't blame him. His new wife-to-be was a real stunner. The fact that shy Zack had scored a former exotic dancer still tickled the shit out of him.

Joaquin led Cori carefully up the three steps. With everyone in their places, the preacher began. By the time her brother gave her away to Zack, the sniffling had already begun, tissues dabbing here and there. Jesus.

At least the air conditioner came on, and a collective sigh of relief burst from the guests. In his coat, however, it would take forever for him to cool off. And he still had the reception at Zack and Cori's house to suffer through. For a long moment, he actually considered skipping out after the wedding.

Shea probably didn't want him around. Didn't care—

And then he caught Shea staring at him. Unmasked longing pooled in those big brown eyes. Or was it wishful thinking?

Either way, he knew there was no way he'd chicken out. Not now. He had nothing to lose and everything to gain.

He shot her his best smile, and when she returned it, lips

curving slowly upward, he wanted to shout out loud. Because, he suddenly realized, she hadn't sought her date out in the crowd. Not once.

But she'd been watching him. *Only* him.

That had to mean something good. Had to.

Tommy, my man, you're still in the game. Don't quit now.

Shea might have come to the wedding with the ultra-polished middle-aged dude in the thousand-dollar suit.

But he'd be fucked sideways if she was leaving with him.

4

Shea hoped nobody expected her to comment later on the preacher's lovely words. If so, she'd have to bluff her way through. The old man's voice faded to a monotonous drone as she devoured the sight of Tommy standing just a few feet across from her. All six delicious feet of him.

His dark suit hugged a body hardened by physical activity, emphasizing his broad shoulders and narrow hips. His chest and abs were rock-solid underneath his white dress shirt, toned and lean rather than bulky. The sculpted body of an athlete—a football player if she remembered correctly. Right this second, she found it hard to hold the jock label against him, though God knows she had good reason.

For one wild second, she wanted to push the jacket off his shoulders, tear off the staid tie, and rip open his shirt to get her first real gander at the golden skin waiting for her touch.

No! He's too young for me, too much like an eager puppy. He can't possibly have enough experience to know what he wants in life. He probably plays the field, breaks hearts left and right. I'd be better off with an older, more settled man, like Forrest. Right?

A trickle of sweat rolled between her breasts that had nothing to do with the heat in the chapel.

Her eyes swept past his hips to mile-long legs she imagined opening to cradle her inside, snug and secure in his heat.

Oh, God! Don't go there.

She shifted to relieve the uncomfortable ache between her thighs and gave her attention to his face. The man was quite simply beautiful. He had the face of an angel, with high cheekbones, full lips, dusky brows arched over crystal blue eyes that sparkled with mischief most of the time. Now they caught her gaze, smoldering hot, not allowing her to look away.

His smile took her breath away, made her pulse hammer in her throat, every silly girlish thing she'd ever read. Never had she felt anything like the way his nearness made her quiver inside—even back *then*—and it frightened as much as it excited. Still, she found herself smiling back, nerve endings tingling, as though her mouth, her body, had a will of their own.

The wedding was over before she knew it, Zack kissing his bride, and the private moment she and Tommy shared was broken. Or perhaps not so private, standing before a chapel full of guests. But it was strange how everything else had disappeared, as though they'd connected without physical contact.

The wedding party turned and filed out, and she wasn't sure whether to be thankful at the absence of the tension between them. Tommy Skyler disrupted her hard-won safe world, and part of her hid, terrified and trembling at the implication.

The other part desperately longed to live again.

In the foyer, she released Howard's arm and sought Tommy. Now that they were free from the biggest part of their duties, it would seem unfriendly not to at least speak to him. But before she could take a step in his direction, a hand caught her elbow.

"There's the prettiest woman in the room," a pleasant voice said.

Shea half turned to greet her date, surprised at having to squelch a stab of annoyance. She mustered a smile for Forrest, but was unable to return the compliment, no matter how much she genuinely liked him. Because the sexiest man in the room had just been greeted by a knockout, leggy blonde in a strappy, barely there summer dress . . . who was now hanging on to his arm.

And planting a kiss at the corner of his mouth.

Her heart froze. Tommy brought someone else. Had she honestly expected him to mope and pine alone all afternoon? *Yes, dammit!*

She tore her gaze from the perfect, striking couple with a massive effort. "Hey, you. Nice wedding, don't you think?"

Forrest curled his fingers around hers and brought them to his lips. "Absolutely. I love weddings. There's something about the promise of a new beginning that gets to me."

The right words from the wrong lips.

Now what on earth made her think that? Forrest was a very attractive man. Light sandy brown hair, earnest hazel eyes, a nice enough build. He stood a bit over six feet, and his body was a bit soft, especially around the middle, but he wasn't heavy. He was an important man with a stressful office-type job, so he likely didn't take care of himself the way he should.

"Yeah, they get to me, too," she said, aware of him waiting for a response. "Thanks for bringing me. I know this isn't exactly what you had in mind when you asked me out."

His puzzled expression cleared. "Are you kidding? I'm having a great time, and we still have dinner to look forward to, just the two of us."

"Yes, we do." But her mind strayed to another invitation,

issued by a man who wasn't safe at all. One who made her feel scraped raw after every encounter.

Was he going out with the blonde tonight?

"Shea, are you all right? You seem preoccupied." He glanced across the now-crowded foyer in the direction she'd been staring.

"Hmm? Oh, yes! I'm fine." She waved off Forrest's concern. "Oh, look, they're waving the wedding party back in to take the pictures. It shouldn't take long; then we'll head out to the reception, okay?"

"Fine with me. Unless you'd like to skip the reception and get an early start on our evening?" A trace of hope colored his voice.

"I thought you loved weddings," she teased. "Just telling me what I want to hear?"

"No, I do! I just thought . . ." He trailed off with a shrug.

"Well, it was a nice idea, but I couldn't possibly skip out on Zack and Cori on their big day. I hope you understand."

"Of course I do." Leaning down, he kissed her temple. "We'll stay as long as you like."

"Thank you." She smoothed the lapel of his suit, noting he didn't smell nearly as good as Tommy, nor was his chest very firm under the fabric. "I'd better go in and get the photos out of the way."

"I'll wait out here."

As she made her way to the chapel doors, she noticed Tommy's date standing alone near the entrance. The girl met Shea's eyes, her gaze unflinching, curious, but not hostile. She acknowledged Shea with a nod, which Shea returned before striding into the chapel. Okay, that was strange.

The photo session was a half hour of sheer torture, being near Tommy yet knowing they weren't together. Her brain went places she'd rather not go, agonizing over what this girl meant to him. What they might do later. Or had already done.

When the photographer was finished, Shea practically fled, allowing Forrest to ensconce her in his Escalade. They took off for Zack and Cori's place and if he noticed she was upset, he didn't mention it. Instead, he distracted her with small talk.

"Will there be dancing?"

She shot him a grateful look. "Dancing, food, beer, and wine. Wait until you see the place. I helped them get stuff ready yesterday after the rehearsal, and it's fabulous. They've got two big canopies outside, one to shade the dance floor and stereo equipment, and one for the sitting area, where the food will be laid out."

"Sounds like fun."

"Firefighters never do a party halfway, I've learned."

He laughed. "So I've heard. Now I'm doubly glad you asked me along."

She eyed his profile. "No offense, but you don't seem like the let-loose, party type."

"None taken. It's the stuffy image associated with us city boys." He gave an exaggerated sigh. "What's a guy to do?"

In spite of herself, she began to relax and enjoy his company. Forrest was a dear, likable man and deserved her attention since she'd agreed to spend the day with him. She would not let her libido drown the voice of good reason.

Screw me twice, shame on me.

Forrest turned down the winding drive and whistled. "Pretty spread. Look at all this front acreage! I can see why they wanted to have the reception here instead of the banquet hall."

"Yep. No rent, except for the tents and fans, and plenty of room for all of the guests to park and enjoy themselves."

"Let me guess—the firemen are cooking the food and bringing the booze."

"Are you kidding? Cori said Zack suggested he hire a caterer to save everyone the trouble and the guys almost staged a rebellion."

"I'll be glad to help them man the grills or whatever they need. Good thing we're all changing clothes."

Shea thought of her own shorts and T-shirt in the back of the Escalade and couldn't wait to get comfortable. A hot July afternoon and peach silk were in no way compatible.

"That's nice of you. I'm sure Zack will appreciate it." She tried to picture Forrest dressed down, hanging out with the others, and the image wouldn't gel. He was a nice man, but as he'd admitted himself, the typecast role of city official tended to stick.

But when they arrived, he jumped right in with enthusiasm, making himself useful to Zack's firefighter friends who hadn't been in the wedding party and were already at work. A handful of them glanced at him in amazement, a couple in disgust. Which wasn't surprising considering what Shane told her about Forrest being so tight with Sugarland's budget. Apparently the police department wasn't the only entity feeling the financial squeeze.

In her opinion, blaming Forrest for trying to soften the blow of the economic downturn really wasn't fair. At least nobody was rude to him, however, and soon the men were cutting up and having a good time.

Satisfied no major disasters loomed on the horizon, Shea retrieved her clothes from the Escalade and went into the house. Upstairs, she peeled off the now-sticky dress with a heartfelt sigh, then pulled on her denim shorts and pink baby-doll shirt. She hung up the dress, slipped on a pair of sandals, and hurried back to the party.

Things were getting into full swing now, guests arriving

steadily, already having fun. The stereo was blasting out "Brick House" by the Commodores, getting folks into the proper mood to do the bump and grind on the dance floor. Shea didn't realize she was tapping her foot and grinning at their antics—until she spotted Tommy and his blond babe among the people gyrating close together. Her arm was around his neck, their foreheads nearly touching.

Shea's smile fell like a rock.

Abruptly, she turned away, the pain in her chest so real she might've been stabbed with an ice pick. She needed to be somewhere else, anywhere she didn't have to see them, but couldn't think where. Just then, Zack's '67 Mustang appeared—decorated with streamers and shoe polish—sparing her from making a decision. As the guests began to cheer at their arrival, Shea jogged over to meet her friends.

Zack emerged, dressed in jeans and a short-sleeved blue shirt and looking completely besotted. He hurried around to Cori's side, opened her door, and helped her out. Shea hung back, not wanting to intrude on their first moments home as husband and wife. However, the instant her best friend saw her standing there, she squealed and closed the short distance, grabbing Shea in a big hug.

"I know I told you a dozen times this morning, but I'm so happy for both of you," Shea said, throat tight.

"Thanks, girlfriend. This might not be my first rodeo, but I know I finally found the right man."

"That you did. He's wonderful, sweetie." And after the horror of Cori's first marriage and the subsequent dangers, nobody deserved happiness more than Cori and Zack.

"Don't I know it!" Her friend pulled away and beamed at her. "So, are we ready to rock out, or what?"

Shea laughed. "Just don't party too hard or you'll be too tired to enjoy your wedding night."

"No worries, I plan to save plenty of energy. Why waste a

night's stay at a place as gorgeous as the Opryland Hotel, right?"

"Absolutely." She knew Cori and Zack were taking off later to stay at the famous hotel, then heading to the airport in the morning to fly to Cape Cod for their honeymoon. Cori had wanted to go to the Caymans but Zack vetoed leaving the country while she was pregnant. "Is Howard locking up the house for you?"

Cori nodded. "He and the other guys are cleaning up tonight. Everything's in good hands."

"Super."

Shea noted Zack hovering behind his new wife, positively vibrating with happiness. She stepped past her friend and wrapped him in a bear hug. "Treat her like a princess, or I'll think up some horrible punishment. Nurses know all sorts of gross things to do to a person."

"I think her brothers would probably beat you to the draw," he said, making a face. "Anyway, she's safe with me."

"I know, I'm just teasing. Go see to your guests, you two!"

With a wave, the blissful couple joined the crowd, accepting more well-wishes. Watching the festivities, she felt an almost unbearable wave of loneliness wash over her, despite her effort to stave it off. Weddings ran a close second to Christmas as far as leaving a person's emotions stripped bare. At least during the holidays she had Shane to remind her she had someone to love and be loved by in return.

"Shea?"

She started, and spun to see Tommy standing less than two feet away. So close she detected his earthy cologne and a hint of sweat. So potently male he made her head swim.

His smile was uncertain, his blond hair artfully mussed like he'd just rolled out of bed. After a long, leisurely bout of sex.

"Um, hello." *Great going, idiot. That's sure to impress him.*

She stared at him, startled. *Did* she want to impress him?

"Hey," he said softly, tucking his hands into the pockets of his cargo shorts. "Having a good time?"

The picture of him plastered to Breast Enhancement Barbie a short while ago beat her like a sledgehammer. Damned if she'd let on how much it hurt.

"Oh, sure." The words weighed heavy on her tongue. Because despite her best efforts, the best part of her day was standing right in front of her. "Are you and your girlfriend enjoying yourselves?"

"Who, Daisy?" He paused, cocking his head. "We're having a blast."

"Daisy? As in Daisy Duke?" She snorted, unable to keep the green monster from her tone. "Where'd you meet her, the Waterin' Hole?"

"We've been buddies since high school." The corners of his mouth lifted. "And that's Officer Daisy Callahan. She works with your brother."

She latched on to the term "buddies" like a lifeline. Holy Moses. Who would've thought the woman built like a brick shithouse and worthy of the cover of *Vogue* was a cop? Not to mention a friend of Tommy's. *Way to make a total fool of yourself, Shea.*

"I . . . well, that's nice," she said, fumbling for something to say. "She doesn't look much like a police officer."

"Don't let her appearance fool you. She's tough as boot leather and has the temper of Satan."

"Charming."

"Actually, she can be when she sets her mind to it."

Shea did *not* want to discuss Daisy's charms, or Tommy's knowledge of them. "I'll take your word for it."

Tommy smirked. "Oh, don't take mine. See for yourself."

He flicked a hand toward the edge of the dance floor, where Daisy was sidled against Forrest as though stuck to him with Velcro. She giggled animatedly at something he said, and ran a long, manicured nail down the front of his shirt. Poor Forrest looked ready to burst into flames.

Worse was the knowledge that Daisy's flirtation with the man didn't bother her at all.

"Oh, I get it." Fisting one hand on her hip, she glared at Tommy. "You brought your friend along to run interference."

He grinned at her, completely unrepentant. "I'd say that makes you a quicker study than your so-called date, wouldn't you? Tell me something. Why would you waste another second of this perfect day on a jerk who's so easily distracted by another woman's attentions?"

"I don't believe it," she said, incredulous. "That's so underhanded."

And sort of . . . wonderful.

"All's fair, as they say."

"Well, Forrest isn't going to fall for your machinations."

"Forrest *who*?" His expression revealed only mild curiosity.

"He's Forrest Prescott, the city manager."

"Thought he looked familiar," he said, unimpressed. "Anyway, seems like he already *has* fallen for my scheme."

"What?"

Sure enough, Forrest and Daisy were on the dance floor, working up a sweat to an upbeat Madonna song. Shea crossed her arms over her chest, unsure whether to be relieved or annoyed. She looked at Tommy, trying to appear unfazed by the whole conversation.

"So? Doesn't mean anything."

"You're not nearly as upset by your sweetie's defection as you should be if you were serious about him."

"He's not my sweetie—he's a friend." Dammit! And damn

him for appearing so frigging happy about it. She clamped her mouth shut.

"Aha! Then you won't mind dancing with me. It's only fair, seeing as how my date deserted me for yours."

She hesitated. God, she needed to give in to him like she needed another ten pounds on her hips.

Cocky, beautiful son of a bitch.

"One dance."

The sly catlike expression of satisfaction on his face almost melted her panties. "Uh-uh. No stipulations except enjoying yourself. Come on!"

Grabbing her hand, he pulled her into the throng and spun her to face him before she could protest further. He made it appear easy, just to throw caution to the wind and let loose. To move to the music with fluid grace, uninhibited, every lean sinew flexing as though making love.

Like liquid, molten sex.

"I'm not that great a dancer," she said, raising her voice to be heard above the music. Trying to match his graceful moves, she felt like a dork.

One strong arm snaked around her waist, pulled their hips together. He rocked against her, his unmistakable hardness pressing into her belly. "Believe me, you're doing fine."

Her cheeks blazed. She wasn't some simpering virgin—far from it—but the man caught her off guard at every turn. And Tommy *was* a man, not a boy. No doubt whatsoever, if there ever had been.

As they moved, the friction of their bodies setting her on a slow burn, she watched his face. Studied the nuances. There was no trace of the young, carefree charmer in evidence now. In his place was a man she'd never seen before. A man completely confident of his intentions, his crystal eyes dark with desire. One who made her blood quicken, her soul cry out to answer his unspoken challenge, to be his.

The fast song ended, abruptly snapping her from the spell. Thinking to make a quick getaway, she stepped back, but he caught her hand.

"This next one, too. Please?"

The soft, pretty opening to "My Wish" by Rascal Flatts began, one of her favorite songs. She paused for a couple of beats and, apparently taking her hesitation as a yes, he enveloped her in his arms. Began to sway gently, big hands spread over her back, chin resting on top of her head. In spite of her qualms, she felt herself melt in to him, soaking up his strength.

Warm. Intoxicating. Incredible.

Like coming home.

"God, it feels so good to finally hold you," he whispered into her hair.

She didn't answer. Couldn't, not when her senses, every barrier she'd erected between them, were under toe-curling assault. Searching for the right response, she lifted her head to meet his gaze.

Instead, his lips brushed hers. A sensual glide that wasn't a tentative question, but a warning. Electrifying her to the core.

His fingers brushed down her cheek. "Pretty baby."

And he claimed her mouth then, kissed her like a man kisses a woman when he means business. When he wants her no matter the cost, above all others. Whatever it takes.

His tongue tangled with hers and she whimpered, unable to help herself. He tasted so good and she wanted to slide under his skin, stay there forever. Wrapped up in him. The party, the guests, vanished as the kiss went on and on. It might well have been the two of them locked in their own world, free of doubts and unwanted baggage. For the first time in more than a decade she felt protected and safe.

But she'd been wrong before.

The memory was a bucket of ice water dousing her ardor. Reality intruded, along with fear. Cold, familiar companions who never failed to remind her what happened to stupid girls who dreamed too much.

She gave Tommy's chest a forceful shove, and he stumbled backward, blinking at her in a daze. Confused, emotions frazzled, she shook her head and in reflex, wiped her mouth with trembling fingers. "I—I'm sorry. I—I'd better go . . . check on Forrest." Which was precisely the wrong thing to say.

Hurt flared bright, then cooled as his eyes went flat. "You do that, baby. And when you figure out that stingy, pencil-pushin' sack of shit can't give you what you need? Call me."

Then he did something he'd never done before—turned and left her standing there, gaping at his retreating back.

His absence, his anger, left a horrible ragged hole where passion and the rightness of being in his arms had been moments ago. She longed to call him back, or go after him, but didn't know if he'd accept her apology. Besides, what could she say, really?

He might listen to the truth and even understand, but she wasn't ready to tell it. Might never be.

Ducking her head, she jogged blindly for the house, praying nobody noticed the tears dripping off her chin.

This wouldn't do. At fucking all.

It was like watching a slow-motion train wreck, his careful plans derailing and stacking like dominoes. Broken and useless.

No. *He'd* be the one broken if he failed, and the possibility—certainty—made him shudder. No use thinking about that. Negativity was counterproductive.

He had a commitment to see through, and his own nest to feather. *Can't lose sight of the prize. There's too much at stake.*

Taking deep breaths, he forced himself to calm down as he watched the dejected blond guy leave the dance floor. Relax. One way or another, he'd achieve his goals.

No matter who he had to crush under his heel to see them to fruition.

5

Joseph Hensley puttered in the tiny kitchen, heating a can of chicken noodle soup on the stovetop. Microwaves made your food taste like warmed-over shit, in his opinion. Made the edges weird, like hot rubber. Young-uns were so impatient these days, wantin' every damned thing yesterday. Never waitin' for the best in life, always in a rush.

Just like Will. Where in the hell was that boy, anyhow?

Probably off at that highfalutin city job of his, as usual, never mind that it was the weekend. Always runnin' like the white rabbit in *Alice in Wonderland*, his nose buried in his stopwatch.

Which was how dumb rodents ended up as roadkill.

He snorted, switching off the burner and moving the pan aside. Will thought he was so smart, but he'd have to live a long fucking time to best his grandpa. Did the boy honestly think Joseph didn't know the Big Secret? Couldn't guess why Will never had a gal around, didn't have friends over for beers and ball games on the television?

Joseph took his soup bowl in shaking hands—goddamn this fucking Parkinson's disease anyhow—and shuffled to the rickety square table in the breakfast nook. He sat down and dug into the savory broth, shoveling in spoonfuls, hardly aware of the mess he made. Didn't the boy understand that Joseph wouldn't hold his . . . *orientation* against him?

Didn't he realize he couldn't keep secrets from a man who'd seen about every stinking, rotten thing the world had to offer? Once upon a time, he'd been like Will—brash, young, nose to the wind. Invincible.

World War II had cured him for good.

Joseph didn't get everything Will did, but he loved his grandson unconditionally. Always would. He just had to—

The bleating of a cell phone interrupted his thoughts. Seein' as how he didn't own one of the damned things, Will must've left it at home again. He was starting to see why, too, because the annoying gadget sounded off constantly. Two, three, sometimes four times a day. Which was mighty strange, since nobody ever came by to see Will, and the boy never asked after friends who might've called.

Making up his mind, Joseph stood with a grunt and made his way to the couch, where he located the small device trapped between two cushions. By the time he plucked it from its hiding spot, the thing had stopped ringing. But it would start again. It always did.

All he had to do was carry the phone to the table, eat his dinner, and wait. He might be old, but he wasn't stupid. He hadn't survived being a tail gunner in the war, decorated with a cedar chest full of medals, by being a pussy. And this, he suspected, might be war of a different kind.

As he figured, the phone shrilled a greeting five minutes later. Eyeing it, he flipped it open and waited. He'd learned the value of patience on the correct end of a B-17 Flying Fortress.

"Hensley?"

"Yep." No lie there.

"You sound funny."

"Not feelin' too good." Also the truth.

"Whatever," the man said, sounding as though he was in a hurry. Sweating, maybe. There was a lot of noise in the background. "Have you been getting my messages? I need that next job done in a week, tops. We have to keep things rolling."

Nothing too alarming there. "Or?"

"Don't fuck with me, asshole," the man snarled. "You're in this up to your balls, same as me."

He stiffened. "Am I?"

"Damned straight you are, no pun intended." The stranger barked a nasty laugh at his own joke. "You flake out on me now, you little faggot, and my contact will make you sorely regret messing with the big dogs. Got that?"

"Yep."

"Next week. Don't let me down."

The man hung up and Joseph did the same, dropping the phone onto the table as it shook from his gnarled hand. "Oh, Will. What have you done, boy?"

He stared into the waning light, long after the remnants of his soup had gone cold.

Joseph Hensley might be tired, his old body giving up the ghost, but it seemed he had one more battle to fight.

And win.

"Where's Sean?" Tommy eyed the hungry group seated around the station's kitchen table waiting for his version of breakfast. He just hoped it would be edible this morning.

"Running late," Eve muttered, scowling into her coffee mug. "As usual."

"Maybe we should chip in for a new alarm clock for his birthday."

Nobody laughed at Julian's lame joke. They all knew why the captain was late, and nothing but a stint in rehab was going to fix him. Which he'd stubbornly refused to do, insisting he could handle his problem with the bottle. Alone.

"It's been a year and half since the accident," Eve continued, as though Julian hadn't spoken. "Something has to be done."

Tommy flipped the pancakes and shook his head. "Like what? Can't help a man who doesn't want to be helped."

"Maybe he *can't* be helped." This from Clay Montana, who normally worked as FAO on B-shift. He'd jumped at the chance to earn some OT this week while Zack was on his honeymoon.

The silence fell like a shroud. Wasn't this everybody's worst fear? That Sean wanted to sink and nothing would stop him? Honestly, if Tommy had learned that his entire family burned to death in a fiery car crash, that his baby girl died screaming for Daddy . . . Jesus, they'd have buried him long ago.

"Maybe if we staged another intervention—"

Julian cut off Eve's suggestion. "No way. Are you forgetting what a disaster the first one turned out to be? He won't listen."

"He's right," Six-Pack said, face grim. "I put my ass on the line with that one, and it backfired."

She slammed her fist on the table, startling the others with the temper normally reserved for her sparring matches with the captain. "Then what the hell are we supposed to do? Just let him drown?"

"Did I miss the memo inviting me to my own fucking performance review?"

Aw, hell. Everybody looked toward the doorway, where Sean stood, arms crossed over his chest, good and pissed. His eyes were bloodshot, making the green of his irises pop.

Tommy turned off the heat under the bacon and took a deep breath. "I brought it up, sir. I asked where you were and everybody's worried about you. Can you blame us?" He met the captain's glare without flinching.

Sean's harsh features softened, but not much. "No, I can't. But I'm here now, so anybody who's got something to get off their chest can do it to my face. Well?"

Seconds ticked by from the kitchen wall clock, the only sound save for Tommy sliding the last of the pancakes onto a plate. Watching, waiting for the man to detonate.

Christ, are we having fun yet?

Eve stood slowly, face pinched with anger. Worry. "I've got plenty to say. In your office."

"You'll say it here. God knows you'll all talk about it later anyway," Sean said, giving a humorless laugh.

"Fine." She rounded the table as the others stared, like witnesses to catastrophe. "You're late for the third time in two weeks, a transgression you'd have called any of us on the carpet for by now."

"Granted," he agreed, mouth tight. "I apologize to all of you."

But Eve wasn't finished. "It wouldn't be that big a deal if it were anyone else, but you? We all know you're stumbling in here either half-drunk or hungover—"

"Just a goddamned minute," he hissed, stepping into her space. His face was parchment white, red flags staining his cheeks. "You're crossing the line, Marshall."

"I'm thinking of this team, something you're damned well not doing." She closed the distance further, getting in his face. Not giving an inch.

"I have *never* come to work drunk," he said hoarsely. "This team is all I have, and I'd never place any of you in jeopardy."

"You wouldn't mean to, but that's how accidents happen, Sean." Leaning in to him, she sniffed at his neck. "I can smell the whiskey oozing from your fucking pores. You might be sober at the moment, but you're hungover. Tired. You're going to make a mistake, and when you do, someone's going to get hurt. When that happens, none of us will be able to save you from the city brass. Or yourself."

Sean fell quiet and, for a long moment, gazed into Eve's earnest face. No one breathed. Not even Howard had ever dared to lay it all on the line quite this way in front of the entire team, the failed intervention aside. Here, at work, it took on a whole new level of seriousness.

"Maybe I don't—"

The high tone of the intercom stopped Sean from saying something he might not be able to take back, and deflated the almost painful tension in the room. The rest of the group around the table shoved back their chairs and rose, and everyone started for the bay as the computerized female voice related a call to a structure fire, close to downtown.

Tommy wiped his hands on a kitchen towel, pitched it onto the counter, and shot a last, forlorn glance at the abandoned breakfast.

For once, his meal had turned out perfect.

Clay pulled the quint into the empty parking lot near the building and whistled. "Mother Mary, look at that bastard burn! Three alarms, baby!" Baby came out *bay-bay*, Austin Powers style.

Despite the thick atmosphere in the cab, Tommy suppressed a snort of laughter. Their resident cowboy couldn't be more different from Zack's quiet authority. Montana was just a little bit crazy, a tad off. But in a likable way.

"Did you take your medication this morning, cowboy?" Eve asked with a grin as they all jumped out.

"Nah. I gotta work, and that shit aggravates my multiple personality disorder." Heading around the side to yank out the preconnected hoses and work the valves, he gave her a wink. "Figured you guys would want to know for sure which one of me showed up today."

Tommy did laugh then, along with Eve. The guy was a ball of white-hot energy, and funny as hell. He must run circles around B-shift and keep them in stitches to boot.

"Skyler, you and Marshall take the roof," the captain called. Clearly, he wasn't in the mood for Clay's humor. "Six-Pack and Salvatore, take the hose around back."

Eve hesitated, frowning at the squat, two-story building. "Sean—"

"Get moving, dammit."

She turned away, muttering under her breath. "Prick."

The four of them sprang into action, Tommy and Eve each grabbing an ax from the quint and hefting the ladder. The FAO from Station Two shut off the hose aimed at the roof, and a pair from their team and from Station Four entered the building in the front with more hoses.

Tommy and Eve jogged for the back of the building and placed the ladder against the back wall of the structure, giving it a shake to be sure it was secure.

"I don't like this," Eve said. "I've got a bad vibe."

"We don't have to go."

"He'll chew our asses."

He didn't have to ask who she meant. "But we'll be safe. Why get killed over an old, empty building?"

She hesitated for a beat, then sighed. "Our guys are inside. If it's unstable up top, we need to know."

"All right, a quick check. If it sucks, we're outta there. Ladies first."

As she began to climb, Tommy squashed a twinge of trepidation. Better the roof than going inside the burning structure, though some of his friends would argue differently. He'd never told a soul how he hated the claustrophobic feeling he got from a dark, tight, unfamiliar space. Add smoke and fire, boiling heat, and the scene was something right out of *Dante's Inferno*.

Most of the time, their jobs involved assisting the community in other ways—accident victims, medical emergencies, school fire prevention awareness. Helping people rocked.

This kind of stuff? Sucked hairy donkey balls.

Glancing up, he got an eyeful of Eve's ass bouncing under the edge of her heavy coat. Not bad, even in the less-than-flattering fire pants. The sight didn't trip his trigger the way it used to, though. Before Shea.

Oh, no. Not going there.

He pushed her out of his head and focused instead on keeping his weight centered, slightly forward, balanced. The Air-Pak was like an anvil against his spine, trying to pitch his tall frame backward. Eve seemed to have no problem, shimmying upward like a spider monkey. As strong as Eve was, he admired how she handled every aspect of her job, given that every one of them outweighed her by a good fifty pounds of muscle.

In truth, for all their good-natured teasing, the woman intimidated him a little. If she got wind of that, she'd ride him into the ground. And not in a pleasurable way.

When Tommy reached the top and hoisted himself over the ledge, Eve was already busy circling the roof. Stepping carefully, she scoped the area, still damp from the attempt to cool off the surface.

At first glance, he could see the dousing hadn't been enough. Little ripples, bubbles, were forming under their boots. A chill chased through his blood. "Eve, let's go." He keyed the mic hooked to his coat and began walking swiftly back to the ledge. "Cap, get everyone out. She's not gonna hold."

"Copy that."

Relieved, Tommy let out a breath—

Just as an ominous rending noise tore through the air behind him, punctuated by a screech.

He spun, just in time to see one of Eve's legs disappear through a gaping hole in the roof.

"Tommy!" Her lower half was swallowed, dangling over the inferno as she scrambled for purchase. Black smoke belched from the ragged hole. Arms straight out in front of her, ax in one fist, she clung, eyes wide with terror.

Tommy ran, slowing his steps as he eased toward her, gently prodding the surface with the head of his ax. One wrong move, one quirk of the bitch called fate, and they were both dead.

Sweat rolled down his temple, and not only from the heat boiling under his feet. Carefully, he stretched out on his stomach and crept toward her, much like a person would on a frozen lake trying to rescue a victim without sending them both through the ice.

"Oh, God," she moaned. "Hurry!"

Incredibly, his mind locked down. Sharpened to the one task he must not fail—to save his partner. Laying the ax aside, he stretched toward her. "Let go of your ax, too, and give me your hands, sweetheart."

She did, and they locked their grips around each other's wrists.

"Don't let go of me," she whispered, mouth white despite her bronzed skin color.

"Not a chance, my friend. Look at my eyes. Focus on me."

"Okay."

A strange, eerie calm settled over him as he began to inch backward. Part of the roof crumbled under her stomach and they slipped, but other than a harsh gasp, she made no sound. Just continued to do as he'd asked, gazing at him with complete trust.

No more time. He had to get them off this death trap.

Without letting go, he shifted, getting on his knees. He dug in, threw his weight backward, hauling for all he was worth. Eve slid out of the hole and onto the roof, and he pulled her backward several feet before helping her up.

"Can you walk?"

"I think so." But she grimaced as she took a step. "Damn. Must've sprained—"

The building shook.

"Shit!"

Tommy lunged, grabbing her and tossing her over his shoulder in a fireman's carry. If he'd ever moved faster, even when he'd dodged the biggest, baddest defensive linebacker on the field, he couldn't recall when. Before his brain caught up with his actions, he was over the ledge, making his way down the ladder a hell of a fucking lot quicker and smoother than he'd gone up. Carrying an extra load, no less.

Who was squeaking in protest at the upside-down view, dangling like a sack of potatoes two stories off the ground.

"I'm gonna be sick," she announced.

"Not on my coat, you don't."

He thought he heard a laugh, but it might've been a grunt. No way to be sure.

Before he knew it, they were down. He stepped off at the bottom and let Eve gently to the ground in front of him. In a flash, they were surrounded by the whole team, plus a few guys from the other stations, demanding to know what happened. Sean foremost among them, wearing an expression Tommy had never seen on his rugged mug before.

Naked fear.

"What the hell happened?" Sean rasped.

"Eve fell through the roof," he said. And Christ, here came the shakes. Delayed, but bearing down hard.

With that announcement, Sean paled. He spun and stalked toward the ambulance with Six-Pack and Julian, where they sat her in the back, removing her boot to take a look at the injured ankle. Tommy trailed in his wake, trembling like a racehorse on crack.

Sweet Jesus, he'd almost lost a colleague. And a damned good friend.

One thing he knew for goddamned certain, and the truth didn't go down easy. This wasn't what he signed up for when he joined the fire department. Not by a long shot.

And he didn't have a single clue what to do about it.

The lady firefighter had been injured.

Another innocent person hurt so he could live as normal a life as possible. Stay well for a few more years. Perhaps indefinitely.

Will's stomach churned. He hated this. Hated lying to Grandpa, to his coworkers, his few friends. He loathed the position he'd put himself in on all fronts. Yes, he had done this. Had been reckless and ruined his own life, then ruined others' in order to save his own hide.

It was like juggling axes and saws. Blindfolded.

What would Grandpa say if he knew the whole sordid truth? The stress and shock would probably kill the old man outright. Picturing his disappointment lanced Will's chest, the pain almost physical.

Grandpa couldn't find out. Ever.

Putting the old man out of his mind, or so he told himself, he reached into his jeans pocket, fishing for his cell phone—which he'd left at home. Again.

He couldn't say he was real sorry about having to make his call later. Much later.

Will was just about to leave when one of the firefighters across the street glanced in his direction. The man, striding for the ambulance where the lady firefighter was being checked out, paused a beat. Stared at Will.

Right at him.

Will pulled his ball cap low over his eyes and walked off. *Casual, man. Easy, like some bystander checking out the action. Moving on.*

He was halfway down the street before he chanced a look over his shoulder and breathed a sigh of relief. The firefighter wasn't paying attention to him anymore. No one was.

A few more jobs, then he was getting out. He'd have enough stockpiled to pay for his meds, and Grandpa's, for good. No more struggle and worry.

That was what he told himself at night, when he couldn't sleep.

When his demons promised to hold his reservation in hell.

6

Shea placed the dust rag and Pledge under the sink, then washed her hands, letting her mind wander to the day ahead. Tidying her small apartment hadn't taken long, maybe an hour. Funny how she lived for her days off, yet when they arrived, she had no clue what to do with them once her chores were finished.

"I could try getting a life," she told Miss Kitty, who wound around her ankles yowling for food. She gave the big gray Persian a rueful smile. "Or we could just be old ladies together—how's that?"

Miss Kitty wasn't impressed. Tail waving like a banner, she stalked over to her food dish, sniffed, and glared expectantly back at Shea.

"No, ma'am, it's not time for dinner."

Which was met with another pitiful howl. And as always, Shea was helpless to resist such a heartfelt plea. When and if she was ever lucky enough to have children, she'd probably spoil them rotten.

The old pang of loss made her ache briefly. Not as bad as it used to be, dulled by the passing of ten years. But a part of her all the same, old scar tissue nobody else could see except Shane.

Fishing in the pantry, she got out the Tupperware container filled with dry cat food and poured some into Miss Kitty's bowl. The howling ceased as the feline crouched and proceeded to crunch, apparently happy.

"If only everyone had it so easy, huh? Just holler for what you want and then sleep all day in the sun."

And boy, she was talking to her cat. Or herself. Either way, she had to get out of here for a bit or go stir crazy.

In her bedroom, she dug out a pair of loose athletic shorts and a tank top, and changed out of her jeans and T-shirt. Tennis shoes completed the ensemble, and she was ready to go for a walk.

Not for the first time, she wished she had a dog to take along. They made good companions.

Or a man.

A gorgeous man with blond hair and blue eyes.

"Argh!" Striding from the room, she grabbed her keys off the kitchen counter and left, locking the door behind her.

Not being able to talk to Cori this week was frustrating. Happy as she was for her friend, she could use some advice. *Female* advice, preferably from someone who knew Tommy a little, which counted out Shane on both fronts. There were some things a woman didn't want to get into with her brother, no matter how close their relationship. Besides, Shane didn't need another reason to nose into her business more than he had lately.

Shea started down the sidewalk to the scenic path surrounding the property. She wasn't much for jogging, but she did enjoy a brisk walk. It helped clear the mind. Usually.

Today her thoughts tumbled one after another, giving her no peace. Saturday's wedding reception took center stage again, despite her repeated attempts to block it in the last few days. All she could see was Tommy's hurt expression. Tommy, turning to leave her alone, staring after him, torn. The awful scene was on a loop, driving her insane.

When you figure out that stingy, pencil-pushin' sack of shit can't give you what you need? Call me.

Even if she did call, what would she say?

Watching you walk away turned my whole world dull and colorless. I need you so much I can't sleep. I want you more than I've ever wanted any man, and I'm scared to death.

And then he'd want to know why.

He'd be kind and understanding, she had no doubts whatsoever. He'd want to help her move on. What he wouldn't understand is not being able to help when he was part of the problem. Indirectly, but still. She knew Tommy well enough by now to know he'd be hurt by her lack of trust. He'd take it personally.

Hadn't he already been hurt, though? He obviously felt rejected and was confused by her mixed signals.

"You're not any more confused than me, buddy." She sighed, picking up the pace. The day was getting hot at barely eleven, sweat rolling down her back and between her breasts. She tried to concentrate on her surroundings, her tennis shoes slapping on the pavement, and conjured a song with a good beat to hum as she went. Next time she'd have to bring her MP3 player and earbuds.

After making a circuit around the entire complex, she started for home. What next? Maybe a pint of Ben & Jerry's Chunky Monkey to completely negate the benefits of her walk. Or perhaps a drive to the Cumberland River, down to the dam. Her pantry was on the bare side, too. She could use a few groceries, but didn't really feel like—

Her thoughts ground to a halt. Across the parking lot, a familiar man walked from the breezeway leading to her apartment toward a dark blue Chevy truck. His head was down, one hand digging in his jeans pocket, pulling out a set of keys. As she hurried to close the distance, he unlocked the driver's door, swung it open, and got in.

"Tommy! Wait!"

He hesitated. To her relief, one long leg appeared, followed by six feet of lean, luscious male. He leaned just inside his open door against the frame, tucking one thumb into the pocket of his jeans, and peered in her direction. His expression was unreadable, and that made her more nervous than if he'd been angry.

Well, she'd wanted someone to talk to, and here he was, in the flesh. She just hadn't expected the object of her angst to show up at her doorstep. She jogged over and stopped a few feet from him, giving him a smile she hoped didn't betray her attack of nerves.

"Hi there," she said, breathless.

"Hey. Came by to talk, but didn't get an answer."

"Yeah, I was out for a walk. Been feeling cooped up, I guess."

He tilted his head, making no move toward her. "I'm surprised."

"Why?"

"I'd have thought Mr. City Manager would be keeping you plenty busy."

Fisting a hand on one hip, she stared at him. "If you really thought so, why are you here? To hurl more barbs at me about Forrest? You'll note that I haven't called you, and a verbal beating isn't exactly the way to change my mind."

Tommy hung his head and was silent for a few moments. When he looked up, his expression was contrite. "I'm sorry. That's not why I came, but I can't seem to filter what goes from my brain to my mouth where that guy's concerned. Picturing you with him . . . you *know* it's driving me crazy. But that's not my reason for stopping by."

She waited while he gathered his thoughts before continuing.

"I came by to apologize for my behavior on Saturday," he said quietly. "There's no excuse for leaving a lady standing there the way I did. I was rude and I hope you'll forgive me."

Never had she seen Tommy so serious, and something about his demeanor put her on alert. Dread curled in her veins. "Of course I do, not that there was ever a question of forgiveness. I hurt you, too, and I'm sorry. I know how you feel about Forrest and I can't change that."

His laugh was unhappy, and he ran a hand through his hair, making the sunlit strands poke in every direction. "Can't you? I guess that tells me what I need to know, but since I'm a masochistic bastard, let's hunt this down and shoot it. Do you have any feelings for me at all?"

"I do," she whispered. "We're friends, aren't we?"

A spasm of pain flashed in those incredible eyes. "In the same way *he's* your friend? Someone mildly interesting to pass the time with over wine and boring conversation?"

"No. Have you forgotten our dance? Our kiss? You're much more than that to me."

Stepping close, he brushed his knuckles down her cheek. "I haven't forgotten one second of how good it felt to hold you, but I wasn't the one who pulled away. You don't *want* me to be more, do you? I just keep pushing against your walls, and to tell you the truth, baby, my hands are starting to bleed. Do you want me gone for good? Look at me, tell me to leave you alone, and I will. I swear I'll get in my truck, drive off, and never bother you again. Is that what you want?"

He meant every word. Leaving would tear him apart, but he'd do just that. For her.

No more Tommy? His smiles, his laugh, his zest for life. Gone. And if she let him go, the next woman wouldn't make the same mistake. A woman even more stunning than Daisy Duke. In his arms. His bed. The idea made her sick.

Turn the tables, and she had a whole new appreciation for how he'd reacted, seeing her with another man.

"Pulling away was a knee-jerk response and it's my problem, not yours." Taking one of his hands, she linked their fingers, loving the rough calluses. The hands of a hardworking man. "I need you in my life, and the way you make me feel . . . it's wonderful, and it scares me, too. There are issues I believed I'd dealt with long ago, before you. Bad stuff."

"Like what? Talk to me, Shea."

"One day, okay? For now, can you be patient with me a little longer?" *Please.* She didn't want to get into this today, when things were so raw between them.

"Honey, I'm not going anywhere unless you make me," he said, squeezing her hand and drawing her in to his warm body. "This is your show, all the way. I'm here for you, whatever you need. Just don't keep dribbling me like a basketball. If you can promise me that, I've got all the patience in the world."

He kissed her nose, and she smiled. "No more dribbling, I promise. You have no idea what you do to me."

"Nope. Maybe you'd better show me."

Reaching up, she curled her fingers behind his neck and brought his head down. Captured his mouth, loved his groan of surrender. Loved being the instigator for a change, his strong muscles tense with desire, body trembling against hers.

She explored his mouth, tasting a hint of beer almost masked by peppermint. Beyond that, a flavor unique to him, heady and masculine like his spicy scent.

His arms went around her as he leaned back against his truck, legs spread, snuggled her in right where she longed to be. Like before, she was struck by the overwhelming sense of *rightness*. As though she'd been made for this man, and her entire existence had been only that—marking time until she met the man brave enough to crack her safe shell.

"God, if we keep this up I'm going to embarrass myself," he said huskily, cupping her face.

His erection burrowed into her tummy, hard and hot. Insistent. Being plastered against one-hundred-percent-potent, aroused male sent signals of appreciation to every nerve ending. One word and she'd have him in her bed, sliding inside her, fucking her into the mattress.

Lord, she was wet. She hadn't been celibate over the years, but her desire for this man was completely different. She'd never felt like she'd die if she didn't rub her naked body against his, skin to skin. She wanted to roll all over him, mark him as hers.

"Want to go inside?"

He nodded, lips curving upward. "I'd love to. But I'm not going to jump your bones—yet. I don't think we're ready."

"Speak for yourself!"

Deep down, though, she knew he was right. She'd learned a harsh lesson before. What was it about Tommy that made her toss her common sense out the window?

"Well, I'm physically ready. No hiding the truth." His slow grin was devastating. "I'm not, however, willing to mess this up."

"I thought you said this is my show," she pointed out.

"It is. Which is why I'm not going to let things go too far. Not today."

"Huh? Then how can you say I'm in charge if you're telling me no?"

"Because you didn't try to convince me," he said gently. "Not really. When you're truly ready, you'll know. You'll be absolutely certain, and we'll both be on the same page."

"Oh."

The truth dawned and she stared at him, seeing him in

a new light yet again. He could've taken advantage of her vulnerability, sated their lust, knowing it might hurt them in the long run. Yet he hadn't.

"Sweet, wonderful man." She gifted him with a slow kiss. "Are you for real? Never mind. I can tell you are." He was still rock hard and surely in pain.

He laughed, shook his head. "I have an idea. Why don't we grab a burger or something? Talk for a while."

"I'm a nasty sweat ball, so if you'll wait while I take a quick shower, you're on."

"I happen to like you sweaty. Makes it easier to slide into home base." He waggled his brows, making her laugh.

"Yuck. I'm showering, and that's one fetish you can cross off your list, *dude*."

Stepping back, she turned and started for her apartment, giggling at his loud protest.

"Hey! I haven't said that word around you in forever!" He hurried to catch up. "My friends have almost coached it out of me."

"Good. But don't change another thing, all right? I like you just the way you are."

"Seriously?"

"Yes. What about me? Is there anything you'd change?"

"Are you kidding?" He sounded taken aback as he fell in step beside her. "You're the most perfect woman I've ever met. You're smart, beautiful—"

"I wasn't fishing," she said, color heating her cheeks. *Liar.*

"Doesn't matter if you were. That's how I feel and if you change one hair on your head, I'll be upset."

"Hmm. I guess the purple-dyed Mohawk is out, then."

"Unless you want me to sport a matching one."

"Definitely out."

She pulled her keys from her shorts and let them inside,

breathing a sigh of relief to be in the air-conditioned space. "Jeez, it must be a hundred and ten outside. Want something to drink while you wait?"

"No, I'm good, thanks." He glanced around. "Nice place. Bigger than mine, and brighter. You've got more sunlight than I do."

She winced at the reminder that she hadn't invited him in on their previous date. The first time they'd gone out, he'd simply picked her up at the hospital and they'd had a burger together. Very casual outings, like today, but they hadn't discussed much beyond work, favorite foods, movies, and such.

Today might shape up quite a bit differently.

"Thanks," she said, pleased he approved of her humble abode. Padding into the kitchen, she dug a bottled water from the fridge. "I've enjoyed living here. Nice neighborhood, not far from work, and the apartments are only a few years old. Rent's not too steep, either, compared to some."

"I like it. I've been thinking about getting a nicer place, so maybe I'll search in this area."

"Cool. I think you'd like it here." She twisted the top off the bottle, took a long drink, and wiped her mouth. "Make yourself at home. I'll only be a few minutes."

"Hurry, or I might have to come in after you."

She figured he was teasing, but hurried anyway . . . even though she was tempted to stall and prod the lion, so to speak. Probably a bad idea.

So she sped through her shower and dried off quickly, then changed into fresh blue shorts and a white, summery tank top. Casual, she reminded herself. Burgers and fries. She could do this.

Once finished, sporting a touch of makeup, she walked out to find Tommy flipping through her latest *People* magazine, Miss Kitty sprawled on his lap like a furry rug. The feline head-butted his arm, demanding attention, and he paused to give her a scratch. The sight was too cute, and her heart melted a whole lot more, if possible.

"Ready?"

He looked up, eyeing her in approval, the heat unmistakable. "I am. You're way too pretty to be seen with me, though. I should buy you a steak dinner instead of another plain old burger."

"Oh, hush. Nobody thinks I'm pretty except you, and burgers are great with me."

"I'll bet Shane thinks you're pretty."

She rolled her eyes. "He's a brother, and they don't count."

Tommy went still, the color leaching from his face. "Yeah, they count," he said softly. "Don't ever take his opinion for granted."

"I—I don't. I was making a silly, clichéd brother joke, that's all." Crap, what just happened here?

His smile appeared forced as he rose, setting Miss Kitty aside. "Shall we?"

"Um, sure."

This time, she grabbed her purse and water along with her keys and they were off. Tommy took her hand and led her to his truck, opened the passenger door, and helped her inside.

As he walked around the front to his side, she noted he still appeared stiff. The set of his mouth was somewhat flat, his expression upset, much as he tried to hide it.

When he got in, however, he shot her a real smile that eased the knot in her chest. Whatever was wrong, he wasn't angry with her.

He pulled out of the parking lot, glancing over briefly. "Can I ask you something without making you mad?"

"I hope so." When he didn't laugh, she sighed. "Sure, go ahead."

"Did you go out with Prescott after the reception?"

"I did," she said, studying his reaction carefully. His knuckles whitened on the steering wheel and his eyes flashed, but his tone was even.

"I see. How did you two meet, anyway?"

"He was at a police charity thing with some of the city councilmen, and Shane introduced us. Listen, Forrest is a friend. Yes, he'd like for there to be more. But there *isn't* more, and I told him so that night. How could there be, especially after . . ."

After you held me and we danced, kissing like we needed it as much as air to breathe.

She didn't have to say it, but he heard it all the same. His hands relaxed on the wheel, and so did his shoulders.

"Thanks. You didn't have to tell me, but I'm glad you did."

"You can't convince yourself to be attracted to someone if you're not. It doesn't work."

His brows furrowed. "Is that what you tried to do with him?"

She hesitated. "I guess. Didn't do any good."

"I don't get it," he said, puzzled more than upset. "I mean, I know he's a better catch, being a big shot—"

"No! Don't ever think that because it's not true. You can't possibly believe I'm that shallow."

"Of course not. I'm sorry. Scratch what I said."

Gazing at his profile, she wondered how to put the issue to rest. "Can we call it temporary insanity on my part and leave it for now?"

"Sure, baby."

The endearment warmed her. He'd called her *baby* more than once, and it gave her a sense of belonging. Made her feel special.

In minutes, he pulled into the parking lot of Stratton's and shut off the ignition. Locals had feared the new McDonald's would put the longtime icon out of business, but so far both had thrived. Stratton's had the best burgers, shakes, and ice cream she'd ever tasted, and her stomach rumbled in anticipation.

"Better get you fed, tiger," Tommy said, grinning.

"Fat and carbs? Bring it on!"

"I like the way you think. Besides, we can always work it off."

Yeah, she could just imagine how. She might have serious trust issues, but she wasn't made of ice.

Inside the fifties-themed eatery, they found a table and sat across from each other. Almost instantly, menus appeared and they glanced through the choices, though Shea's mind was more on the company than the food.

"Cheeseburger for me," she said, laying her menu aside.

"Me, too. I'm not picky when I'm hungry, which is all the time."

"Good thing you're a fireman, then. According to Cori, you guys can cook like five-star chefs."

He laughed, shaking his head. "A total myth, I assure you. Until recently, the guys wouldn't let me cook anything but hot dogs. Pathetic, but I'm learning."

"Hmm, maybe you need more practice. You could always fix me dinner . . ." She trailed off, toying with her napkin.

"Good Lord, I want to impress you, not give you indigestion."

"I'm not worried. I could even help, if you wanted," she offered. His face lit up and he beamed at her.

"In that case, you're on! I work tomorrow, off Thursday and Friday. When's your next night off?"

"I work seven a.m. to seven p.m. through Saturday, off again on Sunday."

"God, we have crazy schedules. Let me think. I work Saturday and then I'm off Sunday and Monday. I'll get off at seven a.m. on Sunday, go home and crash for a while. Why don't I bring the stuff for dinner to your place Sunday afternoon? We can make it early since you have to be at work Monday morning."

"Sounds good. Want to come over around four?"

"It's a plan."

The busty, middle-aged waitress took their order with a big, flirtatious smile pointed firmly in Tommy's direction, much to her annoyance. To his credit, however, his gaze didn't stray lower than her face and he didn't seem to notice the sultry looks thrown his way.

Finally, the older woman moved away and Shea blew out a pent-up breath. "How do you stand it?"

"Stand what?"

"Nothing." He couldn't possibly be so oblivious to his sex appeal. Could he?

"Oh, that," he said, waving a hand in dismissal. "She was being obvious, wasn't she? I mostly ignore it, while trying to be polite. The guys tease me a lot about my resemblance to Brad Pitt and I'll admit I ham it up some, but I honestly don't see it."

Her brows crawled into her hairline. "Then you've had your eyes pecked out and eaten by crows, buddy."

"Gross." He made an exaggerated face. "My appetite is a goner."

She couldn't resist teasing him. "For a man who claims he's always hungry, that's quite a feat. Should we go?"

"Well, maybe it's not completely gone."

"Thought so."

They fell silent and she basked in his company, content. A fleeting, uncomfortable thought that nothing was ever this easy flitted through her mind, but she dismissed it. They were due for a little fun, dammit.

"I'm sorry I wigged out on you earlier, when you said

brothers don't count." His gaze dropped to the table. "I used to give my brother hell for nosing into my business, giving his opinion where it wasn't wanted or needed. Now I'd give anything if he could tell me what he thought about anything at all."

Oh, no. "What happened to him?"

"Donny was a Marine. He was killed in Iraq over three years ago."

7

Shea's eyes widened, and Tommy could've kicked himself. What the hell had made him reveal something so personal? So fucking sad?

"Christ, what a downer, huh? Please forget I said anything."

But she laid her hand over his, her pretty face filled with sympathy and understanding. "Shane and I know plenty about how it feels to lose close family. Our parents were killed right after we graduated from high school, and while it was a different situation, I can relate."

"God, that must've been so hard on you both, and being so young, too," he said, taking her hand. "At least I had my folks, and they had me. We're still pretty tight, in fact." Except for the fact that he'd never be Donny, especially in his mother's eyes.

"It was hard, but Shane pulled us through. Our parents left us a piece of property on the Cumberland and he sold a tract to keep us afloat while we figured out our careers. But what you went through . . . I can't imagine losing Shane. Though I try not to, I think about how dangerous his job is. I could open the door any day to find one of his buddies there, telling me he's sorry."

He nodded. "I hope you never have to know how it feels."

The dull horror, knowing Donny didn't die quick. That he was tortured for days before being beheaded. Like a part of Tommy bled into the scorching desert sands, and died with him.

"Your parents, are they coping?"

"As well as can be expected, I suppose. They were so proud of Donny. He was in the military for the long haul, was convinced he'd retire a general. And I believe he would have."

"What about you?"

"Me?" The question surprised him.

"Yes, *you*. You said Donny was in the military for life. What were you doing back then? Already planning on being a firefighter?"

Their sodas were set in front of them, but he barely took note.

"I was a star quarterback for the Alabama Crimson Tide," he heard himself say. "I was up-and-coming, with NFL scouts salivating over the day I'd finally enter the draft. The whole works."

And voicing it aloud, he was shocked by how bitter he was that his brother's death had derailed his dreams. That his parents had been so cocooned in their own grief, they hadn't noticed their remaining son floundering. *That nothing I do pleases Mom, and hasn't in three years.*

Wasn't that selfish? He felt like a complete bastard.

"Wow, being scouted by the NFL? Exciting stuff. What happened with that?"

"Life happened. I'd just started my sophomore year, and after Donny died, I went home to be with my parents. We needed each other."

"And, what? Were you kicked out of school for being gone too long?"

"No, I just never went back."

"Why not?"

"My brother came home in pieces. After that, not much else seemed important for a hell of a long time."

The waitress brought their plates piled with burgers and fries, but suddenly Tommy's stomach was queasy. He took a bite, all too aware that his brother could never enjoy such a simple pleasure again. Good food, a terrific lady. So much to remember never to take for granted.

Shea picked at a fry, regarding him with compassion. "It's a testament to how strong you and your parents are that you were able to survive and move on. Look at you, a successful firefighter. I think that's pretty special."

So much for not taking any aspect of his life for granted.

"We survived. Moved on, not so much. There will always be this huge hole I can't fill no matter how many construction workers I rescue or fires I put out. I think—no, never mind."

"Please, tell me," she said earnestly.

He almost delivered a lie to avoid the disappointment he was sure to see on her face. But if he hoped to gain her trust, she had to hear the truth.

"I think maybe I gave up football and became a firefighter for the wrong reason. I'd lost the heart to play ball because I thought it wasn't worthy of Donny's memory. How important is a game when there are guys dying for our country? I was determined to be as big a man as him, larger than life. Save the world, make a difference." He gave a self-deprecating laugh. "What a joke, right?"

But even that wasn't the whole truth behind why he'd given up his dreams of playing pro ball, and he knew it. How could he tell her that he hadn't felt worthy in his parents' eyes after Donny's death, especially his mother's? That he'd do just about anything if they'd think as highly of him as they did his dead brother?

Instead of disappointment in Shea's eyes, he saw nothing but understanding. The knot in his gut eased some.

"You're being way too hard on yourself. You do make a difference, every single day," she insisted. "Because of you, that construction worker went home to his family, and that's an awesome thing. As far as your football career, you did what you had to do at the time. How were you supposed to feel? To act? Give yourself a break."

"Thanks, Shea. Nobody's ever put it to me that way before."

"Perhaps because you never talk about it?"

"Perceptive as well as beautiful." He liked this, connecting with another person who got him. The glow loosened his tongue enough to voice his deepest secret, dragged from the darkest corner of his heart. "I wish I could go back, make those choices all over again. Be the man I was supposed to have been, before I threw it all away."

"Haven't most of us said the same at one point? But think of all the lives that would've been impacted if you'd gone back to school. That worker might've died the other day, and he's only the beginning."

Tommy thought of Eve nearly falling through the roof into the inferno below, and it chilled him to think what might've happened if he hadn't been there. Not to mention all the lives that wouldn't have touched his. "Maybe you're right. I also wouldn't have met my friends at the station, or you, which is unthinkable."

A smile teased the corners of her sensuous mouth. "So if you had a time machine, you wouldn't ditch me?"

"No, but I'd go back and tell my brother not to go out with his unit that day. To plead a stomach virus, anything to keep him from getting captured and going through the hell they subjected him to before he died."

Her voice was gentle. "And from what you told me, this larger-than-life macho guy wouldn't have listened."

"Probably not," he conceded. "The what-ifs are enough to drive me insane."

"So you can't go back, but you *can* go forward. If you're not happy, make a career change," she suggested, steering the topic from his greatest sadness.

"Just like that?"

"Why not? You're young, and I mean that in a good way. You can still reinvent yourself, which is an opportunity most people don't have or don't take."

He shook his head. "It's too late for college ball."

"Then go to the Titans' training camp as a walk-on next spring. Guys do it all the time."

"Few are chosen, if any." All the same, a thrill of excitement chased though him.

"Why not you? If you were as good as you claim . . ."

"Hey, I'm better!" He returned her impish grin.

"Well, there you are. What's to discuss? Give it a shot."

"I might do that." Now that it was a real possibility, the thought scared him a little. What if he wasn't as good as he was three years ago?

And what if he only wanted it because he couldn't have it, like a child who'd broken his favorite toy?

"It doesn't have to be football," she said, as though reading his mind. "What are your other interests?"

He pondered the question for a few moments. "I like to solve puzzles. The mysterious, real-life kind. Like this suspicious fire we worked at this abandoned office building on Sunday. The power had been turned off months ago, so the odds of it being accidental were pretty low. Arson was called in to investigate and, sure enough, they found traces of gasoline used to start the blaze."

"You sound really excited about the sleuthing part of it."

"To me, it's fascinating putting all the pieces together to try to come up with a clear picture of who broke the law and why."

"Is Arson a special division of the police department? Since it involves criminal activity, I've never been too clear on that."

"That's an easy assumption, but no. It's part of the fire department, at least in our city. The arson investigators are certified by the state and work under the fire marshall in the Fire Prevention unit."

Shea nodded. "I've heard their cases will sometimes overlap with one Shane or his detectives have open, I just wasn't sure where they were housed. They work together closely when necessary. Do you think that's something you would enjoy?"

Suddenly his future seemed rife with possibilities. "I know so. It gives me a ton to consider. The thing is, I don't have a clue what it takes to get into Arson, whether I have to be a certified peace officer or what. I know firefighters sometimes make the move, but it means applying for a whole new job."

"I'm not sure, either, but if you want I can ask Shane," she offered.

"That would be great. Thank you, sweetheart."

"My pleasure."

The word *pleasure* uttered from those sultry lips did things to his groin. Naughty things that took his mind completely away from sad memories and lost opportunities. Now his focus was fixed solely on the woman who made his world a brighter place just by being there, caring about him.

He wanted to hold her close and not stop with a kiss. Peel her down to the skin and learn what made her tick.

What made her scream.

"Why are you staring at me like that?"

"Like what?" His tone was the epitome of innocence.

"Like you're a cheetah and I'm an antelope—oh, never mind," she said, blushing.

"Roowrrr." He bared his teeth, doing his best cheetah impression.

She giggled and they settled in to finish their meal. After talking with her, the rest of his burger went down much easier. She made him feel damned good, warmed a place inside him that had been cold for years.

When they were done, Tommy paid the check and they left. He helped her into the truck and for a few seconds, considered driving them around for a while. Maybe he'd take her out to the land Julian purchased, show her where his friend and Grace planned to build their dream house.

Something told him that might be pushing things a little, appear as though he was dropping hints or something. Best to not wear out his welcome, leave her looking forward to this Sunday.

At her door, he cupped her sweet face and gave her the lightest of kisses. Allowed their bodies to brush just enough to electrify.

Since today was a day for truths, he decided to impart one more.

"Shea, I want you to know . . . I've never wanted to wait before, with any woman." He brushed her lips in a soft kiss. "I never cared, before you."

Grandpa had been acting strange.

Not that anybody but Will would notice, the change in the man was so subtle. Hell, he might be imagining the sideways glances, the frowns of puzzlement, the way the old man lingered around Will more than usual. Stayed up late, rose early. Might be.

But he doubted it.

Grandpa had that *look* he got whenever he told stories of his glory days in the service. Only he wasn't telling any lately, a worrisome detail in itself.

Will sighed and booted up his computer. As the machine blurped and gyrated, he peered over his shoulder to where Grandpa sat in his favorite chair, remote in one hand, watching *Wheel of Fortune*. Will suppressed a snort.

How ironic. The old man could soak up that crap all he wanted, but Will had the real fortune at his fingertips. Or a fine fucking start on one, anyhow.

Blood money. The words curled around his throat and he shook them off.

Satisfied his grandfather wasn't paying attention, Will opened the Internet and chose his bank's Web site from his favorites. He started to log in, but couldn't remember his damned password. These days, a person had to remember a zillion numbers, log-in names, and passwords to get by. Annoyed, he dug through his top desk drawer until he found the bank envelope he'd written the information on. There.

He laid the envelope on the desk and logged in, then chose his savings account, unconcerned that Grandpa might see the screen from across the room. The old man couldn't spot a fly at two paces anymore. What did concern him was the idea of a double cross, always a hidden threat. If the deposit hadn't been made—

"Yes." Like clockwork, as usual.

Will stared at his balance, more money than he'd ever hoped to see in his sorry, godforsaken life. Six figures. At less than a quarter mil, it wouldn't last long in the face of Grandpa's eventual need for nursing home care and the astronomical cost of his own meds. But it was a good beginning.

Not wise to linger. He moved a bit to his checking account to cover bills, then closed the account. With nothing else to do, he distracted himself for a while with a few rounds of Minesweeper.

He didn't know how long he'd been playing when his cell phone rang, vibrating on the coffee table.

"Better get that, Will," Grandpa said, voice gruff. "Some pecker has been calling fifteen goddamned times a day, and he's starting to get on my nerves."

Alarm kicked him out of his chair, and he moved toward the offending instrument. "How do you know it's a guy?"

Grandpa shot him an indecipherable look. "Figure of speech."

"Oh." Grabbing the phone, he flipped it open and strode for his bedroom. "Hello?"

"Baby's got a new pair of shoes," the man said by way of greeting.

"I saw."

"Where's my gratitude, Willie-boy? Especially since you fucked up by making the cause of the fire obvious."

He hated that nickname with its snide double entendre, the way this asshole said it. "That will take care of itself. It will appear random and they can't prove differently."

"Lucky for you."

Even though I'm doing all the work, prick.

From down the hall, he thought he heard a creak of a floorboard, the old man moving around.

"Was there something else you wanted?" he bit off.

"The next job. I want it done soon."

"For double my fee. That one's too dangerous."

"Are you high? I'll give you an increase of twenty large."

Give? Fucker. "Seventy-five."

"Thirty."

"Sixty."

"Don't piss me off, Willie-boy. I know how bad you need that money for your precious medicine. Getting sick would be a bitch, huh? Who'd take care of dear old gramps?"

Oh, God.

"Fifty, or you can hire someone else." He almost broke into a sweat over the bluff, and the long silence that followed.

The man laughed, a nasty sound. "You keep telling yourself that. I doubt you'd want to find out exactly what becoming unemployed would entail. But you've got balls, Cinderfella, and I can admire that. As long as the bossman approves, fifty more on top of the regular for the next job and the one after. That last one's going to be the biggest of them all."

Something in the man's tone made him shiver. "I fail to see how."

"You'll get the details when you need them. For now, just concentrate on doing the job."

Before he could ask another question, the line went dead. Pompous fuckers.

But they were the fuckers with the money.

He laid the phone on the nightstand and was about to go get a shower, when suddenly he straightened. "Oh, shit."

His log-in and password. God, he'd left the envelope sitting out on the desk, in plain view. Trying not to look panicked, he strode back down the hall to the living room—and breathed a deep sigh of relief.

Grandpa's chin was on his chest, eyes closed, the remote now dangling from his hand. Sound asleep.

"Thank Jesus."

Quietly, he tiptoed to the desk and hid the envelope, far in the back of the drawer. Out of sight, out of mind. Better yet, after Grandpa went to bed, he'd move the paper some-where safe.

He couldn't afford to make a mistake like that ever again.

Joseph listened to his grandson move about the room, heard the boy's soft exclamation. The desk drawer opened and closed, papers moved, something placed inside. Then the drawer slid closed again, the sound furtive.

When Will moved out of the room again, Joseph cracked an eye open, turned his head, and peered at the desk. His eyesight might be failing along with everything else, but he could see the white envelope was gone. Hidden from view, the log-in and password to his bank account was something Will obviously hadn't wanted him to see.

"Too late, my boy," he murmured. "When the war was on, I memorized more confidential data than there are stars in the sky. I've forgotten more shit than you'll ever know."

Tomorrow, Will would leave for work.

And Joseph might just find a clue as to what the holy hell was going on around here.

Tommy stretched out on the sofa in the station's TV room, feet on the coffee table. Four more days until his dinner date with Shea, and it seemed like an eternity. He'd give her a call later, get his fix to hold him over.

"Hey, *amigo*. Isn't it your turn to clean the bathrooms?" Julian strolled in and flopped down on the other end of the sofa.

"Hell, yeah," he grumbled. "I'll do it later."

"Just sayin', is all. Man, what are you *watching*?"

Tommy grinned. "*Young and the Restless*."

"Holy Christ, my *madre* stays glued to that crap." His friend made a face like he'd bitten into a lemon. "How old is that *chica* who's been on there forever, like a hundred and forty?"

"Yes, but it only equals twenty-five in soap years."

"Except for the characters' kids. The ones who were born last year are dating this year."

"For a dude with an attitude, you sure know a lot about soaps."

"Fuck you, man. Change the channel before my eyes start bleeding."

"You wish, and okay." He smirked at Julian, then switched the channel to CNN. "Better?"

"Much, thanks. Now I can be depressed on a reality-based level."

Tommy rolled his eyes. "So, other than interrupting my rare moment of peace here, what's up with you? How are the plans for the house coming?"

"Slow, but sure. Grace wanted us to design the house ourselves so it would be unique. Being the macho man of the house, I said 'no' because of the cost and how much longer it's going to take."

"Let me guess—you got your balls handed to you."

"Sautéed and served on a platter. Limped away whimpering *yes, ma'am* just so I could live another day."

Tommy chuckled at the picture of how his friend's mandate went over with Grace. "I could've told you how that argument was going to end. My parents have been happy together for thirty years because my dad figured out the secret early on—just do what the hell she says and give her flowers on her birthday, your anniversary, and Valentine's Day."

"Heard that. Thank God I have a quick learning curve."

Where his friend was concerned, this was true in more ways than one. Hard to believe this was the same man who, a few weeks ago, kept everyone at arm's length with his cocky attitude.

"Oh, I've got good news," Julian said, breaking into his thoughts.

"Grace is pregnant?"

"No way. I'm not letting her drink the water around here just yet." His tone and stupid grin told Tommy he was joking. "Seriously, though, it's almost as good. My baby brother, Tonio, is moving to Sugarland!"

"Hey, that's cool," he said, ignoring the pang in his heart. Damned if he could begrudge a man for being happy about his brother coming to town. "He's a cop, right?"

"Narcotics officer," he said proudly. "He gave the San Antonio PD notice, and I'm helping him hunt for an apartment. He'll be here in about six weeks."

"That's great. I'm happy for you. How's your mom taking it?"

"Hard. But she's got our four sisters to help her through the transition."

"Maybe you and your brother can talk her into moving here, too."

"Nah, she'd never leave San Antonio. It's her home. But I'm sure she'll visit when she can, especially after Grace and I get the house built. There will be plenty of room for the family."

"Sounds like everything's coming up roses for you these days. I'm glad."

Julian linked his fingers across his flat stomach and fixed Tommy with his dark gaze. "What about you? Roses or thorns?"

"A little of both. I apologized to Shea, took her for a burger. We had a great talk and things are looking up."

"Ah! You forgot to put saying you're sorry on your female to-do list. Very important. So are you guys dating, or what? Or just getting some on the side?"

Anger, hot and swift, rushed to the surface as he slid his

feet off the coffee table. "It's not like that with Shea, so watch your mouth. Unless you'd like your spine removed with my bare hands—"

"Whoa, easy, buddy." Julian gripped his shoulder. "I was totally kidding. It's like that, is it?"

Tommy blew out a breath, and calmed somewhat. "Sorry, I guess I'm touchy where she's concerned."

"Gee, ya think?" At his scowl, Julian held up a hand. "I hear you. I'm the same about Grace."

"Didn't mean to snarl. Anyway, I'm not sure exactly what we're doing yet, but I don't want to mess this up. When we're together we've got this incredible chemistry, but it's taken forever to make headway with her."

"I hear you on that, too," Julian agreed. "Remember the hell Grace put me through, chasing her until I almost gave up?"

"Yeah, but this is different."

"How so?"

"She's gun-shy, and it's more than being focused on her career. She wants me, but something is holding her back. She's hinted at something bad in her past, but won't confide in me."

"So her relationship, or whatever, with Prescott . . ." He let the sentence hang, like a question.

"In my opinion? It was a duck-and-cover maneuver on her part, though I believe it was unconscious at first. A way to avoid the real thing."

"Wow, Dr. Freud."

"I think it's Dr. Ruth."

"Whatever. As long as she gets rid of Malibu Ken."

"You don't care for him, either?" Not caring for him was an understatement on Tommy's part.

"Not when he's within fifty yards of my girl, I don't."

"And his policy sucks."

"But we've got kick-ass flowers in the medians around town."

"Oh, absolutely. He's taming Sugarland, one pansy at a time," Tommy said in a mock announcer's voice.

They kept straight faces for about two seconds before busting out laughing.

The man could open a damned arboretum as long as he steered clear of Shea.

And if the fool wanted trouble?

He'd get it, Skyler style.

8

Forrest Prescott glared at the phone, condemning the man on the other end to the deepest bowels of hell.

Not that it helped, because the phone continued to ring. And would, until he answered. He picked up the handset and snapped a greeting.

"Why the hell are you calling me here? What do you want?"

"Aw, now, that's no way to speak to the buddy who put you in office," the familiar voice drawled. "Having a bad day?"

"My credentials put me here, and my day was fine until you phoned. Don't you have anything better to do than to harass your contacts?"

"Employees," the man corrected, sounding smug. "And as a matter of fact, I do—make money. I'm thinking my coffers are a tad shy of what they should be, given the initial payouts. Can you shed any light on the situation for me, Prescott?"

Oh, fuck. What had tipped him off? He'd been meticulous about covering his tracks to the point of paranoia.

He'd have to bluff his way through the danger zone.

"You have the paperwork. The figures match."

"Papers can be faked."

Sweat trickled down his temple. *Do not show fear, or you're meat for the morgue.* "I don't have to tell you the economy is in the crapper," he said coldly. "Values are down, investments worth a fraction of what they were when accumulated just a couple of years ago. Be patient and you'll have the capital you need."

"Don't pat me on the head, you arrogant little cocksucker," his nemesis snarled. "If I wanted to make a bad investment I'd open a whorehouse in Utah. Get the next assignment rolling so we can all enjoy the benefits. And, Prescott?"

"What?"

"I find out you're fucking me over, so to speak, you'd better shell out for the best plastic surgery and fake ID money can buy. Hide in the darkest corner of the earth, and pray I don't find you. Because when I do, I'll feed your dick to you in pieces. Bank on it."

The bastard hung up and Forrest did the same, hand shaking. If his contact discovered proof of his skimming, the man would kill him without a second of remorse. Might anyway, when he no longer required his assistance to achieve his goals in Sugarland.

Forrest considered making another call, for about two seconds. No, their contact no doubt had this and other lines tapped. They'd have to be extremely careful.

His thoughts turned to Shea and his failure on that front thus far.

He was infuriated that his plans were being disrupted by a pretty boy barely old enough to shave. If he couldn't win Shea over soon, the kid would have to be removed. A distasteful, but necessary, measure.

One way or another, Forrest would take what belonged to him.

Shea checked her appearance in the bathroom mirror for the third time. Hair up or down? Unruly as it was, subduing the curly mass into a ponytail was seldom worth the battle. Down, then.

She studied her figure critically, eyeing the trim black shorts and red top. She wasn't fat, but she'd never had a cheerleader's body. In her opinion, she was an average-looking woman with an average build, nothing special. Not like Tommy, who was even more stunning than the jock she'd been enamored of all those years ago.

Much to her sorrow.

An attack of nerves was forestalled by a knock on the door. "Oh, boy. Come on, girl, it's Tommy, not the Big Bad Wolf."

Reaching for calm, she headed for the door as the knock came again. Giddy excitement bubbled in her veins like champagne, but out of habit, she still peered through the peephole in the door to make certain it was Tommy.

"Oh, no." The bubbles popped. Unlocking the door, she opened it, already contemplating how to get rid of him. "Forrest, what are you doing here?"

"Bringing the loveliest woman in Sugarland *these*," he said, thrusting an arrangement of flowers at her.

A huge vase of white gladiolas that would look perfect spread across a casket.

"My, they're . . . impressive! Come in," she said, taking the heavy vase and stepping aside. Crap, she had to get him out of here before Tommy arrived!

"I thought you might like them." Forrest closed the door behind him and smiled as she placed them on the coffee table. "You look very pretty. In fact, it would be a shame to allow you to languish here all evening, looking so fine and nowhere to go. Why don't we go grab some dinner?"

"Well, actually—"

"Nothing fancy, just a steak or maybe some seafood."

"I have to work tomorrow." She could've slapped herself. That was so weak. *Just tell him!*

Of course, he pounced on the poor argument. "We both have to eat, so why not together? As friends. No expectations, I promise."

"Forrest, that's very sweet of you, but the truth is—"

And that's when the second knock sounded.

Dammit! "Excuse me." Giving the man a sheepish smile, she steeled herself, not bothering to look first, and opened the door.

"Hey, beautiful!" Tommy stood on the threshold, clutching a modest bouquet of daisies in one hand and a sack of groceries in the other. "I picked these for you. They're from my mom's garden."

He couldn't have sounded more proud if he'd grown them himself. Shea faltered, and realized she was staring. "Thank you, they're absolutely perfect. Come in."

"You're welcome." He beamed at her and strode inside. But when he came face-to-face with Forrest, his smile froze. His attention strayed from the other man to the massive spray of gladiolas and back again.

Can anyone say *awkward*?

"Um, Forrest dropped by to say hello. Isn't that nice? Say, I don't think you guys have officially met." *Shoot me now.* "Forrest, this is Tommy Skyler. He's a firefighter. Tommy, this is Forrest Prescott, Sugarland's city manager."

"I know who he is." Tommy gave the man a nod. Though his tone was neutral, the shards of ice in his eyes made it perfectly clear how he felt about the other man's presence. "Good to meet you, Mr. Prescott."

"Same here, and you can call me Forrest," he said genially. Once Tommy set the groceries on the kitchen counter and gave the daisies to Shea, Forrest offered Tommy a handshake. "It's always great to meet some of our city's finest young men outside the rigors of the job. Sugarland appreciates all you do, believe me."

Tommy clasped his hand briefly, then nodded. "Yeah? Then how about voting the fire department a raise?"

Forrest stared at him a beat before giving a good-natured chuckle. "If only it was so easy. Grant the fire department a raise and the police department would demand one, too, followed by every city employee down to the garbage collectors. Where would these funds come from?"

"The flower budget."

Forrest blinked at him. Tommy shot the man a charming grin, but crossed his arms over his chest and widened his stance in a clear challenge. If he was spoiling for a heated debate, Forrest didn't bite, to Shea's immense relief.

Letting the issue drop, Forrest gestured toward the grocery bag in the kitchen. "It seems I'm interrupting. Shea, dear, why didn't you just tell me you were expecting company? I would have left right away."

"Well, I tried, but I didn't have time," she said. Embarrassment was rapidly becoming annoyance. "I wasn't trying to be dishonest."

"Oh, of course not! I'd never imply you were." He seemed sincere. "On that note, I'd better go before I wear out my welcome."

As he headed for the door, she heard Tommy mutter, "Too late."

She hurried to see the older man out—mostly to make sure he was gone. He turned to give her a hug that lasted a few seconds longer than it should, and she firmly pushed out of his embrace. "Have a nice week."

She hoped he got the message. Whether he did or not, she couldn't tell.

"You too, honey. I'll call you this week. Skyler, nice to meet you."

"Highlight of my day, Forrest," Tommy called, rustling through the grocery bag.

Shea practically shoved the poor man out. "Talk to you later!"

"You bet." He gave her a quick peck on the cheek and an indecipherable look before turning and walking away. After locking up, she heaved a sigh and padded into the kitchen. Tommy was busy removing items from the bag for their dinner, acting as though nothing unusual had happened.

"I hope you like what I brought. I was going to go healthy, but then I thought that sounded boring and—"

"Tommy."

"—really, who the hell cares if it's all fancy, right?"

"Tommy." Moving to his side, she put an arm around his waist and laid her cheek on his shoulder. "I didn't invite him here."

Some of the tension left his body. "I know."

"I really was trying to tell him I had plans before you showed up."

"I know that, too."

"And I love the daisies," she said, holding them up with her free hand. "They're very pretty."

"I'm glad you like them. They're not expensive like *those*," he muttered, nodding toward the living room.

"You know why I like yours best? They're much more thoughtful, because they came from your mother's garden and you picked them." Standing up on tiptoe, she kissed his cheek. "Know why else?"

"Why?" He turned, put his hands around her waist and drew her close, careful not to crush the blooms between them.

"Yours don't look like they were stolen from a funeral home."

She liked his throaty laugh, seeing him finally relax. She liked his kiss even more when he lowered his head and took her mouth as though he had a perfect right to do so. One palm strayed to his chest and rested there, feeling the rapid tempo of his heart under hard muscles.

He drew away first and she almost whimpered.

"Why don't we get dinner going, then cuddle on the couch?" he suggested with a wink. "I brought a DVD if you're interested."

"Hmm. Food, a movie, cuddling, and kisses . . . is this some sinister plot to win me over?"

"Of course it is! What kind of stupid man do you take me for?" Leaning over, he pressed against her and whispered, "My mom even helped me with the recipe."

"Ooh, now I know you're evil, pulling out the 'mom' card!"

"It was either enlist her help to woo you, or risk giving you food poisoning, cutie." His knuckles brushed down one cheek. "So I took one for the team and got my mom all excited because I like someone enough to actually try to cook for her."

His warmth and the spicy scent of his cologne were creating lots of tingly places. All over. "So you don't cook for your dates often?"

"Never. You're my guinea pig."

"I—I'm impressed."

"Don't be just yet. I brought Tums."

She giggled and poked his flat belly to find it tight as a drum. Nice. "It can't be that bad, especially since your mom lent a hand."

"We'll see. At least the guys at the station don't complain much anymore when it's my turn in the kitchen."

Shea took a glass vase from underneath the sink, put the flowers in water, and placed the vase on her dining table. Tommy busied himself removing the rest of the stuff from the bag, including a bottle of Chardonnay, already chilled.

She glanced at the label and was pleasantly surprised at his choice.

"Wow, this is really good wine. You can't even buy Ledson in stores."

"I can't take credit. Dad orders it online from the winery and gave one to me before I came over. Should we open it?"

"Definitely. Wine this fabulous was made to be enjoyed," she said, smiling at him. "I'll get the opener and a couple of glasses."

"Thanks, I forgot about bringing an opener. Um, I also forgot a rectangular dish for the casserole. Do you have one?"

"You're off the hook on both counts. Got it covered."

After fetching two wineglasses from the cupboard, she grabbed the electric wine-bottle opener from its charger. In a couple of seconds, she had the cork free and poured them both a glass.

He waved a hand at the opener as she put it back. "That's a nifty gadget. Even my folks don't have one of those."

"I love mine. Now you know what to get them for their anniversary or Christmas. So, what are you making?" Opening a nearby cabinet, she found the dish he needed.

"I hope you like Mexican chicken casserole," he said, sounded unsure. Perhaps a little nervous. "It's shredded chicken, green chilies, onions, tomatoes, and two kinds of soup. I already made the filling and brought it in that plastic container; then I layer it with corn tortillas and cheese."

Her stomach growled in approval. "That sounds wonderful! What can I do to help?"

"Turn on the oven to three fifty, then sip your wine, relax, and talk to me."

"I can do that." She handed him the dish and sipped her wine, watching him go to work.

Holy cow, it was glorious to have a man wait on her for a change. To do something special that required some effort. Anyone could make a reservation at a restaurant, but this? How wonderful was it that he'd gone to his parents, accepted his mother's assistance with their meal, picked flowers, and brought a gift from his dad?

And he'd never gone to all this trouble for another woman.

She'd have to be dead not to notice how sexy he was, plus how heroic in doing his job, but she'd never once realized Thomas Wayne Skyler was a *good* man, down to his soul.

The kind who'd never harm a woman he'd done all of these things for tonight, or any woman.

"Shea? Are you all right?"

"What? Oh! Yes, I'm great."

He'd paused, frowning, a tortilla in hand. "Are you sure?"

"Positive. I was just thinking this is really nice. Nobody's ever done this for me before. The only constant man in my life has been Shane, and if either of us cooks it's usually me. If he does the inviting, we go out."

The furrow on his brow smoothed and he resumed his task, apparently pleased. "Then it's a good thing I came along, isn't it? Every lady should be properly spoiled. Dad says it's the secret to a happy life."

"Your dad is a wise man," she said in a mock-serious tone, then grinned. "I adore him already. And his son is pretty cool, too."

"Thanks." Tommy ducked his head and kept working, but she could see the smile curving his lips.

Shea perched on a bar stool and watched, admiring the play of his muscles under the black T-shirt, his blond hair shining under the lights. And his tight ass in those jeans was a sight to make a girl cry. You could bounce a quarter off those buns.

Just as he got finished, the oven beeped to signal it was hot, and he slid in the dish. "Okay, thirty minutes. How about we take the chips and salsa into the living room—unless you don't like having food in there?"

"Are you kidding? What's a good movie without munchies?"

"Good deal."

He grabbed the stuff, including a DVD case, and followed her into the living room, eyeing the flowers Forrest brought. She moved the heavy vase to the farthest end table practically hidden in a corner, then got the player ready and squinted at the case.

"What did you bring?"

"This romantic comedy with Sandra Bullock that came out last year. It's supposed to be funny. Plus, she's really hot." He waggled his brows.

"And here I thought you were a romantic, and you're actually lusting after another woman," she teased, taking the disk from him.

"Busted. But if it's any consolation, the guy who plays her love interest isn't too bad. Not that *I'd* know, but Mom has a crush on him."

She put in the movie and got it started. When she turned, Tommy was sprawled on her couch. He lifted an arm in an invitation she was powerless to refuse. She sat next to him and he put the arm around her, snuggled her close. She burrowed in, resting her head on his chest, listening to the steady thump of his heart. Her palm skimmed across his stomach and snaked around his waist.

He was solid. So right. She forgot all about the munchies and reveled in being with him like this, hardly aware of the movie or the delicious aroma from the kitchen, until the timer dinged on the oven. He hadn't seemed to want to move, either, which suited her just fine.

"Guess I'd better check on dinner," he said, stretching. "You stay right here."

"I need to show you where I keep the plates and silverware."

"Nope, stay put and I'll find it."

"No arguments from me. I think I like being queen for a night." She sat up, disentangling herself from him.

"More than one night if I get my way." He shot her a smoldering look as he rose and headed to the kitchen.

But not before she caught a gander at the bulge in his jeans. Proof that he wasn't the only one affected by them being wrapped around each other.

She heard the oven open and close, utensils rattling. He wasn't gone long, and he returned carrying two plates piled with the steaming dish. The mouthwatering sight of the food made her temporarily put on hold her hunger for the equally delicious man serving it.

He set the plates and forks on the coffee table, opened the jar of salsa, and gave her a nervous smile. "Ladies first."

She'd heard the jokes about his cooking and knew that the great aroma didn't mean it tasted okay. No matter what, she'd eat the meal he'd prepared. The last thing she'd do was hurt his feelings.

"Okay, here goes." She lifted a forkful and took a bite. "Oh, Tommy, this is really good!"

He blinked at her. "You think so? Really?"

"I mean it, this is wonderful," she said honestly. "You cook like this often and you'll make me fat."

"Awesome! I mean not that you'd get fat, because you won't, but because I did it," he said, obviously proud of himself. "My mom didn't help me that much and I managed to make something you like."

"You'd better believe I do. And now that I know how handy you are in the kitchen, look out." Leaning over, she kissed his cheek. "I'll have you chained in there as my slave labor."

"Chain me anywhere you want, baby."

She flushed at the suggestion in his tone and looked away, concentrating on her casserole. The movie was lost on her by now, but she didn't mind. She spent her time savoring dinner and reveling in his nearness, amazed that she could be alone in her apartment with any man for an extended period of time without the old sense of discomfort. Tension. Sometimes fear.

But never with Tommy. Not in the physical way, at least, because she knew he'd never hurt her. No, her struggle was more with herself these days. Learning to trust her own judgment again wasn't easy.

Shea cleaned her plate and Tommy went for seconds. When he was finished, he took the remains of dinner and put the dishes in the sink.

"I'll clean this up later," he said.

"I'll help you. Let's not worry about it for now. I'm feeling lazy."

He sat beside her and reached out, cupping her chin. "How lazy?"

His voice, smoky with promise, set her blood on fire. She wanted him so much, was tired of denying herself real pleasure with a man she burned to have in her bed.

Dare she take the ultimate risk?

"Only lazy when it comes to cleaning the kitchen, which is a job I hate. Being with you is a different story," she said softly, running the pads of her fingers over his sensual mouth.

He closed his eyes as though drinking in her touch. "How so?"

"Remember when you said you've never cared enough to wait?"

"How could I forget?"

"Well, I've never cared enough to spend all day dreaming about what it would be like to just let go," she whispered, nuzzling his neck. His groan answered her question before she asked. "Do you want me? Because I've never wanted anyone more."

"Oh, God. Tell me I haven't died and gone to heaven."

9

Tommy leaned into her, cupping the back of her head, his mouth hot. Demanding. Shea arched into him and skimmed her hands over his shoulders, nipples hardening against his wide chest through the fabric of her blouse.

Oh. Oh, my.

Stolen kisses were no longer enough. Not with this man. She wanted everything he was willing to give. Truth be told, she always had, no matter how much learning to trust again terrified her.

He pulled back, searching her face. Desire laced his deep, husky voice. "Are you sure?"

She traced a finger along his lower lip. "Oh, *yeah*."

Giving her a lopsided smile, he stood, scooping her into his arms in one smooth motion. She laughed, reached up to stroke his face, happiness blooming in her heart and spreading to her toes. Other places, too.

In her bedroom, he placed her gently on her bed, then straightened. His pale blue gaze never leaving hers, he shed his shirt and slid his jeans off along with his boxer briefs, kicking them away. Shea drank in the sight of his naked body like a woman dying of thirst. Clothed, he was the sexiest man she'd ever seen. Wearing nothing except a grin, the man was a pagan god.

Lord, she'd waited forever to see him. All of him. She

studied his startling crystal eyes set in the planes of a handsome, angular face, thick blond hair framing it and brushing his neck. Probably a bit longer than the fire department would like, but she loved it and wouldn't change a thing.

She let her gaze drift leisurely to his broad shoulders and strong arms. He wasn't ripped, but perfectly formed of lean muscle and raw bone. Graceful as a jungle cat. A very light sprinkling of hair, a shade darker than on his head, covered his chest, trailing downward in a vee past flat, hard male nipples.

Finally, she allowed her attention to roam to his impressive erection, savoring the sight. Heat flamed low in her belly, between her legs, as she stared at his engorged cock jutting proudly from a nest of dark blond curls. The feeling was so miraculous she could have cried for joy, frigid as her body had been during her few encounters in the years since—

No. No place for sadness here. Only goodness.

"Like what you see?" His smile told her he knew the answer.

"I want to touch you."

His eyes went dark, feral. "You're overdressed, baby. All's fair."

Hands shaking, Shea pulled her tank top over her head and pitched it to the floor. What would he think of her body? Would he be pleased? Those were frightening questions she hadn't considered in ten years, because she hadn't given a damn what her lovers thought. How had she survived the utter coldness inside?

Next went her bra, but as she reached for the button of her shorts, he laid a hand on her arm.

"Oh, no, you don't. My turn." He climbed onto the bed to sit next to her. He undid her shorts, slid them slowly past her hips, down her legs, and off. "God, you're beautiful."

Shea's face heated, though the compliment pleased her to no end. "I don't think I'll ever get used to you saying that."

He stroked her belly, making her quiver. "But you *will* get used to it, I promise."

"You're pretty darned gorgeous yourself."

Fascinated, Shea reached out to touch the broad head of his cock, swirling it with one finger as a drop of precum beaded the tip. Encouraged by his sharp intake of breath, she became bolder in her exploration, wrapping her hand around the base.

"Yes." He leaned back and closed his eyes, spread his long legs to encourage her journey.

She pumped him slowly, enjoying the texture of silky, baby-smooth skin over steel. Next, she moved her hand to cradle his testicles, familiarizing herself with the feel of his heavy sex. Marveling that such a powerful man could be reduced to jelly with a caress.

"Sweetheart," he gasped, removing her hand. "I'm not going to last."

"So don't."

"I want this to be good for you, baby." He stroked her cheek, some unfathomable emotion etched on his face.

"It will be. Love me, Tommy."

He lowered her onto the pillows and stretched his big body over hers, settling between her legs. His erection pulsed against her belly as he captured her lips in a sizzling kiss, tongue licking into the seam of her mouth. Teasing, tasting.

He broke the kiss, moved lower, repeating his attentions on her breasts. "Perfect. So perfect . . ."

His teeth grazed one nipple, tongue doing delightful things to the hardened little pebble. Sending wonderful shocks to every nerve ending. When he suckled the other nipple, she came undone, pulling at his shoulders.

"Tommy! I need you inside me."

"Patience, baby."

When he moved off the bed, she frowned in puzzlement. Bending, he picked up his shorts, fished in the pocket, and removed a condom. Even before coming over this afternoon, he'd considered her protection. Instead of being put off by the idea that he might've believed he was going to "get lucky," she was touched. This wasn't just any guy.

This was the man she was quickly falling for, head over heels.

He returned to the bed, laid the square packet aside, pushed her legs apart, and knelt between them, devouring the sight of her spread before him. Instead of feeling scared, she felt cherished. Liberated. He slid a hand between her thighs, fingers brushing the dark curls there. Carefully, he parted the lips of her sex and pushed one finger inside her, stroking in and out, smearing the dewy wetness to prepare her. Lengthening the strokes, he rubbed her clit, setting her body ablaze.

Too long since she'd felt so alive.

"Now, please!"

"Tell me if I do anything you don't like, and I'll stop. Okay?"

The heartfelt words melted the last of her trepidation, if there had been any left. "Don't worry. I will. But I doubt that'll happen."

Quickly, he tore open the package with his teeth and sheathed his erection. Covering her body with his, he guided the head to her opening and began to push inside. The stretch burned a little and she must've made some involuntary sound because he froze, expression worried.

"Am I hurting you? I'll stop—"

"Don't you dare! I'm . . . it's just been so long."

His face relaxed. "I'll go easy, angel."

He did, pushing deeper by inches, letting her adjust to him. His concern brought a rush of tears to her eyes. The slight discomfort became a flame burning brighter and pleasure unfurled. A sense of freedom and completion she'd never known with any other man. She wrapped her arms around him, skimming her hands over the muscles in his back as he seated himself as fully as possible.

"Feel me?" he whispered into her hair.

"Yes." She raised her hips, urging him on.

He began to move, long, tantalizing strokes. "You're mine, honey."

"Oh, Tommy, yes!"

He held her against his chest, made sweet, beautiful love to her. Sheltered her in the safety of his arms, his body covering her like a warm blanket. She'd come home. This wasn't just sex with a gorgeous man, but she hesitated to say the words.

His tempo quickened, his thrusts filling her harder. Deeper. Faster. But even as he drove into her, taking them to the edge, he was careful not to hurt her, protecting her while moving with powerful strokes. Hurtling them higher, higher—

His release erupted, his big frame shaking. She followed, the orgasm shattering her control, the waves pounding her senses. He shuddered again and again, until he lowered his forehead to hers, spent and breathing hard.

She lay unmoving, loving his weight on top of her, his musky male scent teasing her nose—the scent of them mingled together, so right.

Shea wanted to say the words. Longed to hear them returned. She came very, very close to blurting the truth, but years of caution and a healthy dose of reality held her back. Now wasn't the time, when this change in the relationship was so new.

Even though it was a damned fine change.

Thinking of his manly growl a few moments ago made her smile. *You're mine.*

One-hundred-percent pure, satisfied man. Not exactly a declaration of undying love, but her heart thrilled at the memory. Those words had come from the depths of his soul, and she cherished them.

For now, that would have to be enough.

"Stay with me," she said, eyes closing.

"I wouldn't want to be anywhere else. Sleep, baby."

As Tommy rolled to his back and settled her head on his chest, she did.

Bright and early Monday morning, Joseph awoke to the telltale noise of his grandson moving about in the kitchen.

About time. Since the other night, the boy had been as jumpy as a long-tailed cat in a room full of rocking chairs. Hadn't left the house but once, and only for a run to the grocery store.

Not enough time for Joseph to take a look-see at what Will might be up to. It was like the boy was afraid to let his old grandpa out of his sight, afraid he might've seen something important the other night. Which he had.

Will's cell phone had been conspicuously absent as well, and Joseph cursed himself for mentioning how often it rang. He'd like to take another look at the received calls, jot down the numbers.

"What a paranoid old bastard you are," he muttered, sitting up on the side of the bed. "You ought to be ashamed of yourself, spying on that boy."

Except he wasn't. He'd been on this earth a helluva long time and his instincts hadn't failed him yet. There was a fox in the henhouse someplace, and he'd damn well smoke it out whether Will wanted him to or not.

Speaking of smoke, he smelled something good.

Pushing out of bed with a pained grunt, he scratched his balls and reached for his pants on the end of the bed. He pulled them on and shuffled out of his room without bothering to check himself in the mirror. Wasn't much on his shriveled frame worth looking at anyhow.

In the kitchen, Will stood at the stove, flipping bacon, dressed for the day in a pair of worn jeans and a button-up shirt. Joseph paused, struck as always by what a handsome young man his grandson had sprouted into. Despite being a smidge on the thin side, Will had inherited the tall, solid frame of Joseph's ancestors. He had a square face and strong jaw minus the bulbous nose of the Hensley men, thank God, and a wealth of dark brown hair that drove the women wild.

Too bad the boy couldn't care less.

"Smells good," Joseph said by way of greeting. "Got enough there for me?"

Will turned, flashing him a wan smile. "Always. Toast?"

"And apple butter." He sat at the table, bones creaking, and wondered when the hell he'd gotten old. The decades had a way of sneaking up on a man.

"You're too predictable, old man," Will said with undisguised affection.

"Huh. When you get as old as me, you'll have earned the right to be predictable. Surprises don't necessarily agree with a body that's been around as long as mine." He sent his grandson a meaningful look. "Know what I mean?"

Will faltered under his gaze. "I . . . sure, Grandpa. I'll get your coffee."

The younger man opened a cabinet and removed a mug. As he poured the brew, his hand shook, splashing some onto the counter. He replaced the pot on the burner, mopped up the spill with a dishrag, and brought the mug over, setting it in front of Joseph.

"Here you go."

"Thank you, boy." He blew on the surface, took a sip. "Good and strong, like always."

"You're welcome."

Will went back to tending breakfast, fishing the bacon from the skillet and starting the toast. He put the bacon and apple butter on the table, then fetched the plates and forks, setting the table. Finally, he sat down opposite Joseph, swiping his forehead with a sigh.

"No eggs for yourself?" Joseph liked eggs, but his stomach didn't. No reason why Will shouldn't enjoy them, though.

"Not today. You want a ride down to the senior center when I leave? I can pick you up at lunch and bring you home."

Joseph put a couple of slices of bacon on his plate "No, thanks. I think I'll just hang around here and watch TV. Been meanin' to get to that birdhouse I'm making for Miss Margaret, too. Might take you up on the offer tomorrow."

He hated lying, even for a good reason.

"Whatever you want. If you need me, call me on my cell phone." Will's mouth tightened and he dug in to the bacon. "Remembered it this morning, so it won't bother you."

"Good to know." Son of a bitch.

They finished their breakfast in uneasy silence. Secrets simmering along underneath the surface of politeness tended to be cancerous. Especially with his grandson sitting over there sweating, wondering what Grandpa knew. Joseph snorted, almost tempted to lay the cards on the table. He could *tell* Will what he knew, call him out. The boy might get flustered enough to spill what was going on . . . but most likely he'd die before admitting to a thing.

He was a lot like his grandpa in that regard.

In the end, Joseph simply bided his time while Will cleaned his plate. The boy cleared the table and put their dishes in the dishwasher, then grabbed his keys.

"Need anything before I go, Grandpa?"

"No, Will. You go on ahead and be the big-city building inspector while I lay here like an old rug." He regretted his teasing when Will's expression crumpled, filled with dismay. "Shit on a shingle, I'm kidding, boy. I put in my time, worked my ass off for over fifty years, so I'm due for some rest, don't ya think?"

Will laughed, the sound strained. "Damn, don't do that to me. I hate leaving you here alone all day; you know that."

"I'm far from helpless, so don't you fret. Now get going before I boot your skinny butt out the door, and don't think I can't still do it."

"All right, I'm going. Take your medicine."

"Out!"

"Crotchety old fart."

There was no real annoyance in Will's tone, however. He simply chuckled and let himself out, trotted across the porch and down the steps to the sidewalk, footsteps fading.

Joseph listened as Will's white truck, one of the city's vehicles, started and backed out of the drive. He didn't move from the table until the rumble of the truck's engine could no longer be heard.

Even then he didn't move too fast, and it had little to do with his age and physical infirmity. More like dread sitting like a stone in his gut.

He sat down and booted up the machine, waiting as it went through the warming-up process. Once the main screen came up, he logged on to the Internet and selected the site for Will's bank out of the favorites tab. His hand shook, wiggling the mouse, his disease acting up and making it difficult to get the cursor where it needed to be, but he finally clicked on the correct icon to log in to see account balances online.

His fingers trembled over the keys. For about two seconds, he considered letting it go. He was about to commit a gross invasion of privacy, over something Will might come to him about on his own if Joseph was patient.

In reality, his sixth sense told him different.

He typed in the log-in and password he'd memorized from the paper, hoping Will hadn't changed it since the other night. The possibility hadn't occurred to him before now.

Hitting *enter*, he waited, tense. After two seconds, he was in, Will's finances at his fingertips.

First, he studied the checking account. Nothing there beyond the normal transactions, deductions for groceries, bills, medicine and such. A couple of automatic deposits from the city for Will's paychecks, one recent transfer from savings. More medicine.

"Wait a minute. More medicine? What for?" Joseph frowned at the screen, but the notation only revealed a check to the pharmacy Will always used. A large fucking check.

What in God's name did his grandson have filled that cost so damned much? Whatever it was, it didn't belong to Joseph. Medicare paid for most of his medicine for his Parkinson's.

Dread curled in his gut. Became real honest-to-God fear like he hadn't known since the last time he'd had a Japanese Zero on his tail and a shortage of ammo. He clicked on the savings account, uncertain what, if anything, he'd find.

Nothing could have prepared him for the figure of Will's balance.

"Son of a . . ."

Two hundred sixteen thousand, four hundred twenty-nine dollars. And thirty-three cents.

Almost a goddamned quarter million. Large deposits had started five months ago. Four of them, fifty thousand each. No way to trace where they'd come from without more help—

and that kind of help would probably involve getting Will into trouble. No, make that *more* trouble.

There was nothing else to be learned here. Joseph logged out of the system and stared at the screen for the longest time, then lowered his face into his hands.

"What have you done, boy?"

Joseph tried to plan his next move, but he couldn't think right now. He was so damned tired.

But he couldn't leave this world yet. He had a grandson to rescue.

Tommy awoke to sunlight filtering through the blinds, illuminating an unfamiliar bedroom. What?

His sleepy brain cleared a little as he spied the lump under the covers next to him, and he smiled.

Him and Shea. Last night.

Making love to her hadn't been a dream.

Sitting up carefully, he glanced at the digital clock. A quarter to six. Shea had to be at work by seven, and he figured she'd appreciate some coffee in her system when he returned to wake her up.

Unconcerned with his nakedness, he slid out of bed and padded to the kitchen. Coffee he could do, with little fuss. Filter, grounds, water. No problem.

He got the coffee going and walked back into her bedroom and stood over her. She was lying curled on her side, innocent as a child. Fine wisps of brown hair fell into her elfin face. Her rosebud mouth was parted in deep sleep, fingers of one hand tucked under her chin. And that, he thought, was where her similarities to a little girl ended.

At some point she must've gotten cold, because she was wearing his black T-shirt. The material rode up to her slim waist and one slender leg rested atop the bedspread, bent slightly at the knee. Sweet little nipples poked at the shirt, begging for his tongue. The round curve of her bottom invited his cock to come out and play.

Who was he to refuse such a delectable invitation?

His erection had gone harder than the nozzle of a fire hose, straining away from his body. This scrap of a nurse had turned his world upside down. Twisted his heart inside out.

Soft. Beautiful. All woman. All *his*.

He climbed into bed and spooned her from behind. Enthusiastically. She shifted, wiggling her rump against his eager cock.

"Mmm."

He bent over her, raked her hair aside. Kissed the pink shell of her ear, nibbled. Breathed her warm scent. French vanilla mixed with his own musk. *God.*

He slid a hand under the T-shirt, splaying it across her flat belly. She was so small next to him, his fingers stretched almost the width of her abdomen. Football hands. The thought made him smile. He loved the way she fit against his body, like an all-knowing higher power handcrafted her perfection especially for him.

His fingers traveled upward, found the taut pebbles of her nipples. He took one, rolling the peak between his thumb and forefinger. She moaned, arching her back, skin heating to his touch. More kisses at the vee of her neck and shoulder. Tasting and playing with her breasts.

"Oh, Tommy. You're going to make me late." She rolled to her back, blinked up at him. Huge brown eyes were glazed with arousal. Needing, wanting him.

"No, I won't. Trust me, baby."

He flung the bedspread out of the way, then grabbed her panties. She must've put them on when she borrowed his shirt. Why the hell did women wear them to bed when they only got in the way? He worked them down her legs, tossing them to the floor. The T-shirt followed, Tommy dragging it over her head. She lay on the pillows, gazing at him with desire that rocked him to his toes.

"Spread your legs." Lips turned up, she did, erasing any concern that she might not be game. He knelt between her thighs, trailing kisses from the inside of one dainty knee to her pouting sex. "So pretty and pink. Already wet for me. I could come, just looking at you."

She whimpered, raising her hips a bit. With a low chuckle, he obliged, his fingers parting her. His tongue flicked her folds, dipped inside. He lingered, taking his time, like a man enjoying an ice-cream cone.

"God, you taste so good."

"Oh! Please!" She fisted her hands in his hair, urging him.

Gladly. He tongue-fucked her for a few strokes and then fastened his mouth to her sex, suckling the sensitive nub. Eating a woman was one of life's finest pleasures, this woman in particular a dream come true. She came undone, bucking beneath him. The sight of her, mindless to everything but his touch—*his*—nearly made him lose control.

Suddenly she found her release, and holding back his own was the hardest thing he'd ever done. She was wild against his mouth, sweet honey bathing his tongue.

"Oh, yeah. Beautiful," he whispered.

When the last of her shudders stilled, he moved to her side. Bent and kissed her lovely mouth. Then he quickly fetched another condom from his shorts, glad he'd brought more than one.

She sat up a bit and wrapped her hand around his rampant erection, licked and sucked the tip. "Poor baby. We need to do something about this."

"Oh, we are," he promised, low and dark. "But if you keep that up this is going to be over in two seconds, and I want inside you."

"All right, but next time I get to taste you all I want." The wicked little gleam in her eye made his cock jump.

"Deal. I want you on your hands and knees. I'm going to fuck you from behind, sweet girl."

"Feeling a bit naughty, are we?"

"Nah, this isn't naughty. Later, I'll tell you some of my dirty fantasies. Maybe we can even pick one to make a reality."

"Sounds intriguing." With that, she rolled to her hands and knees. "What are you waiting for?"

"Jesus." He looked his fill. Savored the sight of his woman ready to give herself to him this way. Unruly hair cascading around her face. Knees spread, the pink lips of her sex, pouting and slick from his attentions, ready to welcome him inside.

He sheathed himself and ran his fingers along her slit, spreading her. Christ, he wasn't going to last. Grasping her hips, he guided the tip of his penis to her and thrust home. Buried his cock to the hilt. Her heat surrounded the throbbing length of him like a glove, squeezing, driving him mad. *Not yet . . .*

"Look at you," he rasped. "Beautiful. Mine."

She began to push back into him, stroking him in time with his thrusts. "Yes! Oh, God!"

He surrendered control. Gave himself over to the beast raging to do her. Hard, wild, nasty. He pounded into her with long strokes. Thrusting faster. Joyous, feminine cries reached his ears, erasing any lingering doubt he might've had about taking her so roughly. He might tread the razor's edge, but he'd never, ever hurt her.

The beast stood no chance against such heady stuff. With a hoarse shout, he impaled her one last time. Held her close, buried so deep he actually felt them connect in more than just a physical sense. His release rocked him to the core. Branded him as hers, for always, if she cared to keep him. Her climax milked him on and on.

Covering her like a blanket, he remained inside her for a moment, sweating and shaking. He'd never come harder or been drained more thoroughly in his life. Not that he'd been a total horn dog in the past, as his dad maintained, but still. He'd never before shared a shattering awakening, a fusing of hearts with the woman he loved.

Oh, God, I love her.

He just hoped his feelings weren't all one-sided. Only time would tell, and it was too soon to let that particular cat out of the bag.

With regret, he pulled out of her and took a few seconds to dispose of the condom in her bathroom. When he returned, Shea was sprawled on her back, glowing with the wattage of the well fucked. He was pretty darned proud of himself.

"You are a bad, bad man," she said with a grin. "I am *so* going to be late."

"It was for a good cause." He smiled and crawled up next to her, giving her a kiss on the nose. "And as a peace offering, I made coffee."

"I suppose I can cut you some slack." She was silent for a moment, then arched a brow at him. "Dirty fantasies, huh?"

"You have no idea."

"Suppose we continue this conversation tonight, after I get off?"

Hope flared brighter than ever before. They were making progress at last.

"Why don't I drop you off, pick you up at seven tonight?"

She bit her lip. "If you're sure you don't mind . . ."

"Of course not. I've got some errands to do and I'll be back to get you. If you're able to get off any earlier, just call and I can be there in minutes."

"Sounds good, thanks. And, Tommy?"

"Yes, baby?"

"Bring your clothes for work in the morning—if you want."

Yes! "Honey, I can't think of anything I'd like more."

10

"Shea, darlin', you're late," Dora said without looking up from her chart. "That ain't like you."

"Sorry, I was . . . detained." A bubble of laughter fought its way out despite her effort to squelch it, and Dora finally glanced at her.

The older woman gaped. "Lordy mercy, you're lit up like a torch! Who is he?" she hissed, grabbing Shea's arm and steering her to a more private alcove. "I'm not even gonna bother to ask if he's good!"

Shea beamed at her friend. She couldn't help it. "You know the blond firefighter who was brought in the other day, the one from the scaffold collapse?"

"Yeah, the hottie who saved the construction worker." Dora's eyes widened and she waved dramatically. "No! Seriously?"

"Yep. One and the same."

"Holy Moses! Your fairy godmother got anybody for me?"

"I don't know, but I'll ask."

"Is this where I get to call you a bitch?"

"If it makes you feel better."

"Bitch!" She gave a hearty laugh and wiped a hand over her brow. "Wow, I feel great now."

Shea hugged the other woman's shoulders. "You are too much. I really am sorry I'm late. I don't make it a habit."

"I know. In this case, you're forgiven. Lord knows you're due for some major happiness, girlfriend," she said, her tone softening. "So how are things with him, really? And I don't mean the awesome sex."

"Dora . . . he doesn't know. I'm just not ready to get into all of that with him. Not yet."

Dora patted her arm in a show of support. "Then you won't. Not until you're comfortable sharing it with him. Don't let him or anyone push you. Ya hear?"

Shea swallowed hard and blinked at the sting in her eyes. "I won't."

"Now don't go gettin' all weepy and shit. We've got work to do!"

All day long, her mind turned toward Tommy's incredible lovemaking. The way he made her feel cherished, as no other man had ever made her feel. They had a real connection, the chance at something solid.

If only she didn't ruin their blossoming relationship with fear and doubts.

By agonizing over ghosts that wouldn't rest.

After dropping Shea off at Sterling, Tommy drove with no particular destination in mind. Just a vague sense of unrest. For no reason, his mind drifted back to the conversation he and Shea had in Stratton's. Her encouragement for him to try a new profession. Reinvent himself, if he wanted.

Did he? He'd just earned his paramedic status a few months ago. He liked his job, his friends. He was set for an entire career. But did he want to be a firefighter for the next thirty or forty years?

He was at a crossroads, and while he hated the uncertainty that he hadn't chosen the right profession, he was immensely grateful he was questioning his choice now rather than twenty years from now, when it was too late.

Truly questioning, and considering his options.

Because of Shea's support.

It was like a burden lifted from his shoulders. He hadn't felt this free in over three years.

For the first time, he felt as though it was okay to say, *Maybe I took a wrong turn. Got off at the wrong exit.*

It was all right to live, even though Donny hadn't. Maybe that was the most startling revelation of all.

Without paying attention to where he was going, he found himself at the burned-out hull of the office building they'd worked the other day. The one where Eve had nearly fallen through the roof.

An arson job.

Who would want to do that to an abandoned building, and why? Bored teenagers? Or someone with a darker motive?

A puzzle. And he loved puzzles. The prospect of being able to solve an arson crime excited him like nothing had in ages. Regular crimes, like burglaries and drug running? Forget that shit. Those were crimes that had to be solved on a human level. But arson? The clues were science, pure and simple. The arson investigator's job was to present the evidence and let the detectives handle the arrest.

Tommy parked, noting that another vehicle, a nondescript Ford sedan, was parked nearby. Until he knew for sure the other person had business here—*like you do, idiot?*—he'd have to be cautious.

He got out of his truck and walked toward the shell of the building, a chill going down his spine. Some sick fucker had torched the place on purpose, and his partner had nearly been killed. He'd dearly love to find out who, and corner the asshole some dark night.

Ducking the yellow tape, he walked as close as he dared, studying the places where the fire seemed to have done more damage than in others. Some spots inside the shell were blackened and charred, others almost untouched.

"The tape is there for a reason."

Tommy jumped and spun to face a dark-haired man who appeared to be at least ten years older than himself. He wasn't quite as tall as Tommy, but his body was fit and compact. His expression was curious rather than unfriendly, and Tommy gave him a smile, walking over to meet him.

"I know, sorry. Tommy Skyler, Sugarland Fire Department," he said, sticking out his hand. "My station worked this call, and my partner almost fell through the roof."

With that information, the man's countenance completely changed from wary to open. He clasped Tommy's hand and whistled. "You guys got a live one, all right. Is he okay?"

"*She*, and yes, thanks." He let go of the other man's hand and gestured toward the building. "I've recently become interested in this end of things. You know, after the fire engines have gone home. I think it would be cool to help catch the perpetrator rather than just cleaning up his mess."

The guy laughed. "You're kidding, right? A couple of the men I work with would give their eyeteeth to be firefighters. One made the high score on the written test but couldn't pass the physical agility. I don't know why you'd give up the excitement of being a fireman for a boring career in investigations." The new speculation in his eyes, however, belied his words.

"The grass is always greener, I suppose."

He smiled. "I guess so. Oh, I'm Mark McAllister, by the way."

"Nice to meet you, Mr. McAllister."

"Just Mark. So is this just a passing curiosity, or are you truly interested in finding out about the Arson team?"

"I'm really interested. I'd like to find out more, see if I even have what it takes to make the move."

"You know it's not lateral, right? AI is a whole different ball game."

"I figured as much. I'd still like to check it out."

Mark considered him for a moment, then removed his wallet and extracted a business card. "Tell you what. Why don't you come by my office whenever you get a chance and we'll talk? I can go over some of the nitty-gritty with you if you want."

"You'd do that?" Tommy took the card he offered, and a thrill of excitement went through him.

"Sure, why not? If one of our boys on the front lines is itching to get into the Fire Prevention Division, I say everyone wins. Come on by. Just call first to make sure I'll be there."

"Cool. I appreciate it."

McAllister turned and started for his car, and Tommy got the distinct impression he was being given a hint to leave. He couldn't blame the guy, really, for not wanting someone here messing up the crime scene or possibly getting hurt.

Tommy unlocked his truck and McAllister waved. Tommy lifted a hand and got in, and it didn't escape his notice that the other man didn't drive away, but made a call on his cell phone. A delay tactic to make sure Tommy was gone?

"All right, I'm outta here," he said with a half grin.

As he started his truck and drove away, he swore he could feel the man tracking his progress. Maybe he had some doubts about whether Tommy's story was legit, and even now was checking him out.

That was okay. The man's mind would be set at ease, and with any luck, Tommy had made an inroad.

One that might prove valuable in the long run.

Tommy spent the rest of the day running a few errands, including packing a duffel and bringing his regulation navy pants and shirt on a hanger so he could change for work in the morning.

It occurred to him that Shea could stay at his place instead, but maybe she felt safer on her own turf. Whatever made her more comfortable was fine by him.

Shea was waiting when he pulled up, and he grinned at the sight of her dressed in scrubs with little cats printed all over them.

"What?" she said as she hopped in and shut the door.

"I guess plain, ugly green is a thing of the past," he said, gesturing at the pattern on her uniform.

"Not entirely. The guys don't go for cute patterns, so they tend to stick with the puke green unless they work with kids."

"Ah. I stand corrected. They're cute, anyway." He glanced at her before pulling onto the road. "Not as cute as you, though."

"I'll wear them every day, then."

"I prefer you out of them, actually." His cock agreed, twitching in the confines of denim. Seemed like he was perpetually horny with this woman around. No complaints, though.

"Is this where we talk about fantasies? Seems like I recall some hot-to-trot guy mentioning certain perversions . . ."

"Hey, you say that like it's a bad thing." He huffed in mock indignation.

"Not at all. I am curious as to what some of yours are," she said, running a fingernail down his arm.

He shivered, and he actually felt his nipples tighten. Shit! "Damn, baby. You're going to make me wreck the truck." He tapped a finger on the steering wheel. "I did start this topic, didn't I?"

"You most certainly did. Spill it, buddy."

"Okay . . . one of my top fantasies is two girls and a guy. Me being the guy, of course," he said with a mischievous grin.

Shea gave an unladylike snort. "Yeah, that's *so* not going to happen, unless you're willing to participate in one of mine—two guys and a girl. Guess who gets to be the girl? *Moi!* And the guys have to kiss."

"No way," he muttered. "I mean, to each his own, but *dude*."

"Ha! I knew I could do it!"

"What?"

"Get you to say *dude*," she said, laughing. "You haven't said it in ages."

"That's mean, Shea Ford." He shot her a curious look. "So you weren't serious? About the two guys?"

"Well, sure I was. But I'd give up the dream for you," she said sweetly.

He laughed. Man, he had his balls in a vise with this woman. He couldn't tell if she was teasing or not, but surely she was pulling his leg. "I'd appreciate that, baby. Guess the two women thing is a bad idea, too." He thought for a few seconds. "Okay, another one is a naked picnic on the beach."

"Tempting, but we're curiously out of beach in Tennessee."

"There's always the man-made one down by the Cumberland River Dam."

"Um, nope. Too crowded, and I don't want to have to explain to my cop brother why he had to bail me out of jail. Next."

"All right. I'm going to piggyback on the last idea and tell you I've always wanted to have sex in a public place. Not in front of vast multitudes, but somewhere dark and mysterious. Maybe another couple is watching, and it gets them hot." Jeez, can a guy die from his cock being strangled in his pants?

"Oh, my." She sounded intrigued, her voice low and husky. "Like where? There's that getting-arrested thing . . ."

"I'm not sure. We could go to a club in Nashville and find a dark corner to fool around in."

"That sounds risky on way too many levels. Cross that off."

"Oh, wait. I know. There's this young couple who moved next door to my parents, and my dad says they're always going at it like bunnies by their pool. And my folks are going out of town for a few days next week."

He let the statement hang and glanced over to see her staring at him, eyes wide, lips parted. She looked equal parts shocked and titillated.

"Would you really want to?"

"Honey, I'm a guy. The evidence doesn't lie. What about you?"

Her gaze strayed to his lap and back to his face. "I—I don't know! It sounds so—so naughty! And, wow, I've never—"

"Me neither," he said, hoping to put her at ease. He'd really blown her mind. "Like I said, they're only fantasies. If you don't want to, no worries. I'd never do anything to make you uncomfortable."

The reminder seemed to settle her somewhat. "I appreciate that. But I never said I didn't want to."

Oh, man! Yep, she was going to kill him. But what a way to go.

"Cool. Whatever you want, baby, all you have to do is ask. If you're pleased, I'll be pleased. That's the way it works."

"You're something else, you know that?" She took his free hand as he turned onto her street, rubbing at the calluses on his palm. "I don't know why I ever thought you needed to grow up."

He winced. "Sheesh, put it right out there, why don't ya?"

"That wasn't very graceful, was it? What I'm trying to

say is that I'm glad I'm finally getting to know the real you," she said softly. "And I like what I see. A lot."

A strange new feeling wound around his heart like a vine, hugging it close. "I'm glad, because I've liked what I've seen all along."

"I gave you such a hard time the night we met, and since then. I'm sorry."

He parked the truck and turned to face her, cupping her chin. "No regrets. Let's concentrate on here and now."

"Sounds good to me."

She leaned into him, sending his senses tumbling with a kiss. Gentle as a feather, her lips nibbled his. An affirmation of their growing bond. Her breasts pressed against his chest, soft and warm. Her scent shot a jolt of need straight to his balls and squeezed.

"Let's take this inside," she said, pulling away.

"Good idea." He grabbed his uniform hanging behind his seat and the duffel in the truck bed. Once inside her apartment, he laid his stuff on the couch and pulled her close. "Hungry? I should've asked if you wanted to stop and pick up something."

"I thought we'd heat up some of your casserole later. Right now, I'm starving for something else."

"What might that be?"

One small hand skimmed down his chest and belly, pausing at the snap of his jeans. "You're not that innocent. I think you can guess."

His pulse sped up as she unsnapped his jeans, eased down the zipper. Before meeting Shea, if any of the guys had asked him if he thought being seduced by a woman in kitty-cat nurses' scrubs was sexy, he would've laughed.

As she hooked her fingers in the waistband and pulled down his jeans along with his boxer briefs, and hit her knees in front of him, he had to admit she could've been wearing a clown suit and it wouldn't matter. Having her mouth on him was all that did.

His erection pointed straight to his goal, already red and leaking because of their discussion on the way over. Reaching out, he caressed the silky curls on her head but managed to stop himself from following his first instinct, which was to yank her head forward and fuck her mouth until he exploded.

He didn't, though it wasn't easy. When she flicked her tongue over the wet tip, however, he was glad he'd refrained. There was a certain heady freedom in surrender, and that concept was new to him. Watching her explore at will was the most erotic thing he'd ever seen.

She suckled the head, tasting, fingers testing the weight of his heavy balls. Manipulating them with gentle pressure. He sucked in a harsh breath and widened his stance as much as the jeans around his ankles would allow, letting her have him.

He was pretty proud of his control, until he watched the length of his cock slowly disappear, enveloped by her wet heat.

"Oh, God," he rasped, hips bucking forward. "Hell, yes. Suck me."

Grasping the base of his shaft, she increased the suction to long pulls. Taking him deep, sliding out. Again and again, tongue stroking the ridge underneath. Her free hand explored behind his balls, rubbing his perineum, an erogenous zone he'd never experienced before.

It felt so damned fantastic, her mouth and hands working him, devouring him, driving him crazy, that he actually whimpered. The wonderful heavy, tightening sensation began in his spine, wrapped around to his groin.

"Oh, baby, shit! I think I'm gonna . . . gonna—"

He was robbed of speech as she deep-throated him, every

inch of his cock being sucked and massaged mercilessly. He was along for the ride now, didn't even try to hold back. His entire body clenched and he shouted, pumping his release down her pretty throat.

"Yes! Fuck, yes!" He shuddered several times, dazed, letting her bring him down easy. Finally she let him go, and he was sorry it was over. "Jesus, that was incredible. Thank you."

She dabbed at the corner of her mouth and smiled up at him. "You're welcome. I've been wanting to do you for a long time, if you must know the truth."

He took her arm and helped her up, then gave her a thorough kiss. "God, I can taste us mingled together. That's totally hot."

"I agree. Anytime you want an encore, I'm your woman."

He traced her lips with his thumb, reading her reaction carefully to his next words. "*Are* you my woman? Are we together?"

"I think it's safe to say we are, yes," she said quietly. But her good mood seemed intact, which he took as a good sign. "I'm not sure where this is going, but I know that much. I don't sleep around, and if I do choose to sleep with a man I care about, I don't date other men."

"I never thought you would, but it's awesome to hear you say it aloud." He could've jumped for joy, but decided he'd better not. "I feel the same way, so you don't have to worry about me catting around. I wasn't raised that way."

"Oh? What about your threesome fantasy?" Her tone was only half-teasing.

"Nothing but fun dirty talk, baby," he assured her. "I am a bit of an exhibitionist, though, so I'm still holding out for putting on a show for my parents' lusty neighbors."

"The idea has possibilities. But do me a favor and don't use the words *parents* and *lust* in the same sentence."

"Eww. Sorry." He looked down at himself and chuckled.

"Crap, I'm still exposed here. You must've melted my brains along with my bones."

After he made himself decent, she hugged him tight. He felt her smile against his chest. "Too melted to go another round later?"

He tightened his hold, kissed the top of her head. "No way. Tonight, lady, you'd better be ready. I plan on making love to you all night long."

"Ooh, promises, promises."

"You bet. Sooner rather than later if you keep wiggling against me like that."

"A long dry spell, was it?"

"Ever since I met you, it has been. I haven't wanted anyone else, and it's been damned lonely," he said honestly.

She leaned back and touched his face. "I'm sorry."

"Don't be. I'm not lonely anymore."

"Me, neither."

He led her to the couch and pulled her down with him, holding her snug at his side. She laid her head on his chest, arm around him in what was fast becoming his favorite position. The ensuing silence was a rare, perfect slice of life, too huge for him to process.

He simply sat and imagined the vines around his heart reaching out to curl around hers, too. Good and beautiful, like water filling cracks in dry, parched earth.

After several more minutes, he stirred and rubbed her arm. "Want me to heat some of our leftovers?"

"In a little bit. I want to sit like this a while longer."

His stomach growled. "If you're going to make me burn all this fuel, you have to feed me."

Twisting in his arms, she rested her chin in the center of his chest and gazed at him with big brown puppy dog eyes, poking out her bottom lip. "Please?"

He barked a laugh and kissed the end of her nose. "That's dirty pool."

"It's ingrained into the female DNA and is an evil form of mind control used to arouse and befuddle the male, bending him to the lady's wishes."

"Well, it works. Damn, what have I gotten myself into?"

"Poor baby." She traced his lips with a delicate finger.

Content to be the object of her sympathy, he sank into the pillows, enjoying her touches. She explored his mouth, his brow. He groaned in pleasure when she sank her hands into his hair, massaging his scalp.

She paused. "How's your head since the scaffold accident? I'm ashamed I haven't thought to ask before."

"Better, especially with those magic fingers doing the trick."

"Does it hurt much?" She peered at the area.

"Not really. Just when I push on the sore spot."

"Then I won't bother it. I'm really glad you're okay."

Studying her, he asked, "Are you okay with me having such a dangerous job? What if I decide to stay at the department?"

"You have to do what makes you happy. I worry, but I'd never let that erode what we have."

He nodded. "I met a man today, Mark McAllister. He's an arson investigator over in Fire Prevention. He gave me his card, invited me to come in and talk."

"Tommy, that's wonderful!" Shea sat up, excited. "Are you going?"

"Yeah. I'm going to give him a call soon, drop by and find out what it takes to make the move. Just out of curiosity, though. It's all preliminary."

"Good for you. Have you said anything to the guys at the station since we discussed stuff before?"

"Not yet. No reason to get them all worked up if it doesn't sound like something I want to pursue."

"Okay. In that case, I won't mention it to Cori. She'd want to tell Zack and the guys would find out before you're ready."

"Thanks, honey, I appreciate that," he said, stretching. "Now will you feed me?"

"If it'll speed your recovery time? Sure."

"On second thought . . ." Standing, he lifted her into his arms. "Let's have dessert first."

Her happy squeal pierced his eardrum as he jogged for the bedroom. Yeah, he could make this a habit.

From now on.

11

"Did you assholes miss me?"

Zack's greeting was met with cheerful backslaps and off-color comments about the success of the honeymoon. From his spot at the dining table, Tommy glanced up from his coffee and gave his friend a wave.

"Hey, man! How's Cori? Did she make the trip okay?"

"Why, yes, Thomas, thank you for asking," Zack enunciated, rolling his eyes at the rest of the crew. "I appreciate it, considering all the rest of the bozos want to know about is how much nooky I got."

"So? How much nooky *did* you get, *amigo*?" Julian leered, making a suggestive gesture with his tongue.

Eve scowled at Julian.

"Enough to write a new, revised version of the *Kama Sutra*," Zack bragged. "And that's all you're getting out of me."

Tommy's brows rose. For Zack, that was saying quite a bit, considering the man had been a shy virgin before he and Cori met one cold, stormy day this past winter.

Julian pointedly ignored Eve. "Sex doesn't hurt the baby?" He seemed genuinely interested, and Zack warmed to the topic.

"Not as long as the pregnancy is progressing normally. Nature cushions the baby really well. He doesn't know a thing is going on."

"That's exactly right," Six-Pack put in, nodding.

"It's not weird for you that the baby is, like, *there* when . . . well, you know," Julian said, fascinated.

Zack shook his head. "Not really. It's gratifying, in a caveman sort of way."

Eve choked, and started for the door. "Good God. I'm going outside before I become ill."

"Wait for me," Tommy called after her, scooting back his chair. "Welcome back, Z-man."

"Thanks."

Tommy rode Eve's heels out the door to the bay, and heaved a sigh of relief. "That's a little too much information for me at this point in my life."

"Same goes." She leaned against the quint, propping one foot on the fender behind her. "I want kids someday, but jeez. Hearing those three discuss babies is beyond weird."

"You want kids?" For some reason, that surprised him.

"Sure, why?"

"No reason, I just never thought of you as the maternal type. No offense."

She gave him a considering look. "None taken. You aren't exactly the first person to say so."

"Aw, don't pay any attention to the guys," he said. "What do they know? I mean, look at them now, all former studs-about-town turned lovesick fools."

Eve's white smile contrasted against her medium-bronzed face. "True, but I wasn't talking about them. My mother is the one with the doubts, though I think she's only concerned about how hard it is, bringing a child of mixed race into the world. She worries about how it affected me. Not my daddy being white, but the fact that he left. Couldn't take the pressure."

Tommy weighed his answer carefully. Never had he heard Eve discuss her background openly before, with such candor, and he felt as though he'd been included in her circle of trust. A precious thing, if you knew Eve.

"I can see how that might've been true over thirty years ago, but now? Attitudes have changed. People are more informed, more accepting of cultural or racial differences. Don't let those old constraints keep you from getting what you want, Eve."

Eve cocked her head and fell silent for a moment, gazing at him as though she'd never seen him before. Not really. "What happened to the cocky kid who, just a few months ago, hurled sexual innuendo at me at every opportunity? What gives?"

"I grew up," he said softly.

Her eyes widened. "By God, you fell in love."

"Yeah. Gives a guy a whole different perspective, I suppose."

Eve gave a quiet laugh and crossed her arms over her chest. "Tell you what. I won't give up on my dreams if you don't."

"Deal. Do I have to guess who your dreams involve?" He might be slow, but he'd put it together.

"I doubt it," she said with a sad smile.

"That battle might not be one you can win, sweetheart. And it has nothing to do with the fact that he's white."

Only that he's a man with a broken heart, and one who can't admit he has a drinking problem.

"I know. But without dreams, we don't have a hell of a lot to look forward to when the sun comes up, do we?"

The statement hit him hard. While he searched for what to say next, the intercom emitted three loud, high tones. Next came the call, one Tommy had never worked before and had, in fact, only seen on the news.

A residence had exploded due to a suspected gas leak, leaving little but a pile of charred brick, wood, and ash. The home was believed to be vacant, but that had not been verified. The HazMat unit assigned to Station Three was on the way to assist.

"Shit," Tommy breathed, jogging over to slip into his gear. "What the fuck is up with all the wrecked buildings around here?"

"That's what we'd all like to know, kid," Sean said in a clipped voice, moving past him to bunk out in his own gear. "I was just talking to the battalion chief this morning. The vacant buildings we've worked aren't the only ones the fire department has seen in the last few months. Disturbing fucking pattern."

Tommy mulled that information over as Zack drove them to their destination. Six-Pack followed in the ambulance, the unit called out because of the possibility of injuries, however low.

When the house—or what remained of it—came into view, Julian crossed himself. *"Jesucristo."*

They all shared the same sentiment. If anyone, including innocent bystanders, had been caught in the blast, they were likely dead.

After Zack parked the quint, they piled out and set to work. Tommy caught a snatch of conversation between Sean and Captain Reynolds of Station Three.

"Gas is off?"

"Hell, yes. Wouldn't send my men in otherwise," Reynolds barked.

"Verifying, that's all."

"Wouldn't need to if you'd keep up with communication."

"John?"

"What?"

"Go to hell."

What the fuck? Tommy shot a glance at the two sparring captains, but was quickly swept up in searching the rubble for bodies. The Search Now team, comprised of off-duty fire-men and local volunteers, arrived with their cadaver dog, which was a huge help. The enthusiastic Labrador bounded all over the property, nosed every cranny that was difficult for his human counterparts to reach, avoiding the worst hot spots, but came up with nothing. Still, the dog was rewarded by his handler for his hard work with his rubber toy, which he shook with vigor, causing some of the guys to smile.

It was easy to be amused by the dog when there were no casualties.

The amusement faded with the arrival of news crews, who obviously had nothing better to report today, body or no body. Tommy and his buddies kept their heads down and let the battalion chief field the questions, especially when one intrepid reporter made the connection between all of the destroyed buildings in the area of late.

Fuck a duck, this was shaping up to be a long day.

Tommy wished he was curled up with Shea, snuggling on the couch or better yet, making love. Twenty-four hours—well, make that thirty-six after she'd worked all day when he got off duty—and he'd be with her again, stealing every moment with her that he possibly could.

Poking a booted toe at a piece of charred wood, he glanced toward the street and the gawkers standing beyond the news vans. Man, what he wouldn't give for an ice-cold soda or glass of lemonade. Beer wasn't an option, but—

Wait a second.

Tommy froze and peered at the crowd, or rather, at some-one in particular. At a lone figure standing slightly apart from the rest, a man wearing a ball cap. Something teased his fuzzy memory. His grandmother would've used the term *walked over my grave*, rest her soul. Whatever the notion was, it re-mained elusive, to his frustration.

It shouldn't have affected him at all, the sight of a man in a baseball cap, hovering at the edge of the onlookers.

But it stayed with Tommy for the rest of his shift.

Joseph felt the fucking earth move, the tremor rattling the windows. A short time later, the sirens came, their wailing giving him the creeps. Whatever was going down might've been on the next street or miles away. No way to tell.

Except to turn on the news. He didn't have to channel surf for long, no more than twenty minutes, before coming across the coverage. One of the big news teams out of Nashville was already there, a male reporter talking in a solemn tone about an explosion in an older Sugarland neighborhood.

". . . rocked this sleepy suburb about half an hour ago. A spokesman for the Sugarland Fire Department stated that the cause of the explosion is believed to have been a gas leak, and neighbors claim the residence has been vacant for several months. Which raises the question, why wasn't the gas turned off?"

The camera cut away to footage of the flattened mess, no longer recognizable as a house. A couple of neighbors were interviewed, exclaiming their shock at such a thing happening, blah, blah. In the background, people milled about, reminding Joseph of vultures hovering over a carcass.

Then Joseph sat up straight. A man had stepped apart from the group of gawkers. He wore a baseball cap. Joseph's vision might be bad and the man a blurred form at best, but it was a form he knew well. That and the hat.

But it was a blink in time, and the clip ended, leaving room for doubt. The man could've been someone else. After all, Joseph hadn't been able to see his face.

The scene flicked back to the reporter, who warmed to his topic with enthusiasm.

"In an interesting side note, this isn't the first building-related calamity to occur in and around the Nashville area of late. In the past several months, a total of nine buildings have either been destroyed or have suffered major structural damage to the tune of tens of millions in insurance payouts. Coincidence, or something more? No doubt, the authorities will seek answers. Mike Hanson, Fox 17 News."

Groping for the remote, he switched off the television and sat staring at the blank screen. Suspicions formed of their own accord, not caring that his first impulse was to reject them as impossible. Facts were facts, and while Joseph only had a handful, the ones he did have were alarming.

Will was hiding some serious shit from his grandpa.

His grandson was being harassed by a scheming bastard.

And the boy, who'd never had two nickels to rub together, city job or not, had almost a quarter of a million in the bank.

Had the man in the background on the news been Will? If so, why was he there? For no good reason, that's what.

So here he was, contemplating what would equal the final gross invasion of privacy, and hating the motherfucking hell out of it. He couldn't just ask Will to explain, because this was too big. He'd either give Joseph a sanitized version or lie outright. The boy would do anything to shelter his old grandpa.

And Joseph felt the same way about Will. That was why he needed the rest of the facts to back him up, then they'd see what to do about cleaning up whatever mess his grandson had gotten himself into.

With an effort he pushed himself up and shuffled through the living room, down the hallway. At the door to Will's room he paused, more afraid than he'd been at age eighteen when he'd boarded a ship for Europe knowing he'd probably die.

Now he was terrified.

Guilty as hell, too. But there was no help for it, not with Will's life at stake. Every instinct that had saved his ass *over there* spurred him on now, warned him that this mission was even more urgent. More important than his own hide.

Steeling himself, he went inside and looked around. Surely if a man hid something in here, it could be found. The bedroom was small, as were all the rooms in the house, the faux-wood furniture cheap and aged. It consisted of a bed, a nightstand, and a dresser, plus one tiny closet. Nothing more.

The most natural place to look as far as he was concerned was the nightstand. A convenient place where a person might shove a paper or some other important item.

He found something there all right—a box of condoms and a small tube of that slippery stuff that made sex more gratifying. Or so the tube claimed. Joseph wouldn't know, and didn't want to contemplate how these things had been put to use, perhaps while Joseph had been at the senior center. Or maybe Will visited his lovers during those nights he "worked late."

Christ. No, he didn't want to know the details, but a part of him was hurt that Will felt he couldn't confide the truth of his nature.

"Bigger fish to fry, old man," he muttered to himself. Not as though that was his most pressing worry anymore.

He slid the drawer shut and tackled the dresser methodically, starting at the bottom, which was hell on his ancient knees, and worked his way to the top. Nothing but shorts, T-shirts, socks, and underwear. He even peered underneath the drawer bottoms and behind the dresser, searching for something that might be secreted there. No damning evidence of shadowy activities present.

Next he checked the bed, specifically under the mattress and on top of the box springs. He was sweating by the time he finished looking, not being used to squatting, lifting, and such. Damn, in his day, he'd carried wounded men almost twice his size all the way to the infirmary without breaking a sweat.

Okay, on to the closet. Nothing escaped notice. Pants and shirt pockets were searched, as well as shoe boxes full of boyhood shit. Scout merit badges and trinkets that meant God-knows-what, and only to Will. One was heavy, and upon inspection, he discovered it to be full of rocks and fossils.

Rocks of all sizes, shapes, and types. Joseph recognized granite and quartz, which was about as good as his rock-identifying skills stretched. Some of the fossils were nautilus-shaped, embedded in rock. He smiled, thinking of the sweet boy who'd saved these treasures. At one time, Joseph had owned a similar, prized collection. God knew what ever happened to it.

Letting the memories take him back some, he dug his hand into the stones, shifting them around, admiring, wondering at the story behind each one. Wishing he could turn back time to the bright-eyed boy Will had been, holding one up proudly for Joseph to see.

Grandpa, look at this!

As his gnarled fingers brushed aside some of the rock, something white at the bottom of the box caught his attention. Too white for the gray color of the cardboard box, out of place. Frowning, he picked at the white and one edge lifted up. A corner of a piece of paper.

With the Parkinson's ravaging his system, grasping the small corner wasn't easy. But he got hold and pulled the paper out to find it was an envelope. One that had already been opened some time ago.

Turning it over, he squinted at tiny writing. A dull sort of panic crawled through his belly when he read the name and address of a doctor in Nashville.

There was only one reason Joseph could come up with as

to why Will would bury something from his doctor at the bottom of a box of innocuous childhood mementos.

The ever-present shaking in his old hands increased as he withdrew the paper from within, let his vision adjust to the print, and read what the fucking thing had to say.

The box slipped unnoticed from his grasp.

The doctor's letter crushed in his gnarled hands, Joseph buried his face in his hands and wept.

Forrest answered the phone, a glass of Scotch in hand. All day and into the evening he'd been dreading this call from Rose. The bastard probably knew he was sweating, and Forrest resented the hell out of it.

"Hello?"

"Your boy made himself visible. On top of the arson ruling, that's two fuckups. This pisses me off," he said coldly.

"He's your boy, not mine. You give the orders."

"You think that'll save your ass when I come calling?"

Forrest's bowels turned to water. "You're coming here again?"

"Eventually. Sooner rather than later. In the meantime, the little dipshit's mistake has put us in a bind. We'll have to wrap this up ahead of schedule. The question is, who's going to pay for the error?"

Sitting in a chair, hard, Forrest sucked down the rest of his drink. "One more job and you'll have more than enough funds, nobody the wiser. Leave Hensley alone."

"What job would this be? And it had better be profitable."

"It will be. There's a warehouse on the outskirts of town. The results will kill two birds with one stone," he said, thinking of eradicating a particular thorn in his side. The prospect almost made him hard.

"When?"

"Soon. Within the next couple of weeks."

"One week. I want my quota met on the jobs and the money, yesterday."

"You'll have it."

"Prescott? Don't disappoint me. My therapist says committing murder is bad for my sense of self."

The other end went dead, and Forrest punched the *off* button. For one second, he longed to hurl the phone against the wall, but it would mean one more mess to deal with.

No. He'd hand the man his quota, and then he was done. Forrest had no clue what the asshole did with the lion's share of the cut, and he didn't care.

Forrest would be the richest SOB this town had ever seen. He'd have everything he wanted, and nobody was going to stand in his way.

Shea clutched a towel around her otherwise naked body, eyeing the pool at Tommy's parents' house. The neighborhood was older, modest but nice, the stately trees the most admirable natural feature. The pool was a welcome touch as well, especially after a long, frustrating day in the ER.

Well, the pool and her equally naked and towel-clad counterpart. Tommy's terry-cloth covering was slung about his lean hips, his chest and taut abs gleaming in the pool lights dancing off the water. Crickets chirped all around them, but nothing moved.

"You're crazy!" Her loud whisper echoed in the silence. "What if they *do* see us?"

Tommy set his beer bottle on a nearby table. "So? They might learn something new."

"Tommy!"

He laughed and moved in for a kiss. Winding her arms around his neck, she decided to go with the moment. Spontaneity hadn't exactly been her strong suit in the past few years, but with this man, it felt right. A bit scary, but right.

They tasted each other, tongues dueling for dominance, though it didn't matter who came out the winner. She figured they both were, in a big way.

"You're sure your folks are long gone?" she gasped, pulling back.

"They're staying overnight at their friends' house in Chattanooga. We're good," he said hoarsely, yanking off her towel and tossing it aside.

"Oh! You didn't!" She tried to sound indignant as she danced aside, shielding herself from view, but the intended scolding came out as an excited squeal.

Tommy jerked off his own towel, leering at her playfully. "Yes, I did! What are you going to do about it?"

She backed up, giggling as he advanced like a beast stalking his prey. "Run!"

And that's what she did. She spun and ran, conscious of how ridiculous she must look but loving the chase. Her sprint around the pool was short-lived, however, as she was grabbed from behind and scooped into his strong arms. One arm around her back and the other supporting her under her knees, he tucked her into his chest, grinning down into her face.

"Gotcha."

Happy, she twined her arms around his neck. "What are you going to do with me?"

"This."

Before she could protest, he sprinted for the deep end of the pool, and leaped. She screamed out of pure unadulterated joy, feeling like she was seventeen again. Free and with nothing but fun ahead.

Because of the heat of the summer night, the cool water was a shock. They plunged underneath together and emerged sputtering and laughing.

"Brat!" she yelled with no heat whatsoever, shoving her wet hair out of her face with one hand.

"You know it!"

She splashed water in his face and he returned the favor, which resulted in a full-scale war, the two of them chasing each other around in the pool. He lunged, catching her in a tackle, dunking them again, then pulling her up and spinning her in his arms to face him.

"Stalemate," he gasped.

"Nope, I win."

"On what grounds?"

"I'm a girl, and if I don't win, I can make your life miserable."

"Okay, you win." His indulgent expression told her he didn't mind.

She wound her arms around his neck and her legs around his waist. For a while they were content to drift around the pool, locked together, savoring kisses and the closeness between them. Tommy fell quiet and she grew concerned, wishing he'd act goofy again.

"What are you thinking?"

"Why do women always ask that question? What if we're not thinking anything and there's just wind blowing between our ears?"

"Come on, tell me."

He waded to the side of the pool and backed up against the wall. She lowered her legs to stand, but kept her arms around him, loving the contact.

For a while, she thought he'd forgotten her request, or had decided to ignore it. Finally, his voice broke the stillness.

"I haven't been in this pool since Donny died."

"Oh, sweetie," she said softly. "Why not?"

"We used to love horsing around out here, in our little oasis away from the world. After he was gone . . . it just didn't seem right."

"To have fun when he couldn't?"

"Yeah. Stupid, I know."

"No." She cupped his chin and looked into those amazing, pale blue eyes. "It's very common to feel that way after the loss of someone close. Shane and I have both been there, and it hurts. Badly."

"It never goes away," he whispered, looking into the darkness. "He was tortured first. They told us what was done to him and I see it in my nightmares. How terrified he must've been."

Oh, God. "What did they do?"

"You don't want to know, and I don't think I could repeat it."

"Okay." After a pause, she asked, "Have you ever been to counseling?"

His face stilled. "No. I don't want anybody messing around with my brain, telling me how I should feel."

"It's not quite like that—"

"No. That shit worked all right for my parents, but it's not for me. He's just as dead, no matter how I feel."

"Tommy, listen. I've seen what happens to a person when a ravaged psyche doesn't heal. Don't bury your pain until it destroys you." She stroked his cheek, hoping she wasn't crossing the line. "I just want you to realize I'm here, and you're not alone. I'll say it as many times as necessary to get through."

"What happened to you besides losing your parents? How do you understand so much about getting past the pain?"

Shaking her head, she tried to lighten the subject. "Oh, I think that's enough heavy stuff for one night, don't you?"

"You know what I think? I think you're not completely over whatever it is, even though you dispense advice like you are."

That hit her hard, and she struggled not to show how much

it sideswiped her. "I never said I was over anything, and I was just trying to help."

"I know, and I love you for that." He hesitated, damp blond hair curling around his beautiful face, eyes serious. "In fact, I love you, period."

The breath rushed out of her lungs. She stared at him, lips parted, heart in her throat. "I—I . . . oh, my God."

"Baby, it can't be that big of a news flash," he said, looking away. But not before she saw the raw vulnerability he tried to hide.

Her mind reeled. "I suppose I knew, deep down. Tommy, I—"

"You don't have to say anything, okay?" His eyes met hers again, gentle with understanding. "I blindsided you. I'm sorry I put you on the spot, but I won't apologize for how I feel. I can't change it, and I wouldn't."

"No, I'm glad you told me," she said softly, tracing his lips. "I truly am."

"Jeez, what are we doing talking when there's other stuff we could be doing?"

Suddenly, he pushed away from the side of the pool and dragged her toward the steps.

"Where are we going?"

"Over there," he said, pointing to their towels. "We're going to spread those out on the grass."

"Oh? And then what?"

"Why, I'm going to have my wicked way with you. What else?"

12

Shea giggled nervously as Tommy spread the towels out underneath a tree not far from the pool. "You're insatiable."

"Complaints?"

"Not a one," she said, admiring his tight, fine ass as he bent over. His skin gleamed with droplets, clinging to every lean muscle. Yum.

He positioned the towels together and sat, stretched out his legs, and held out a hand. "Join me?"

Slipping her palm into his, she lowered herself to the towel and sat facing him. "This really is naughty. What if the neighbors call the police?"

"They won't. The old lady who lives on that side is ninety and never ventures out. The couple I told you about lives there," he said, pointing. "They're every bit as horny and we aren't doing anything they don't do every other night of the week."

She thought about that, and the idea gave her a wicked little shiver. "Now do I get to find out what's in the duffel?" He'd brought it from his apartment and dropped it with the towels when they came through the gate. The stinker had refused to tell her what was inside.

His grin would've melted her panties—if she had any. "Patience, honey. Now lie on your back and close your eyes."

Curious and excited, she did as he asked.

"No peeking."

"Okay."

She heard the zipper and some rustling around. A snap of a lid? Next, his palm smoothed over her tummy, and down one thigh.

"Put your arms over your head and cross your wrists, like you're bound." She did. "Good. Now spread your legs wider—let me see all of you."

His sensual command plucked at her nipples like a physical touch and they hardened, as much from this game as from the night air on her damp body.

His palm traveled upward to her breasts, grazed the sensitized points as he spoke, low and mesmerizing. "Sweet baby, look at you, all spread and ready for me. I can do anything I want and you'll love it—isn't that so?"

"Y-yes." She wiggled a little, burning. Right there, between her legs.

"You need it so bad. Need me to do decadent things to you right out here where anyone can see." His fingers found her sex, rubbing with just the lightest of touches, designed to drive her crazy. "I thought I saw a curtain move over there. Just imagine them watching while I play with you."

"Tommy," she whimpered.

"Yes, baby? Need me to do something about that ache? God, you're wet. So slick, I'm not even sure I need this, but it'll add to the experience."

His fingers disappeared and she heard a squirt. Then they returned, rubbing something slippery along her sex, all over her clit. As he rubbed, it warmed under his ministrations, transforming every spot on her body into a massive erogenous zone. She was lost to what he was doing to her, his control.

"Ooh." She moaned as a finger slipped inside, spreading the moisture.

She loved being bared to him, and this naughty tryst made

her wonder about herself. He'd said he was a bit of an exhibitionist, and it seemed he wasn't alone.

Her nipples were pinched, oiled, and she arched her back with a gasp. He played with them for a few moments, and then moved between her spread thighs.

"Lift your legs and bend your knees, but keep your legs spread, out to the sides," he said, voice husky.

She complied, imagining what she must look like, offered to him this way. "I want to open my eyes so I can watch you."

"No. Keep them closed, just feel."

More oil dribbled on the exposed lips of her sex and he worked it over every crease, teased her throbbing clit. Some of the oil streaked downward, between her cheeks. His hand followed, smoothing the liquid all the way to—

"You're not—"

"Shh, relax. Open to me, sweetheart," he murmured. "Trust me, give yourself to me."

His seduction was too much to resist. So naughty. Forbidden.

One well-oiled finger dipped inside the small opening. Twisting slowly, stretching. She felt him move without removing his hand and suddenly his breath puffed against her slit.

"There you go, baby. You're all mine. So pretty, writhing on my hand, begging for more. And you do want more, don't you, my love?"

"Please, more!"

"More what?"

"Your fingers and your m-mouth. Tommy . . ."

The feeling of fullness increased, burning a little, as he added a finger or two. It was strange, but it felt good, too. Made her feel connected in more than a physical way. Why?

The truth washed over her in a wave of desire.

Submitting to this man, belonging to him, made her complete.

His hot tongue licked her slit. Just the tip and nothing more. Teasing, like a feather. Light enough to drive her insane as he worked her hole, turning her into a ball of mindless sensation.

"You want my mouth, honey?"

"Yes, dammit!"

His chuckle floated in the darkness. "Anything for my girl. You'll have my mouth, and I'm going to eat you until you come so hard you melt. But I won't be finished with you just yet."

"Tommy!"

"Know what I'll do to you next? I'm going to fuck you, honey. Right here," he said, twisting his fingers. "I'm going to fuck you until you scream, and you're going to come for me again."

With that, he lapped at her sex, tasting. True to his word, he ate her like a starving man, leaving no spot unattended. The storm built fast and she tried to hold back for a bit, but when he latched on to her clit and began to suck it like a piece of delicious hard candy, she came undone.

Forgetting about his order to keep her hands over her head, or not really caring, she reached down and buried her fingers in his hair. Her orgasm splashed over her in luxurious waves and she cried out, riding the pleasure.

When the last tremor subsided, she felt him withdraw, and reached for him automatically.

"I'm just getting myself ready. Not going anywhere. You can watch now if you want."

Shea opened her eyes to see a pagan god kneeling near her feet. Keeping his gaze locked on hers, he opened a foil packet and sheathed his erection. Next, he tipped a bottle over his cock and fisted himself, making the shaft nice and slick.

"Will . . ." She swallowed hard, nervous and already tingling again in arousal. "Will you fit?"

His mouth tilted up at the corners. He looked so sexy, feral, preparing himself in the moonlight. "If I don't, I won't hurt you. Trust me."

"I've trusted you so far, haven't I?"

He didn't answer. Just scooted forward and scooped his hands under her bottom. With little effort, he lifted her up. "Put your legs over my shoulders."

In this position, she was more exposed than ever, if possible. She had a fleeting thought that she should've been afraid, but wasn't. The languid haze spread to every limb once more, as if he had her enchanted.

Spreading her cheeks, he brought the head of his cock to her opening. Began to push, his face suffused with hunger.

"Oh!"

"Doing good, baby." More, inches at a time. "How do you feel?"

"Full," she moaned. "So full."

"Almost there. I wish you could see my cock splitting you wide, claiming your pretty ass." And then his groin was snug against her, balls rubbing her backside. "Ah, yes."

"Move, do something," she begged, clutching the towel on either side of her body. "I need you."

He began to pump, slowly at first, letting her adjust. This was a fire that had never consumed her before and she was helpless as it built. Burned higher.

"Fuck, yeah. Sweet baby."

She thrashed, lost in how wonderful it was to be impaled on him. Owned by him. "Harder!"

Her demand flipped the switch and he gave her what she

wanted. Fucked her with abandon, hips driving like a piston. Keeping her steady with one hand, he reached to her sex and massaged the tiny nub, relentless.

To her amazement, a second orgasm unfurled, shaking her apart. "Oh, God! Yes!"

Tommy thrust deep and held there, throwing back his head with a hoarse cry. Heat warmed her inside, completing the circle. She'd never seen a man more beautiful in the throes of ecstasy.

His cock twitched a few more times, and he gradually relaxed. Came down off the euphoric high and opened his eyes, smiling. "You were incredible."

"Me? You're the gorgeous god who seduced me under the stars. Bad man, you."

"Your man." He slipped out gently and removed the condom, tying it off and wrapping it in a paper towel, then placing it in his duffel to dispose of later.

As he stretched out beside her, she rolled to face him. "You are my man." Reaching out, she touched his face. "And I love you."

His eyes widened and he snatched her into his arms, rolling her on top of him. "Say it again."

"I love you."

He laughed, the sound of sheer joy, and pulled her down for a lengthy kiss. When they broke away he said, "I love you, too. I wish I didn't have to work tomorrow."

"Call in sick. You can do that once in a while, right?"

He sighed. "I could, but I'd better not. We've been swamped with lots of calls lately. But soon, okay? We'll plan a hooky day."

"Okay." Damn. "Hey, Tommy?"

"Hmm."

"Did you really see the curtain move?"

"Yep."

Now that reality had crept in, her face heated. "Do you think they saw?"

"I don't know. Want to wave at them?" He started to lift his hand, but she slapped it down.

"Don't you dare!"

"Just tryin' to be neighborly, honey."

"You're a nut."

"I'm your nut. And hey!" He wiggled his lower half. "I've got two nuts."

She burst out laughing. "Oh, Lord, we'd better go inside before someone calls the police."

"Which probably wouldn't endear me to your brother."

"On that note, we're getting out of here!"

The idea of Shane hearing about this from one of his buddies got her moving. She leaped up and grabbed her towel, quickly shaking off the grass and wrapping it around her.

Tommy did the same. "Shower? Then we'll lock up and go."

"Lead the way."

He grabbed his duffel with one hand, her hand with the other, and pulled her toward the house. Walking by his side was the most natural thing in the world. She still had fears, but she felt capable of dealing with them now. She'd wasted enough precious time and wasn't willing to let doubts steal another second.

With Tommy by her side, she could do anything.

"What the heck are you grinning about?"

Tommy glanced up from the television show he hadn't paid a bit of attention to and looked over at Six-Pack. The lieutenant's big body was sprawled in one of their recliners and the guy was watching Tommy with a bemused expression on his face.

"Me? Not a thing. Just enjoying the program," he said,

waving at the TV. "Who doesn't like reruns of *America's Funniest Home Videos*?"

"Um, this is *Good Morning America*. I changed the channel ten minutes ago, buddy."

"Oh." Well, crap. Might as well come clean. "Okay, the truth is, I'm in love. And she loves me."

"Get out!" Six-Pack said, beaming at him. "Would she happen to be Cori's friend Shea? The girl we met at the Waterin' Hole and the one who took care of you in the ER a couple of weeks ago?"

He couldn't keep the pride out of his voice if he tried. "That's her. She's awesome. The real deal, if you get my meaning."

"I believe I do, having found the 'real deal' myself. Congrats. I mean that."

"Thanks." Tommy studied the older man, tempted to reveal his interest in a career change. He knew Six-Pack would be nothing but supportive, would even keep his confidence if he asked, but it wouldn't be right. Tommy needed to speak with Sean first. As captain, Sean had the right to know before anyone else. "You know if Sean's here yet?"

The good humor faded along with the other man's smile. "Actually—"

The phone rang, and rang again. Six-Pack shifted in his chair. "Everybody's outside. I'll get it."

"No, sit. I've got it." Tommy pushed off the couch and crossed to the phone on the table across the room. "Station Five."

"Uh . . . Skyler?"

"Hey, Cap. Runnin' late?" he asked, careful to keep his tone respectful.

"A bit. Be there in thirty."

Sean Tanner's vocal cords sounded like they'd been through a meat grinder. No doubt, he was hungover.

And late for work.

For the fourth shift in the past couple of weeks.

Tommy's hand tightened on the receiver as the lieutenant's eyes met his from the opposite side of the room. The older man's expression was grim as he shook his head. "I'll let Six-Pack know."

"Thanks. I appreciate it."

Sean disconnected before Tommy could reply. And shit, what could he have said that everyone hadn't already tried?

You've broken every single promise you made to us.

Get help. Before it's too late.

Right. That would go over well.

Tommy set the phone into the cradle and turned to see that Julian and Eve had joined them. A strained silence filled the next few heartbeats, until Tommy cleared his throat and shot his buddies a cheerful grin, hoping to distract them.

"So, what's for breakfast?"

Eve rolled her eyes. "Anything, as long as you're not cooking."

"Hey," Julian said, coming to his defense. "His breakfast the other day was great. We just didn't get to eat it. And he can now follow directions on a box without setting off the smoke alarm."

"Is the damned thing broken?"

Tommy relaxed. *This* was the normal bullshit. Just another day on the job.

Still, he mulled over the captain's losses, not to mention his own. He shivered, thinking of how one man's life can turn—or end—in the blink of an eye.

Fate was an evil, evil bitch. Sooner or later, she'd catch a man unaware. And burn his life to the ground.

With his soul trapped inside.

Christ, feeling love for someone outside family was new to him, and had obviously made him jittery. So far, in his experience, if something seemed too good to be true, it was.

If that wasn't so, Donny would still be alive.

Two hours later, when the call came, he wondered if he'd had some sort of premonition. Station Five was sent to assist on a two-alarm warehouse fire that was rapidly progressing to three. The caller had reported one night watchman inside, who was supposed to have gotten off duty at eight this morning and hadn't been located.

Fuck.

They arrived at the scene and Zack started readying the preconnected hoses while the others looked to Sean for their orders. Sean spoke briefly with the captain of Station Three, and walked back to join his team. Tommy frowned, thinking Sean's coordination seemed a little off, but immediately dismissed the notion. Though the man had problems, he'd never come to work incapacitated.

"What's the plan?" Six-Pack called above the crackling noise of the fire.

Sean stared at the building for perhaps two seconds too long before turning his bloodshot gaze to the rest of them. A tendril of dread curdled in Tommy's gut. He sloughed it off.

The captain shook his head as though to clear his thoughts. "We'll try and douse the fire from there and there," he said, pointing to the sides of the building. "Skyler, Marshall, you two are going in to assist Jones and Valdez from Station Three in conducting a search for the night watchman. Let's get moving."

Tommy and Eve slipped on their masks, turned on their Air-Paks, grabbed a pair of axes, and started for the structure. Tommy glanced around the parking lot and in an instant, something struck him as wrong. He couldn't pinpoint what at the moment, and then it got pushed to the back of his mind. They were in, and had work to do. If the man was still here, they had to find him, get him out safely.

The inside of the warehouse was thick with smoke, flames

shooting to the ceiling in places, spreading rapidly to wooden pallets stacked in clusters throughout the vast space. A high row of windows near the roof let in sunlight and kept the place from being too dark, but they all knew that even in broad daylight, the deadly smoke could render the visibility pitch-black in minutes.

Across the warehouse, he could barely make out the figures of two other firefighters searching as well. One gestured to their side and both of the corners, gave a thumbs-up to indicate an all clear. Eve waved and they made their way to the back of the building, picking carefully through the burning piles.

Sean's voice cut through the noise on their radio units. "North side is clear. Check the west side. There's an office, a break room, and restrooms back there."

Tommy keyed the microphone attached to the collar of his jacket. "We're on it."

In front of him, Eve paused in her trek and looked around, shaking her head. "I don't like this," she yelled over her shoulder.

He knew why, too.

"It's burning too hot," he called, hurrying to catch up. "I smell something, maybe gasoline."

"Think we've got another arson?"

"Could be. Look how the fire is concentrated in spots. Almost too neat, instead of starting in one corner as an electrical short or something, and spreading outward."

"You're good, kid." She turned briefly and from the way the corners of her eyes crinkled, he knew she was smiling.

"Not a kid."

"Yeah, yeah."

The back of the warehouse, along with the office, was empty. They checked quickly, and he thanked God the rooms were small, with few hidden nooks and crannies. The smoke was becoming dense, and they both knew time was of the essence.

As they left the office and stepped into the hallway to try the break room next, a groan shook the structure.

"Shit!" Eve pressed the button on her radio. "Tanner! What's the status?"

The answer was more than ten seconds in coming. "She's holding. Find the guy yet?"

"No. I don't think there's anybody here," she told him, tone rising. "The building is becoming too unstable."

Again the response took too long. "Complete the check."

They were already on it. He and Eve exchanged a worried look, the tension thick as the smoke.

"Will do," she snapped.

With angry strides, she led them to the break room. The silhouette of an old Coca-Cola machine hunkered on one wall, testament to the fact that they were in the right place. Thankfully, there was nothing else to be found.

The walls shuddered. Eve pressed the button one last time. "All clear in back." Pause. "Sean? What's going on with the other team? You want us out?"

Another shudder.

"Fuck this, we're gone," she barked. "Let's move!"

Hurrying, Tommy followed her out into the hallway. As he did, it hit him what was wrong with the scene in the parking lot.

There were no civilian cars. No vehicles that didn't belong to the fire department.

Which meant no night watchman. If there ever had been.

The third time the building shook, Howard whirled and got in Sean's face.

"What the fuck are you doing?" he yelled. "Get them out!"

"What?" Sean blinked at him, pale, almost in a daze.

The duo from Station Three burst from the warehouse, into the clear.

"Pull them out!" one of the men bellowed. "She's gonna go!"

Howard took charge, keying his mic. "Marshall, Skyler, vacate the premises! You copy?"

"Coming your way," Eve said, voice crackling on the other end. "Almost there."

He saw her emerging from the smoke, handing off her ax to Jules and pulling off her mask.

"Thank God."

Of course, at that moment, the walls of Jericho came tumbling down, and pitched them headlong into hell.

Tommy lost Eve in the smoke. One moment she was there and the next? Gone.

He kept moving forward, toward where he thought the entrance should be. Searched for daylight. Vision was shadowy, but he could just make out the interior highlighted by the last of the flames that hadn't yet been extinguished. Just a little farther—

A blow on the back of his head sent him to his hands and knees. Thankfully, his hat cushioned the impact, but it was now lying on the dirty floor in front of him. Stunned, he fought to regain his feet and pushed up. What the hell?

A second blow sent his senses reeling. His knees buckled and everything slowed as the floor rushed up to meet him. He lay prone, the ax next to his outstretched hand. The tank on his back was heavy, but oddly reassuring. He had air, he could make it out of here.

Disoriented, head spinning, he shoved upward once more.

And heard the building give a roar, like that of an enraged beast.

He knew, even before he got to his knees, before he looked up at the ceiling, that he was a dead man.

The walls gave up the ghost and with a mighty crack and a horrible rending noise, the roof plummeted. It came at him like a freight train and he had only a second to raise an arm in front of his face before he was slammed to the floor.

Debris rained down forever, piled on top of him.

Crushed. His body pinned, arms and legs immobile.

Pain. So much pain.

Can't breathe.

A shaft of sunlight broke through from somewhere above him, but his vision blurred. Then the light faded, along with awareness. No more agony.

So silent here. Strange, he'd never thought death would be so peaceful. Shouldn't this moment be more profound?

He was sad for his folks. *God, I'm so sorry.*

Both of their sons taken too soon. They didn't deserve this.

Will Donny be waiting for me?

The idea brought him comfort as consciousness slipped away.

Shea. Baby, be happy.

Awareness shrank to a pinprick, and then the world was gone.

13

Howard started for Eve, and the building let out a shriek. A sound he knew well, one that sent a jolt of fear through his system.

"Run!" he yelled.

As he waved her on, she sprinted toward the quint and safety.

Just as the entire structure collapsed.

Events seemed to unfold in slow motion. Eve spun, half stumbling, as the whole thing caved inward. Her scream went through them like a blunt spear, agonized.

"Nooo! Tommy!"

· She ran, but Howard caught her, dragged her backward. She fought him like a wildcat, no matter that she was no match for his size.

"Howard, let me go! Let go of me! He's in there and . . . Oh, no, no." She spun and launched herself at him blindly.

He pulled her against his chest, unable to take his eyes off the smoldering wreckage. Struggling to comprehend.

"I thought he was right behind me," she sobbed.

When his mind caught up to what his eyes were seeing, reality hit him hard. Skyler was probably dead. *Probably.* The odds had been cheated before.

That slim hope was good enough.

He turned to his stricken team, who stared at the charred

rubble in horror, and shouted loud enough to burst a blood vessel. "What the fuck are you all staring at, goddammit? *Fucking find him!*"

Shocked into action, they scrambled, yelling Tommy's name. Eve started to turn and he grabbed her arm.

"Are you okay?"

"No." Her chin quivered. "But he's my partner and I left him behind. I have to find him."

"You didn't leave him; the building fell on him. A huge difference." But he understood how she felt. He'd feel the same way under the circumstances.

She nodded, her expression miserable. "He should be near the front entrance, where we went in. We were almost outside."

"Okay. Go, help me tell them where to start looking."

At that moment, the kid's PASS device—Personal Alert Safety System—attached to his coat began to emit a shrill alarm, much like that on a car when it's been burglarized. That meant he'd been immobile for much too long, and Howard's heart wrenched.

After Eve jogged over to join the rest of the firefighters and the captain from the other engine company, Howard stalked over to Sean. The older man was leaning with his back against the door of the quint, head bowed, face in his hands.

Without thinking, Howard seized the front of his best friend's coat and shook him hard enough to rattle his teeth. "You're done, do you hear me? Finished."

Sean raised his face, expression tortured. "Howard—"

"Shut up! Just shut the fuck up. Because you were hungover and exhausted, because you hesitated and couldn't make a decision, that young man might be dead," he yelled, getting in Sean's face. "The only reason I'm not beating you to death is it's partly my fault. I stood by and I watched it happen, and I trusted you one too many times."

"Howard, I saw them," Sean whispered.

"Wh-what? Who?"

"My family. Blair, Bobby . . . and Mia. I couldn't get to them." His voice broke. "I couldn't get to them."

Sean slid down the engine, tears streaming down his face.

God in heaven. To his knowledge, Sean had never cried after their deaths. Never. And now he was having, what? A flashback?

So here it was, the final breakdown. Rock bottom. And Howard knew what to do, because he'd coached himself through the motions in preparation for this day.

He retrieved his cell phone from inside his coat and made a call to fire chief Bentley Mitchell, who was supposed to retire at the end of June, and had postponed the event for a few months. Thank God.

After two rings, the man picked up.

"Dad," he said. "I need your help."

After he'd explained the situation, his dad promised to come right away. Feeling no relief, Howard made one more call, this one to Shane Ford at work.

"Ford. What's up?"

"Detective, this is Howard Paxton."

"Hey, great to hear from you! What can I do for you today?"

"This isn't a good call, Shane. You know your sister is dating one of our guys, right? Tommy Skyler?"

"Well, she doesn't tell me a lot about her love life lately, but I'd kind of hoped things would work out." Caution edged into his voice. "Why? What's going on?"

Howard told him. And when he was finished, he said, "I think she'd better hear this from her brother, in person."

"Ah, fuck," he said quietly. "I'll head over to the hospital now. Thanks for calling, Howard."

"No problem. I didn't want her hearing this from the news or some shit."

"Call me as soon as they find him."

"Will do."

Hanging up, he replaced his phone and crouched in front of his best friend. He grabbed Sean's shoulders and shook him. "Look at me. Dad is coming, and when he gets here, you're going to go with him and you *will* do what he says, no questions asked. Okay?"

No response.

"We're going to get you through this. Do you understand? Sean?"

The other man raised his head, green eyes ravaged with pain. "Nobody can help me now. It's too late."

"No, it's not. Don't you quit on me, you selfish bastard," he said harshly. "Don't you dare."

"Howard . . ." He looked away, lost. In a daze.

"I'm here, buddy."

"I want to die."

And there it was. The crux of the matter, naked and exposed. At last.

"Tough shit. We're not going to let you." Torn between his responsibility to the search effort and his duty to a fallen friend, he pulled Sean close, the lump in his windpipe as big as an apple. "I will *not* let you."

"I'm so tired."

"I know." *Oh, sweet Jesus. Help me.*

A throat cleared and he looked up to see Captain Reynolds standing there, sympathy etched on his craggy face. There wasn't anyone in the fire department who didn't know Sean's story.

"I just wanted you to know I've got things in hand. They're still looking, but so far . . ."

"Thanks, I appreciate it. I'll be over there to help as soon as Chief Mitchell gets here."

God, don't let Tommy be dead, please. Sean would never survive, and neither would our team.

"No problem, son," the captain said kindly.

The captain walked away, toward the building, and Howard comforted the man in his arms as best as he could. It wasn't enough, but it was all he had to give.

All that was left to do was continue to be there for Sean.

And pray they all survived the fallout of this day.

"Did Hensley report in?"

Forrest's hand tightened on the receiver. Rose had no idea Hensley hadn't done the job, or that the firefighter's demise wasn't simply an accident, a casualty of their plans, so to speak. And there was no reason he *needed* to know about Forrest's side deal, either.

Best that Rose believe Will was the one buried in the rubble along with Skyler. If they were lucky, he'd never learn differently. He'd just have to get Will out of town before Rose arrived.

"No. It's been too long, so I'm assuming he perished in the collapse along with the firefighter."

His stomach threatened to eject his breakfast, but he held on somehow. He didn't like to lose, but murder was an appalling way to ensure a win. Almost like a cop-out. *Better them than me.*

"Too bad," Rose said, not sounding sorry. "The authorities will find his body and assume he's the missing night watchman?"

"At first. When they realize there was no guard, they'll probably think whoever reported that was wrong and he was a derelict."

"Fine. He can't be tied to us anyway, nor can the money we paid him be traced back to us. We made certain of that."

"True."

They had a maze of safeguards in place to protect their scam. It would take a genius to unlock them. Though the Feds had some pretty smart people employed to ferret out information—no, he wouldn't think of that.

"As soon as I have my money from this job, our association is at an end," the man said. "When I arrive in town, should our paths cross, you don't know me, and we've never spoken in our lives. And you won't get in my way. Is that clear?"

"Crystal."

Ever since the day Jesse Rose had arrived in Sugarland more than two years ago and showed up on Forrest's doorstep sporting a cocky grin, his life had been hell. The bastard had proof in hand that Forrest was skimming money from the city coffers, and had proposed a deal—Forrest's cooperation in a massive fraud scheme in exchange for Rose allowing him to live to enjoy the money. They'd both benefit from the relationship, he'd said.

And they had. Forrest had no idea what Rose did or intended to do with his portion of the money, nor did he care. Thank God Rose would soon be out of his life, and that was enough.

But Forrest's relief was short-lived as the man continued.

"I expect that sum will include the two million you've skimmed off the top of our agreement, plus a twenty percent penalty. I believe that's fair. Besides, you'd have to be breathing for it to do you any good, correct? Have a nice day."

The asshole disconnected and Forrest replaced the handset, slumping in his office chair. "He knows."

Desperation clawed at his belly, sudden and foul. Will had warned him not to cross this man, but he hadn't listened. As with so many other details, he had to have his way.

He had to find a way to distract himself from his current predicament, or he'd go mad. What to do?

The news. Maybe he could learn something more about the warehouse collapse.

Nervous, Forrest flipped on the small television set in the corner of his office, the one he used as city manager to keep him abreast of current happenings in the area.

A feverish search was under way for the firefighter, and hopes were dimming in regard to finding him alive.

With any luck, he'd have a lady to console before the day was done.

"Shea, honey, your brother is here to see ya," Dora said, catching Shea as she left a patient's exam room.

Shea glanced up from the papers she was reading. "Did he say what he wanted?"

"No, but I don't think he's going to leave until he talks to you. Seems important."

He wouldn't, either. He'd make like a boulder in the waiting area until she made time for him, so she might as well see what he wanted and send him on his way.

"All right, thanks. I'll get rid of him."

"Oh, don't hurry on my account." Dora's tone left no doubt she'd be more than happy to keep her brother occupied.

Shea smiled and shook her head, and started down the hallway for the waiting room. She found Shane near the double doors, pacing with a frown on his face rather than lounging in a chair thumbing through a magazine as he usually did.

"Hey, Bro," she said, giving him a peck on the cheek in

greeting. "What's up? I'm not sure I can get away for lunch today, if that's what you were thinking."

"No, that's not why I'm here." When he paused, something in his demeanor set off alarm bells. "Is there somewhere we can go to talk in private?"

"I—sure. This way."

She led him through the double doors, down the hallway past the break room where he ate lunch with her now and then. When they came to a private family consultation room that wasn't in use, she gestured him inside. The expression on his face was one she'd hoped never to see again—filled with anguish for what he had come to say.

"Shane? What is it? You're scaring me," she said, grabbing his arm.

Gently, he took both of her hands in his. "Sis, I got a call a short while ago from Howard Paxton, Tommy's lieutenant. There was a fire at a warehouse, and it collapsed."

Collapsed. She stared at him, processing the word. Then the meaning behind the word. Strange how the little things, like the lines around Shane's mouth, the tick of the clock on the wall, the voices in the hallway, became sharper when bad news was imminent. She'd been here before, like this, with him.

Cold swept through her, but not enough to numb the fear.

"No," she cried, shoving at his hands. But he refused to let go. Her voice rose in panic. "No, don't you tell me anything bad has happened. I won't accept that."

His face twisted with remorse. "Sweetheart . . . he didn't make it out. They're searching, but—"

"Oh, my God." The room spun and she felt him grab her around the waist, guide her to sit in a chair. "What do you mean they're searching? How long ago was this?"

He sat down next to her, not relinquishing her hands. "Howard called about twenty minutes ago, and I rushed right over here. I got the impression that it just happened. The other firefighters got out safely before the building fell, but Tommy didn't. They're looking for him, and Howard promised to call as soon as they found him."

Her lips trembled and she clung to her brother. "They will, and he'll be fine."

Shane didn't say anything else for a long while.

Howard and Captain Reynolds kept the search organized, focused on the front of the building. The tall structure had been reduced to kindling no higher than his knees in many places, not an encouraging sight. Firefighters crawled all over the debris like ants, thankful the fire was out, though they kept a watchful eye for flare-ups.

They were working against the clock now, every single second one more off Tommy's life. The kid had to be about out of air by now, and could easily suffocate. The wail of his PASS device frayed everyone's nerves more with each passing minute, escalating their fears.

Howard was glad his dad had left with Sean a few minutes ago. His friend did not need to be around to witness whatever they found.

"Over here!" Jones, one of the Station Three guys, yelled. "Got him!"

Howard and the others converged on the spot, but had to slow down as they picked their way over the rubble. "Go easy," Howard advised. "We don't want anything to shift and hurt him worse."

If he was still alive, but nobody voiced that.

"He's about four feet down, under some boards and pieces of the tin roof," Jones said, pointing. "I can't see much except part of his coat, but he's not moving."

Julian started tossing shit aside. "Help me make this hole

wider so one or two of us can get down there next to him, free him, and lift him out on the backboard."

"Quick as you can, but careful," Captain Reynolds said.

"Tommy?" Eve called. "Can you hear us? Tommy!"

The lack of response dampened Howard's spirits, and he saw the impact reflected in the faces of the others as they worked, yet no less diligently. If anything, they doubled their efforts, finally widening an opening big enough for two of them to slip down next to Tommy and finish extricating him.

"I'll go," Julian said grimly.

"All right, you and me." He turned to tell Zack to run and grab the backboard and medical kit, but the man was already back with them, waiting to hand them down.

Julian went first and crouched next to the still form, Howard following. Howard grabbed the kit from Zack and peered into the space where Tommy lay, trying to see his injuries. He set the kit aside and they struggled to move boards and metal off him, some of the shrapnel twisted like spaghetti.

Tommy's back was to them, the Air-Pak hanging slightly off center. His blond hair was nearly gray with dust and dirt. Julian reached out and switched off the PASS device, and the silence, the complete stillness, was ominous. Working quickly, they managed to slip his free arm out of the strap holding on the tank, and moved the heavy piece of equipment off to the side. His other arm, however, was still caught under a sheet of metal.

"Let's roll him, easy. One, two—"

On three, they gently turned him onto his back . . . and Howard's heart nearly stopped.

"*Madre de Dios,*" Julian whispered.

The right side of the kid's face was sliced open, filleted,

right through the straps on his face mask. An angry red line traveled from his temple, down his cheek, and curved underneath his jaw, almost bisecting his throat. He was awash in blood. But if they'd hoped that would be the worst of it, nobody upstairs was listening.

"My God, his hand," Howard said hoarsely.

His wrist wasn't just pinned—it was severed almost clean through by a shard of metal the size of a dinner plate. The fact that it was still deeply embedded there was probably the sole reason their friend hadn't bled to death.

Julian pressed two fingers to the side of his neck. "Alive, thank God, but weak. We've got to get him out of here."

"Help me get this mask off."

Howard held his head steady while Julian slipped the mask off and discarded it. Tommy's face was pale, lips parted, lashes resting against his cheeks. He appeared to be barely breathing.

Quickly, Julian put on a neck brace as a precaution, to avoid more damage, if possible. They left the metal in his wrist. It wasn't safe to remove it, except by the surgeon in the OR.

Howard didn't want to think about the road ahead for Tommy, if he made it. Which was far from a given.

Tommy's lashes fluttered and he moaned, pale blue eyes glazed. "Six-Pack?"

"Easy does it, kid. We're getting you out of here."

"Tell my parents . . . I'm sorry . . ."

"Can't do that, cause you're going to be fine. Tommy?"

No answer. His eyes closed.

They ran an IV, strapped on an oxygen mask, and checked his vitals. "He's in shock," Julian said, voice anxious.

"BP's slipping."

Julian grabbed the backboard. With as much care as possible, they worked his Air-Pak the rest of the way off, moved him onto the hard surface, and strapped him down. Ready to go, they stood and lifted their burden, keeping him level. Zack and Eve were waiting to take him.

The others gave a cheer, more as a morale boost than any conviction that Tommy would be fine. A couple of the men helped him and Julian out of the hole, and Howard turned to Captain Reynolds.

"We've got this," Reynolds said, waving a hand at the mess. "You guys go ahead and take care of your own."

"Thanks, I appreciate it." He wanted to say more, but words failed.

"No problem. We'll give you the next clean-up duty."

Howard managed a halfhearted smile. "Done."

"Let us know how he's doing."

Howard nodded and jogged toward the ambulance, where Zack and Eve were loading the gurney into the back. Howard jumped in the driver's seat of the ambulance and Julian rode in the back, monitoring Tommy.

"Goddamn, I'm down two good men."

He didn't envy any of them what lay ahead.

Least of all, Sean and Tommy.

Shea jumped when Shane's cell phone rang. She wrung her hands as he listened, and pounced on him the second he hung up.

"They've found him and got him out, alive."

"Oh, that's wonderful! He's okay, right?"

"I don't know, hon. Howard just said they're bringing him in, and to keep you out of the way."

"What! What does that mean? I can't see him?"

"I'm assuming that's what it means, yes. Here, sit back down."

"I don't want to sit! I'm going out there to wait, and

you're not going to stop me," she declared loudly. "I work here, not you."

"Shea—"

As she marched out, the first person she saw was Dora. "What's going on? Have they radioed in?"

To her credit, Dora didn't even try to feign ignorance or offer her false assurances. "He's going straight to surgery," she said calmly. "He's busted up pretty bad, sustained some lacerations and has some blood loss. He's in shock. It's not good, sweetie."

She felt Shane's palms on her shoulders, his body strong and solid behind her. *Oh, no. He has to be all right.* "Thank you for telling me."

"There's something else—"

Just then a commotion outside interrupted and a gurney burst through the doors, being pushed by Howard and Julian. When she caught sight of Tommy lying there, face slashed, covered in blood, her knees almost buckled. And his hand . . .

"Oh, my God! Tommy—"

She tried to rush to his side, to follow as the others met the doctor and turned down another corridor toward the OR, but Shane held her back.

"You'll just be in the way, sweetheart," he said, hugging her tight. "They need to be focused on him, not you. I'll stay with you, okay?"

"D-did you see him? His face, and his wrist . . ."

"He'll be fine," Shane said, trying to soothe her. "Why don't we go back into the private room and wait?"

"His hand was almost severed, for God's sake! Do you have any idea what that means or what it will do to him? How can you say he'll be fine?"

"I know what it means. But right now, the main concern

is making sure he's out of danger. The rest can be dealt with later."

Having apparently handed off Tommy to the surgical team, Howard and Julian rounded the corner and came toward them. The men shook hands and Howard studied Shea, expression bruised. Weary.

"I'm not going to lie to you. It's bad," he said quietly before she could ask. "If we'd found him ten minutes later, he wouldn't have made it. He'd lost a lot of blood and wasn't getting enough air. As it stands, I believe he'll survive, but there's a possibility he could lose that hand. I don't know for sure, though. I'm not a specialist."

Shea swallowed back her tears. "As long as he's alive, nothing else matters. We'll help him deal with the rest as it comes."

Howard gave a faint smile. "I'd hug you for that, but I'm filthy. He's going to need people around him with positive attitudes." His smile vanished and he wiped his eyes, looking tired. "Speaking of which, I've got to call his parents. God Almighty, I don't want to tell them."

"Want me to call?" Julian offered.

"Nah, I'd better do it. I feel obligated."

Dora spoke up. "You guys are welcome to wait in the private room. There's a phone in there, too, if you need it."

"Thanks," Howard said. "We'll take you up on the offer and stay until we get some word, or until we receive a call."

"Stay as long as you need to. Shea, honey, I'm thinking you're going to be worthless this shift. Why don't you go ahead and clock out, wait with them."

"Thank you, Dora. I'll make this up to you."

"No problem, sweetie. I know you'd do the same for me." Dora gave her a quick hug and hurried off to tend to patients.

Shane sighed. "This could take a while. You might have been better off working to keep busy, take your mind off of things."

"If you really think that, you don't know me very well."

"Yeah, that was stupid. Forget I said it."

"I will." She walked back into the consultation room, wondering how things could be going so beautifully, then turn into such a nightmare.

"Are you going to be all right?"

In spite of herself, she softened at his concern. "Always the worrywart. It's Tommy who's in there, not me."

He cocked his head, studying her. "In some ways, it is you. Why didn't you tell me?"

"Tell you what?"

"That you love him," he said, sounding hurt and trying not to let it show.

"It's not like we were keeping it a secret from anyone." She hugged him, resting her head on his shoulder. "We just admitted it ourselves. I'm not trying to cut you out of the loop."

His sigh was one of relief, his voice filled with affection. "I'd wondered, after our difference of opinion about Forrest Prescott. You're not still mad at me?"

"I wasn't. I was mad at myself. I didn't want to admit you were hitting too close to home." She hesitated. "Deep down, I knew I was settling for a 'safe' man because Tommy frightened me."

"And I know why."

"Yes, you do."

"He doesn't any longer?"

"I'm not afraid of *him*. I'm afraid of me. Or, I was. Maybe not so much now."

"You're putting way too much pressure on yourself. Relax and go with the flow."

She smiled. "You sound like Tommy."

"Smart man."

"You know what? I do trust him," she said in a sudden epiphany. "And when he comes out on the other side of this, I'm going to tell him everything. I know he's not anything like the bastard who hurt me."

"Good for you, sweetheart. I've been waiting a long damned time to hear you say that about someone who can make you happy."

She squeezed him tight. "When are you going to find some lucky woman to make *you* happy?"

He laughed. "They call me the breeze, baby."

"I don't believe that bull for a second."

"Let's get your life in order first, shall we? Then you can meddle in mine. Tit for tat."

"I'm going to hold you to that."

She would, too. As soon as Tommy was okay.

14

Lights flashed overhead, bright. Blinding him.

Disjointed voices spoke in sharp, urgent tones, but he couldn't make sense of what they said. Or where he was.

His body was lifted, moved. Settled somewhere new. The lights stopped spinning, but one was like a giant eye, skewering his brain.

Blurry forms hovered above him, dressed in white. Were they angels? Was this heaven?

If so, the hurting should stop. And he told them so, or thought he did. After all, if pain was supposed to be a distant memory in heaven, he'd gotten screwed.

"H-h-hurts."

Gentle hands smoothed his brow. "I know it does. Easy."

"Mr. Skyler, you're in surgery, and you're going to take a little nap. When you wake up, your friends and family will be here for you, okay?"

What? Surgery?

"Not heaven?"

Which, of course, came out *noth theven?*

"Not today," the kind voice told him. "Count backward from ten, Mr. Skyler."

Huh? Well, all right.

"Ten . . . nine . . . uh . . ."

What came next?

Didn't matter. He was too tired to count anymore, and the figures above him vanished into darkness.

What a weird thing for an angel to ask him to do, anyway.

Consciousness filtered in slowly, marked by sounds. A rustle, quiet conversation. Strange beeps. Smells came next. Antiseptic and cleaner. Familiar perfume as someone leaned close. Vanilla.

Then touch. A hand on his face, his arm. He liked this best and strained for more, though he wasn't sure his message came across.

He drifted, wondering whether he was dead. Or simply waiting to cross over.

That question was answered soon enough, when the agony returned.

He felt as though he'd been beaten with hammers. There was no place that didn't scream in misery. He must've made a sound, because someone was there in an instant, trying to soothe him.

"Tommy? Oh, thank God! Don, he's waking up!"

"Son, can you hear us?"

"Mom . . . Dad."

"Son, do you know where you are?" Dad.

"I—no." He tried to open his eyes, but his lids were so heavy.

Mom's voice drifted to him, choked with tears. "You're in the hospital, baby. You were hurt on the job, but you're going to be fine. Just fine."

This didn't make much sense. He attempted to process this as painful awareness seeped into individual parts of his throbbing body. Automatically, he tried lifting his arm, but it was weighed down as though by a brick. "How? What—"

"Don't worry about that right now. Just rest," his dad said.

Wasn't like he had a choice. He was so tired.

Sleep claimed him once more.

When awareness returned, it was much sharper. So was the relentless pain. His chest and ribs were locked in a vise, his face and hand throbbing.

This time, his lids obeyed and opened, though reluctantly. His bleary vision began to adjust, taking in his surroundings. He was lying in a bed, wires and tubes attached to every available patch of skin. Had someone said something about being injured, mentioned surgery? They must have, but the memory vanished like smoke.

Another fact penetrated his brain—he was surrounded by flowers. Practically a garden, with several balloons dancing around. They made his head swim.

He was in the hospital, then. Had the shit knocked out of him, but he was alive. Okay. He could deal with that.

One issue at a time. Blinking to clear the grit from his eyes, he took stock of himself.

A strange pressure and a sensation of tightness on the right side of his face was bugging him something fierce. Opening his mouth and stretching his facial muscles caused it to pull and sting, and his immediate reaction was to bring his hand up to touch the area.

Problem was, he couldn't move his arm. Hadn't he tried before? Damned thing felt like a rock.

His gaze slid down to where his right arm rested on top of the blankets. His hand and wrist were heavily bandaged, the wrap extending halfway up his forearm. A burn? Must not be broken, or it would be in a cast. He could deal with that, too.

He brought his left hand up instead to feel his face. The IV in the back of his hand pulled, making him wince, but he managed to reach up and brush his fingers over his right cheek.

"Jesus."

The entire right side of his face, extending underneath his jaw to his throat, was covered in gauze. Damn, he must've . . . what? Had a car accident?

No, that wasn't right.

Fire? Yes. Flames, smoke. He was looking for an exit when a heavy object fell on him.

The warehouse! It all came back in a rush. The urgency to get out, the terrifying roar of the building as it fell.

"Hello?" His voice emerged as little more than a croak. Just as he began eyeing the bed, searching for a call button, the door opened with a quiet swish and his dad walked in, carrying a cup of coffee.

The older man's eyes lit up. "Holy Christ, it's good to see you awake. How do you feel?"

"Like a building fell on my ass," he rasped. "What day is it?"

"Still Friday, almost six thirty in the evening. You've been in and out, trying to wake up for a couple of hours." His dad set the coffee on the bedside table and gave his son a careful hug. "I'm glad as hell you're all right."

As his dad pulled up a chair, Tommy saw the suspicious moisture in his eyes that he dashed away. "*Am* I all right? What about these?" He lifted his good hand and gestured to indicate the bandages.

A strange look flashed in the older man's eyes, and was gone. "Don't worry about that right now. We've got plenty of time to discuss it when you're better."

"I'm not better?" Alarm began to niggle at his brain.

"More alert, I mean. You're exhausted and you've been through quite an ordeal, whether you recall it or not. I want you to sleep," he said, the love and protectiveness apparent in his tone.

"I'm not ten, Dad. I know when I need to rest, and I will, after you give me the rundown."

"I'd rather wait for your mother. I took her home to rest herself for a while, but she'll want me to get her soon, especially when I call and let her know you're awake. That sweet girlfriend of yours, too. She went down to the cafeteria to get a quick bite to eat—"

"You're stalling." That scared him more than anything. His dad was the most up-front, honest person he knew, and if he was trying to put off the conversation, whatever had to be said wasn't good.

"Son—"

"Tell me."

The niggle of alarm grew exponentially. He knew that expression on his dad's face, the one that conveyed sadness, worry, and a little guilt for being the bearer of bad news. His dad let out a weary sigh and dropped his gaze to the floor. When he met Tommy's eyes again, he nodded, resigned.

"When the roof fell, a piece or two of metal caught you on the right side of your cheek. Laid you open pretty bad from your temple to your throat. You're stitched from here to here," he said, drawing a line on his own face to indicate the path.

"Oh, my God." He raised his hand again, felt the bandages. "I want a mirror."

"Not yet. There's more. Christ, this is so hard," he said, choking on the words. "You had a piece of metal embedded in your wrist as well. Son, your hand was nearly severed from your wrist. The surgery took hours, but the specialist said they think the reattachment will work, barring infection. You're on heavy antibiotics."

Tommy stared at his dad in shock. "Reattachment? What are you . . . are you fucking kidding me?"

"I wish I were. You're going to need physical therapy, and in time, you might regain some use of it. I'm so sorry, son," he said sadly.

"Regain . . . no. No, I'm a firefighter, at least until I figure out what else I want to do." His voice rose with his panic. "Shea encouraged me to try being a walk-on at the Titans' training camp. She said I could be anything I wanted and . . ."

He trailed off, gazing at the bandaged lump. Concentrating hard, he attempted to wiggle his fingers. Nothing. He looked up at his dad, panic morphing to terror.

"I—I can't work like this. I can't go back to my job, or play football. I can't do shit. It's over, isn't it? Every dream I've ever had. Everything. Oh, God, Dad," he whispered, his voice breaking.

Scooting close, his dad wrapped his arms around him, held him close. Tried to comfort him as he had when Tommy was a boy with hurts that a hug from Dad could fix.

But nothing could fix this. He was done.

My fucking hand was cut off.

And the best he could hope for was to keep it as a permanent reminder of what he'd lost.

"Your life isn't over, son," his dad said hoarsely. "Just going in a different direction. There was something else in the cards for you, that's all. You're going to be fine, and you've got your friends, your mother and me, and that pretty lady to help you through this."

Shea. How could he face her as less than a man? He felt sick.

"What do I have to offer her now? I don't know how I'll make a living and on top of that, I'll be scarred for life."

"Physical therapy will help, and you'll find a job."

"I want a mirror, Dad. Now."

He had to see for himself. To know what he was up against.

Suddenly looking old, his dad went out, presumably to ask a nurse about Tommy's request. He was gone for a few minutes and when he returned, he brought a medium-sized handheld mirror.

"Help me with the gauze."

Tommy held the mirror in his lap while the older man carefully peeled off the edges of the tape at his temple. He lowered the gauze pad enough for Tommy to be able to examine most of the wound.

Left hand shaking, he raised the mirror, turned his head to the side, and angled it to see—and almost dropped it.

"Oh," he moaned. "Oh, no."

He didn't recognize the face in the reflection. A black line of railroad tracks pulled his angry red flesh together and marched down the side of his face to his jaw and beyond. Nobody would ever mistake him for some handsome actor again, would they?

In a word, he was hideous.

The mirror slipped from his hand and plopped onto his lap. His dad silently removed it, retaped the gauze, and waited, anxious, gripping Tommy's forearm to lend his support. Hot, bitter tears slid down Tommy's face and his chest felt like it would explode.

He couldn't be that lucky.

Settling back on the pillows, he closed his eyes, wishing for oblivion. Darkness. He'd longed to be a man Donny would've been proud of, to make something meaningful out of his life. What would Donny say now, if he could?

Maybe his brother was the lucky one after all.

Shea crept into Tommy's room and laid her purse on the rolling table next to a pot of flowers. Mr. Skyler sat at his son's side, hands clasped in front of him, head down.

"Mr. Skyler?"

The man raised his head and gave her a bleary, sad smile. "Shea, you can call me Don."

"Okay, Don," she said, a little nervous. They hadn't spoken much, given the circumstances, but his folks seemed to be nice people who were desperately afraid for their son. "How is he?"

"Sleeping, doped on painkillers. Woke up for a bit and had questions about all of this." He flicked a hand to indicate the bandages. "I answered them as honestly as I knew how."

Shea moved to stand beside him and studied Tommy's pale face, the half she could see. Dark circles were smudged under his eyes and he still had dirt in his hair. But he was here, breathing. Alive.

"How did he take the news?"

"About like you'd expect—badly. He insisted on looking at his face, too." Don appeared miserable. "He was absolutely devastated. I haven't seen him like that since he lost his brother."

"Oh, no." She laid a hand on his shoulder, heart twisting as she gazed at Tommy. "I was hoping to put off his seeing himself a little longer."

"Me, too. But once that boy gets his mind set on something, a team of horses can't budge him." Don met her eyes. "And I'll tell you another thing, he's got it in his head that he has nothing to offer you now."

Oh, God. "That's his emotions talking. They're bound to be all over the place for a while."

"We know that, but he doesn't. Not yet. He'll find another career, other interests, and in the meantime we'll all be here to support him."

"Isn't that nice? I feel so much better."

Startled by the bitterness, the anger, in Tommy's raspy voice, Shea looked down at him. His eyes were open, and the dullness there frightened her even more. Gone was the playful sparkle, the hint of promise.

"Son, we love you and we just want to help—"

"Well, you can't."

Don's expression was wounded, but he stood firm. "You don't think so now, but you're upset. We're here for you, whether you want us to be or not."

"Upset. What a tidy word." His laugh was ugly. "Do I look upset to you? I don't know."

Don gave a resigned sigh and stood. "I'm going to give you and Shea a chance to talk while I run home and get your mother. I know she wants to see you before visiting hours are over."

"Don't bother, okay? I'm tired and I'll be asleep." Tommy stared at the opposite wall, not meeting his dad's scrutiny.

"If you're sure . . ."

"I am. And if you'd take those fucking balloons with you, I'd appreciate it. Tell the nurses to give them out in the kids' ward. Where the hell did all those flowers come from, any-way?"

Don shared a pained glance with Shea, and she could swear he was silently wishing her luck with their surly pa-tient. "You have a lot of friends, son. They're just trying to cheer you up."

"Fantastic. Do you think there's a plastic surgeon with a magic wand hiding in one of those pots?"

Don just turned and busied himself detaching the ribbons on the balloons from the various arrangements. Clutching them, he said, "Your mother and I will see you in the morn-ing. Call if you need anything before then."

His father was almost to the door when Tommy called out.

"Dad?"

Don looked back. "Yes?"

"Thanks for being here," he said, voice anguished. "I'm sorry I spoke to you that way."

His father's face softened. "Never thank me for being

your dad. As for the other, I understand, believe me. See you in the morning."

"See you."

After the older man was gone, Shea took his vacated seat and steeled herself for the conversation to come. She didn't need a crystal ball to see the man in the bed was about to do some serious backpedaling. Anger and confusion fairly vibrated around him, and the wall quickly being erected between them was as impenetrable as a fortress.

She'd spent so long being afraid to love him. Now she was terrified of losing him.

Reaching out, she rested her arm on his pillow and ran her fingers through his hair. "You don't know how scared I was when I found out what happened, and that they were looking for you. When they brought you in, I was there, and I was scared I'd lose you. Thank God you're going to be all right."

"Is that what you think? That I'll be *all right*? That I'm happy as shit to be twenty-three years old and facing the prospect of no job, no future? That I'm thrilled to carry a reminder of my failure on my face for the rest of my goddamned life? Excuse me if I don't leap for joy and praise God that I'm not dead!"

His shout echoed in the small room like a bomb, explosive and every ounce as destructive. His eyes were wild, like a trapped animal ready to chew his leg off to escape confinement.

"Well, you're *not* dead," she said calmly, taking back her hand. "And it's not fair of you to wish you were when so many others might have begged for the second chance you received. Especially your own brother."

He flinched, but his steely tone didn't change. "Don't talk about Donny to me. And what the hell do you know about second chances?"

Grief swept her, and her voice broke. "I know that my baby never got a second chance. I know that I'd give almost anything if she'd had one."

That stopped him cold. "Your—your baby?"

"My daughter. You see, I made the mistake of falling for a football player, the big man on campus. This plain Jane was easy pickings for a guy like him—he crooked his finger and I ran to him, grateful he asked me out. But when things went too far and I said 'no,' he didn't take that for an answer."

"You . . . you were raped?" Tommy looked ill.

"At seventeen. I turned eighteen in a hospital bed, recovering from losing my child and almost hemorrhaging to death. Shane and I lost our parents just a few months later."

"What happened to the baby's father?" he asked quietly.

"He served some time, lost his college football scholarship. After that, I have no idea. And I don't care."

Tommy looked away. "Finally, it all makes sense. Why you were so reluctant to be with me, to trust me." His tone was bitter. "I guess the writing was on the wall, wasn't it? You and me, we never would've worked. I started out as nothing more than a terrible reminder of what you lost, and now? I'm a joke."

"What?" She stared at him, alarmed. "You're not a joke! I love you! I don't care what you do for a living or if you have a scar. Those things don't matter."

"Look me in the eye and tell me I didn't remind you of *him.*"

"Okay, at first you did," she admitted. "But only on the outside, because of your looks and the fact that you're a jock. I was afraid to trust, but that wasn't a reflection on *you.*"

"Well, we don't have to worry about my looks anymore, do we?"

"Don't do this," she said. Unshed tears stung her eyes

and she struggled not to let them fall because it would be like admitting defeat. He was using every trick in the book to push her away and she was losing ground with each passing second. She'd never felt so helpless.

Tommy's eyes filled as well, but he didn't waver. "It's over."

"Tommy, no—"

"At least you still have your fancy city manager with his fine clothes, pretty manners, and his big wallet."

Her heart tore. "No. I don't want him. I want you."

"Get out."

"I love—"

"*Get out!*"

She knew what he was doing, that he didn't mean it. But she fled just the same—pushed from her chair, grabbed her purse, and hit the door running. Maybe later she'd regret allowing him to push her away, but at the moment, all that she could think of was escaping his rage. His endless pain.

She couldn't even call him a coward.

By running, she was a coward, too.

Shea left me.

Driving her away had been too damned easy.

Which meant he'd done the right thing. Saved them both a ton of heartache down the road. Saved the woman he loved from being tied to a man with an empty future. A man she hadn't wanted to be with in the first place, one who brought back awful memories.

He could survive without her. He could.

Alone in the gathering darkness, he covered his eyes with his good hand and wept.

Joseph was usually in bed asleep by now, but the sandman eluded him. So when the phone rang in the living room at an hour when no one usually called, he pushed from the bed and tottered to the door, twisted the knob slowly. He eased the door open and listened, not nearly as ashamed to do so as he would've been this time last week.

"Good, I'm glad this is over. I've got enough to see us through." Pause. "I don't want to know about this, Forrest."

Joseph straightened, every cell on alert. *Forrest Prescott?*

"No, I won't take responsibility for what you did to that firefighter! I never thought you'd actually go through with it! Don't try to divert the issue. What is our contact doing with all that money?"

Joseph braced himself against the wall, hand on his heart.

"None of my business? That's funny. Whatever, man. I don't care as long as I'm out. I didn't get anyone hurt this time and never on purpose. That was your deal." Pause. "Fine. Don't call me."

Will ended the call and Joseph crept into his bedroom, closing the door. Shuffling to the bed, he sat and considered everything he'd seen and heard, for a very long time.

His heart sank as he realized he was backed into a corner. Will needed help and there was only one way out he could figure.

He just had to find the courage to make that phone call.

15

Two weeks. She'd called three times; once while Tommy was still in the hospital and twice since he got home last week. He hadn't answered, or returned her calls.

His rejection hurt so bad she thought she'd die, but she held on to the knowledge that he was, in actuality, rejecting himself. Didn't make the pain any less, but at least it made sense.

She hated to picture him alone in his apartment, in great emotional distress and not speaking to anyone, but his dad had told her that's exactly what he was doing. He'd shut out his parents and his friends. Refused to discuss how he was doing, just waved it off and said he was fine.

He was in pain, and she couldn't reach him. He'd have to make the first move, and that wouldn't happen until he'd come to grips with his situation. He had to decide he was as much a man as before, and let her in. Until he did, it wouldn't work between them.

And he might never come around.

The phone rang and she practically attacked the damned thing, fumbling it to read the caller ID. Her heart sank when she saw the name and number, and she felt foolish for getting her hopes up. Still, it would be good to hear a friendly voice other than her brother's.

"Hello, Forrest."

"Hey, beautiful. Got time for a friend?"

"Of course I do," she said, picking at the sofa cushions.

"I wasn't sure, given the way we left things before."

"I feel bad about that." Which was true. "I never meant to hurt your feelings."

"Oh, it's all water under the bridge. No worries. Speaking of my rival, I wanted to call and tell you I saw on the news about what happened to Skyler, and I'm terribly sorry. How is he doing?"

Rival? What an odd word, out of place with his sympathy. Not to mention that Forrest had never really posed any competition against Tommy.

"Not very well. If you don't mind, I'd rather not get into it." She winced at her sharp tone.

"I—oh, no," he breathed. "You two aren't seeing each other anymore, are you?"

"Change the subject, or I'm hanging up."

He sighed. "I apologize. I just wanted to know if you were free for dinner tomorrow night. As friends. I have to admit, I could use one."

"Yeah? Maybe I could, too," she said, relenting. "I shouldn't have been so short with you."

"We've both been under a lot of stress lately. Why don't we go out and forget about it all for a little while? Please?"

What else was she going to do? Sit around here and mope until Tommy decided to give them a chance? If he ever did.

"Sure, why not? What time?"

"Wonderful! I'll pick you up at seven and we'll go have some Chinese or Mexican. Whatever you want."

"Sounds good. See you then."

"I'm looking forward to it."

For a long time, she sat with the phone in her lap, willing it to ring. She'd much rather spend the evening with the man she loved.

With every passing day, it looked as though she was waiting for the impossible.

He stood on the edge of the precipice, unable to go either forward or backward. Death awaited him in either direction, mocking his puny efforts to cheat it.

Behind him, slow torture. Before him, a swift end.

He knew his choice, and his heart lurched.

He lunged for the edge, and Shea screamed—

Tommy's eyes popped open. He lay curled in his bed on his side, disoriented, gasping, still vibrating from the nightmare.

A pounding noise filtered into his brain as the dream faded, and he gradually realized the sound was part of the real world.

The racket was accompanied by a deep, insistent voice. And whoever was there wasn't giving up anytime soon.

He pushed out of bed and swayed on his feet, dizzy. The pain pills made him loopy and he hated them, but he disliked pain even more. The bruises on his body were healing and while the scar on his face was sensitive, it didn't sting. But his wrist and hand ached like a bitch. He'd been lucky infection hadn't set in, and the skin was pink and healthy.

Lucky. Hah.

Stumbling through the mess in his living room, he tried to be careful where he stepped. Wouldn't do to fall and injure his useless extremity. Then he'd have to get fitted for a fake hand, and how fun would that be?

The pounding increased in volume, as did the yelling on the other side.

"I'm coming, dammit!"

Using his left hand, he fumbled with the lock and flung open the door. Great. On the threshold, looking as though they'd lost their best friends, were Zack, Eve, Julian, and Six-Pack, who was clearly the one doing the pounding and yelling.

"You going to invite us in, or what?" he demanded.

Tommy attempted a smile and a wave, but immediately lowered his hand so they wouldn't see how badly it shook. "Sorry, guys. I was asleep and didn't hear the door at first. Come in."

"*Chingado*," Julian muttered, glancing around in disgust.

Standing aside, Tommy waited for them to file in and closed the door, breathing through his mortification. The very last thing he'd wanted was for his friends to see the disaster of his apartment, not to mention the sorry state of his person.

Tommy studied the place and saw it through new eyes. Pizza boxes, milk on the counter, dishes overflowing in the sink, newspapers, beer cans. Six-Pack found the last and swung his angry gaze to Tommy's.

"Tell me you are not drinking while taking painkillers."

"Not at the same time," he lied. "I've been careful."

The lieutenant, who topped Tommy by nearly six inches in height, was truly a fearsome sight as he stalked forward, muscles straining under his T-shirt. "Jesus Christ! As if I don't have enough to deal with getting Sean well, and now this? I find you living like a pig, not bothering to answer the phone, not eating right, and you fucking stink! When's the last time you had a shower?"

Tommy's face heated. "Nobody asked you to deal with me! I'm not your problem."

"No, you're not," he yelled, poking Tommy in the chest. "You're my friend, you ignorant jackass! Every one of us is here because we care about you."

"And you not being at the station is never going to change that," Eve said softly. "We love you, Bro."

"Aw, damn . . ." His voice choked and his gaze dropped to the floor. "Here I am doing my best to be a shithead and you guys have to go and say something nice."

"But you do stink," Julian said. The others chuckled and he shrugged. "I'm just sayin'."

"I was going to take a shower," he said, embarrassed even if they were his friends.

"Can you manage okay?" Six-Pack asked.

"It's not easy doing stuff one-handed, but I get by. Besides, I'm supposed to work it a little when I'm not wearing the brace."

Zack spoke up. "Tell you what. You go shower while we tidy this place some."

Tommy shook his head. "You don't have to do that."

"We want to," Eve insisted. "Go."

He felt a slight warming in a place inside him that had been like ice for two weeks. "All right. Thanks."

"Don't mention it," Julian said. "Need some help with the bandage?"

"If you don't mind." While the others began to pick up his crap, Julian carefully unwrapped his bandages. When he was done, he didn't even pretend not to stare at the thick, jagged line bisecting Tommy's wrist that matched the one slashing his face and throat.

"Sucks, huh?"

"Yeah, it does. I'm sorry, *amigo*."

"At least I can get it wet now, which was hell when I first got home. Ever try to bathe without getting your face or hand wet?"

"Nope. How did you?"

"My dad came over and helped me."

"You know, if you had a lick of sense, that pretty lady of yours would be here taking care of you instead."

"Don't start with me, Jules. As you can see, she's better off."

"What I see is a fool who doesn't know his ass from a hole in the ground."

"I'm not going to argue with you. I'll be back in a few."

Ignoring their glances, he left them to pick up his place, feeling damned guilty about it but grateful for the help. It took him forever to take out the trash, do dishes, all the mundane things fully abled people did every day. It was exhausting. And it was wrenching, especially for an athletic guy like himself.

In the bathroom, he turned on the water and struggled with his clothes, finally getting them off. The spray felt heavenly and he cursed himself for an idiot for denying himself a simple pleasure he could still enjoy.

Flipping open the lid on the shampoo bottle was a challenge, but after that things got easier. When he was done, he turned off the spray, more invigorated than he'd been in days. His friends' arrival had as much to do with that as the shower, he suspected.

After drying off, dressing in clean boxer briefs, shorts, and a T-shirt was another battle. One of many he had to look forward to, for the rest of his life. Some of his optimism dimmed, but he was determined not to let it suck him down. He'd been in a dangerous place in his head for the past few days, and it scared him.

He did *not* want to wind up like Sean.

Padding back into the living room, he stopped and his mouth dropped open. "Oh, wow. It looks great."

Eve had just turned off the vacuum and Julian was placing the last of the dishes on the drain board. Howard and Zack had tackled the trash cleanup and had filled an entire garbage bag. Everyone grinned at him and he couldn't help but smile back, even though he knew the scar made his face look weird.

"I don't know what to say."

Zack shrugged. "That's what friends are for."

"Start singing like Dionne Warwick and I'm history," Julian said.

Eve ignored them. "Just say you'll call and ask for help before you let it get like this again. And promise you'll take better care of yourself. We don't need this sort of stress."

"I will, promise. I feel bad for making you guys worry when you've got so much else on your plate," he admitted sheepishly. After a pause, he asked, "How is Sean?"

His friends shared a "look" and then turned their attention to Six-Pack. He was always their leader, their rock, even away from the station.

Six-Pack set the garbage bag by the front door and returned to sit on the couch. "Dad took him to that rehab facility where we made the reservation before. They kept a spot open for him. According to Dad, he's detoxing, and it's ugly. I wish I could see him, but he's not allowed any visitors for a few more weeks." Howard sighed. "He might not want to see me anyway."

Across the room, Eve quietly rolled up the cord on the vacuum and swiped at her eyes. Was she crying? He couldn't tell. She straightened and rolled the vacuum down the hallway to the little closet.

Tommy turned his attention back to Six-Pack. "Why wouldn't he want to see you? You're his best friend."

For a long moment, Tommy thought he wouldn't answer. When he spoke, his voice was filled with regret. "When the building fell on you, I didn't realize he was in the middle of a meltdown. A flashback. Before I knew he was sick, I accused him of being responsible for you getting trapped in there. He was lost in a daze, talking about his family burning. I knew then we had a serious problem, but it was too late to take back the shit I said."

"Doesn't make it any less his fault," Julian muttered.

Coming back into the room, Eve rounded on him. "How can you say that? He was *ill*. He didn't know what he was doing."

"And if he'd listened to us when we held the intervention and gotten treatment, what happened to Tommy might have been avoided. Sean might be well by now and Tommy—"

"Guys," Zack interrupted, glancing between the combatants. "Come on. We can drive each other crazy with what-ifs and it won't change a thing. It is what it is."

The pair stopped arguing but continued to glare at each other. Tommy processed what the lieutenant had said; Sean had hit rock bottom and as a result, Tommy's life had been destroyed.

Or at least altered on a major scale.

It was hard not to blame Sean. But he was trying.

As if Six-Pack read his mind, he said, "I know Sean will want to see you when he's released. It will be part of his program to deal with the messes he made, and make restitution. Will you see him?"

"Of course I will. I want him to get well as much as anyone does." No question.

"Good. I'll let him know when the time comes."

"Tommy . . . have you seen Shea?" Eve asked.

Just hearing her name made his heart bleed. "No, and I don't plan to."

"Maybe you should—"

"Do *nothing*. I should do nothing but let her get on with her life, and I don't want to talk about this."

An uncomfortable silence ensued, until Zack spoke up. "Have you eaten anything today?"

At the reminder, his stomach grumbled. "No. I've been asleep most of the day."

"Well, that settles it. Get some shoes on, we're taking you out. Unless anybody here wants to cook?" A chorus of "no way" settled the matter and Zack stood, the others doing the same.

"Oh, guys, I don't know." He stared at them, gut clenching. "I haven't been out since before . . . well, just before."

"People are going to see your face eventually, my friend," Eve said, giving his shoulders a hug. "And truthfully, the scar isn't that bad. Makes you look sort of rakish, like a pirate."

He rolled his eyes. "Oh, for God's sake." But it did make him feel a little better as she went on.

"Might as well take the plunge. You can't stay holed up in here forever like an old hermit."

"Nope, we won't let you," Julian said. "I'll help you wrap your wrist."

They wouldn't allow him so much as a word of protest. In short order, his wrist was done in a fresh bandage, tennis shoes were shoved on his feet, and he was herded out the door.

They'd arrived in two vehicles, so Tommy and Julian rode with Six-Pack in his big black Ford truck, and Eve climbed into Zack's Mustang. Tommy looked around, the afternoon sunlight almost too bright after being cooped up for so long.

"Where are we going?"

Julian answered. "The diner on the square. It's the best place for homemade Southern food."

"You guys had this all planned, didn't you?"

"Yep. Operation Kidnap Tommy, a success," Six-Pack said, grinning.

In spite of himself, he smiled. The awful pain in his chest eased, just a little.

They arrived at the diner and got out of the vehicles, Tommy more slowly than the others. He was still a bit stiff, but he figured at this point it was mostly due to not getting enough exercise rather than from the building falling on him. He'd never been so lazy in his life as he had been in the past two weeks.

Inside, they waited as the hostess grabbed laminated menus for everyone and then followed as she led them to a big booth. She handed out the menus with hardly a glance, and left. Tommy let out a pent-up breath, not realizing until she was gone that he'd been waiting for her to remark on his awful scar.

The cute young waitress who came to take their drink orders, however, did a double take when she saw him. She recovered quickly and didn't comment either, which was good, but neither did she flirt with him like women typically did. That bothered him more than he cared to admit, even if he wasn't looking for anyone else.

He wanted only Shea. Who was better off without him.

What was she doing? Was she sitting alone in her apartment, with nobody for company but Miss Kitty?

He recalled the last time they'd made love, by his parents' pool. How she'd given herself to him without reservation.

How it had all gone to hell.

"Tommy?"

"What?" He blinked and looked across the table at Six-Pack, who gestured at the waitress. While he'd been daydreaming, she'd returned with their drinks and was waiting for his order. "Uh, I'll have the chicken-fried steak, mashed potatoes and gravy, and green beans."

"Rolls or corn bread?"

"Corn bread."

"Okay. It'll be out soon." Sending them all a chipper smile, she flounced off.

Studying each of them, he decided it was time to address the elephant in the room. He pinned Six-Pack with a calm stare. "So when are you going to replace me?"

The lieutenant almost choked on his soda. "Jesus, kid. You're still on leave, and you're recovering. We're not going to make any decisions until *you* do. You're not being tossed out on your ear."

"I know that, but come on, man. I'll be lucky if I ever hold a pencil again, much less an ax or a fire hose." Or a football. The knowledge crushed him all over again. "We all know I won't be going back."

"I was thinking," Julian said tentatively. "Maybe you could work in Fire Prevention. They do training programs, teach classes, and they have arson investigators who get to catch bad guys. I'm not sure, but I don't think your hand would be a problem."

Six-Pack nodded. "It's not a lateral move, but it could be exciting. And I hear the fire marshall is a good guy."

"Actually, I have a confession." He smiled, feeling good about this for the first time in days. "I'd already been thinking about making a change, maybe going over to Arson. I talked to Mark McAllister not long ago."

It was their turn to stare, wide-eyed. Six-Pack laughed, slapping his hand on the table. "Damn, you always surprise me. Good for you. If you want to pursue it, I know Dad will be happy to put in a good word for you. We all will." The others were grinning in approval.

"See?" Eve poked a finger at him. "All is not lost. You can have an interesting, productive career."

"I guess it just didn't occur to me that I still could," he confessed. "I wasn't exactly thinking straight until my nosy buddies barged in and rescued me."

"Well, there you go," Eve said. "So when are you going to fix things with Shea?"

His burgeoning happy mood deflated. "I don't know if I can. I made it pretty clear that we were done."

"Undo it, then."

Could he?

Their food arrived, the waitress setting plates of steaming food in front of them. Tommy faltered, picked up his fork and tried to figure out how best to proceed. And he actually felt the blood drain from his face.

The chicken-fried steak. He stared at his plate, devastated.

He'd completely forgotten he couldn't cut it by himself.

This was what Shea would be getting if she took him back. A man who needed his food cut into squares like a small child.

He couldn't think of anything more demoralizing.

Except glancing away from his food to see Shea sitting at another booth across the diner. Smiling, laughing.

With Forrest Prescott, the motherfucker.

The breath left his lungs. If he'd been bleeding before, he was hemorrhaging to death now, run through the chest with a bayonet. No fire, no building falling and crushing him, could ever compete with the agony of watching her touch Forrest's hand, face turned up, obviously amused by whatever he'd said.

Had they been going out the whole time since Tommy broke things off? Had she kissed him?

Would she invite him home?

"Tommy, do you need help with—shit." Julian obviously found what held his attention. "What do you want to do? Go over there and deck him? I'll bail you out."

He tore his gaze away from the couple and looked around at the worried group. "And what would I deck him with, Jules? My incredibly powerful left hook?" He could barely manage a fork. What a joke.

"Nobody's doing any decking," Six-Pack said firmly. "We're going to eat. Dig in."

The food on his plate might as well be sawdust. But he'd be damned if he'd let this level him—at least on the outside. Picking up his fork again, he angled it and began to saw at the meat awkwardly. His friends knew better than to offer assistance with Shea and her date nearby, and he was grateful.

He struggled with a few bites of everything, but truthfully? He just wanted to go to the restroom and throw up. He'd forced down about half his meal, glad as hell Shea hadn't noticed him, and was almost ready to toss down some money for his dinner and take off on a nice long walk. And he would have, too.

If a man hadn't stopped by Shea's table, apparently to say hello to Forrest.

A brown-haired man in his late twenties or so, wearing jeans and a red ball cap.

It couldn't be.

The man stood with his slight weight on one foot, thumb hitched in one pocket. He fingered the cap, readjusted it as he spoke. His mannerisms, his clothing, his build, were identical to the man he'd seen in the crowd after the gas explosion.

And, he realized, at the scaffold collapse.

Tommy had just been lowered to the ground, someone asking if he was all right. He'd taken a couple of steps, his gaze lighting on the crowd across the street. He'd seen a man in a red ball cap before he'd passed out.

This man, he was almost positive. Every nerve in his body sang, telling him he was right. So what if he was? What could that mean? Sugarland wasn't a huge city, and the guy could have been passing by, gawking like the other people. On two separate occasions.

Tommy noted how Prescott's smile seemed forced, his lips thin. Prescott looked away from the man in the cap for a few seconds, fiddling with his napkin. No, Prescott wasn't pleased to see this other guy. Wanted him gone. Interesting.

Tommy might've been inclined to chalk it up to Prescott just being jealous of his time with Shea, but for some reason that didn't strike him as being quite right. Maybe he was imagining the weird undercurrent between the two men, the barely concealed anger on Prescott's face, mixed with some other emotion.

When Shea asked the waitress for a refill of her soda, and Prescott took advantage of her brief distraction to shake his head at the other man and make a slashing motion across his neck, Tommy knew he was on base. If the man in the hat was just some casual acquaintance, Prescott would have to be nice and do the friendly city manager bullshit. Obviously, these two knew each other pretty well.

And they were up to no good. Tommy's grandmother would've said there was a fox in the henhouse.

Tommy couldn't eat any more, and was hardly aware of the conversation around him. He kept coming back to the men, one of whom he'd seen at two of the area's suspicious disasters. And was acquainted with a man who wanted Shea for himself. That bore thinking about. And perhaps something more.

The man in the ball cap left, and Prescott paid their check. He and Shea departed soon after. The love of his life never once glanced in his direction.

Watching her leave with *him* tore out his soul.

Appetite lost, he attempted to join in his friends' discussion. His mind, however, was trusting his bad gut feeling. Maybe a little Dick Tracy action would get him some answers.

Tommy might not be good enough for Shea, but he'd be goddamned if he'd stand by and let her be charmed by a snake.

16

Shea poured Forrest a glass of wine and did her best to focus on his company instead of her aching heart.

At the diner, she'd felt Tommy's eyes on her, had known the instant he noticed her, as though they had some sort of invisible bond that glowed when they were near each other. When he hadn't approached, she'd been crushed.

How must he have felt, though, to see her with Forrest again? She had no intention of being anything more than a friend to the city manager, but Tommy didn't know that. Had he been jealous? Hurt?

He had no reason to be, if he'd only take a chance on them.

"Sebastiani?" Forrest whispered, close to her ear. "A nice Sonoma wine, though not rare. Unlike you."

Oh, my. That wasn't exactly ambiguous.

Sidestepping him, she held out his glass. "Cheers."

"To us. Friendship."

"Yes." She led him into the living room and sipped her Chardonnay, her brain already working on how to get him out of here soon. She did have to get up at seven in the morning to go to work, so that would have to suffice.

He sat on the sofa next to her, too close for her comfort. "Tell me something. I heard that you and your brother own a piece of property on the Cumberland River not far from the dam."

She blinked at him. She'd mentioned it to Tommy, but never Forrest. "That's true. Our parents left it to us, but how would you know about that?"

"I make it my business to know who owns what in Sugarland, keep track of property values and such. It's just part of what I do. Have you and your brother ever thought about selling?"

"Not really, I guess." She amended that with a wave of her hand. "We did sell a tract after our parents were killed, enough to help us survive until we were set in our careers. Since then, selling the rest hasn't come up as a serious topic because Shane would like to build on his half someday. Why? Are you interested in buying?"

"I might be," he said pleasantly. "It's a prime piece of real estate. Great location with gorgeous scenery."

She considered that for a few moments. "True. Which is probably why I've never really considered selling. And I doubt I ever would, sorry."

Disappointment flashed in his eyes. "Don't blame you a bit. Anyway, I had a nice time at dinner. I eat at the diner quite a bit since it's so close to the city offices, and they have great food."

The tension in her shoulders eased. She was glad he didn't push on the land issue. She thought about dinner and decided to do some probing of her own.

"Nice of that man to stop by and speak with you. What was his name? Will?"

He took a healthy gulp of his wine. "Oh, yes. Will. He's a building inspector for the city. Run into him from time to time."

"That's nice. How long have you known each other?"

"Couple of years. Why?"

"No reason. Just making small talk." Why did he suddenly seem nervous? In the next moment, however, his jitters seemed to be gone, vanished behind a seductive smile.

"Well, the last thing I want to do is talk," he said, placing his glass on the coffee table. He took hers from her hand and put it beside his. "Shea, you drive me insane. I thought I could do this 'friends' thing, but the truth is, I want more."

Uh-oh. "Forrest—"

"Kiss me, Shea." He cupped her cheek. "A real kiss to see if there's anything between us. If there isn't, I'll be just your friend if it kills me."

"I—I don't think so."

"What do you have to lose? Are you saving yourself for a man who doesn't want you? I saw him sitting across the diner, and he didn't even approach and try to be civil to you," he said, moving so that their lips nearly touched. "The man who wants you is right here. Has been all along."

His lids closed and he moved in, planting his lips on hers. She thought of Tommy as his mouth claimed hers, and felt disloyal. As though she'd betrayed him. But Tommy had broken things off.

Forrest smelled good. Manly. He was a handsome man, and an expert kisser. Any woman would be happy to take him to bed.

Almost any woman. For Shea, there was no spark. He wasn't Tommy.

She broke the kiss, worked a hand between them, and pushed him back. "I'm sorry. I can't do this."

"You're a fool to wait for him," he said, shaking his head.

"Maybe so, but I can't change the way I feel. I hope we can still be friends."

Abruptly, he stood. The flash of anger on his face touched a cold finger inside her, but it was gone so quickly she thought she must have imagined it.

"I've overstayed my welcome. I'll call you this week and perhaps we'll do lunch."

"I . . . okay."

Why had she never noticed how Forrest made that sound like a foregone conclusion instead of a heartfelt invite? Something was wrong here and she didn't have a clue what, besides the obvious. She knew Forrest wanted to be more than friends, but this feeling was something almost . . . bad. Sinister?

No, that was ridiculous.

He gave her a peck on the cheek and was gone, leaving her alone with a freshly opened bottle of wine.

And nothing to do but drink it.

Tommy sat in his truck in Shea's parking lot and leaned against the steering wheel, the pain so bad he wanted to die. And not pain from trying to shift gears and then drive one-handed, as difficult as the task might be.

Shea was in Prescott's arms. Accepting his kiss.

At first he was glad she hadn't closed the blinds so he could keep an eye on Prescott. Now he regretted his stupidity.

How can you want him? How?

He tried to reason with himself. If she could fall into the other man's arms so easily, maybe what he and Shea had in the past wasn't special after all. Yes, Tommy had pushed her away, but she sure hadn't let grass grow in the time between lovers.

Then something miraculous happened. She shoved him away. Tommy sat up straight, taking in her stiff body language, her obvious refusal to take things further. Prescott's reaction, his defensive posture, manhood obviously wounded.

"Yeah," Tommy hissed in triumph, thumping the steering wheel. "Take that, asshole. Whatever you're selling, she ain't buying."

Moments later, Prescott exited Shea's apartment, wearing a sour expression and sporting a very unsatisfied hard-on in his neatly pressed pants.

Tommy smiled.

The man jerked open his car door and flung himself inside, revved the engine, and squealed away. Tommy started his truck and followed, wary of keeping a distance. He didn't want to be up in the man's tailpipe, but he didn't want to lose him.

Prescott ran a couple of errands. Drove to a liquor store near Nashville, bought some hard stuff. Stopped at a convenience store. Drove to the river and got out of his car, walking around a nice piece of property and running a hand through his hair in agitation, talking on his cell phone. At just past ten, when Tommy was about to call off his amateur sleuthing adventure, Prescott's next destination proved to be more intriguing.

His quarry drove to Sugarland's city offices and parked. Instead of taking the main entrance, Prescott used a key on his ring to unlock a side entrance, and went inside. Tommy was about to follow when a white city truck pulled up—and the man in the red ball cap got out.

Tommy scrunched low in his seat, hoping the guy didn't notice him there. But the dude seemed oblivious as he entered through the same door as Prescott, without using a key.

Hot damn! It wasn't locked. Which meant they'd arranged to meet. Probably why Prescott had been on his cell phone. More and more interesting.

Once the second guy was inside, Tommy got out of his truck and tried to look casual as he took the same path as the other two. He kept his head up, shoulders back, walking with confidence so that anyone who might see would believe he had business there.

Right. After ten o'clock at night.

Inside, however, he paused and listened to the boot steps fade down the corridor. He followed, keeping close to the wall, knowing that if they saw him there, he was screwed. There was no story to explain his presence that anyone would believe.

He made his way deeper into the office building, anxious. Which way had they gone? He paused and strained to hear, and was just able to make out voices. Moving silently, he rounded a corner and saw a light at the end of the hallway, glowing from under a closed door.

Sweat rolled down his temple, stinging his scarred cheek as he positioned himself beside the door, ear close to the frame.

". . . had no idea you were going to be there. Chill, would you? I didn't say two words to her!"

Shea. Tommy's blood ran cold.

"I'll *chill* when all of this is behind us," Prescott said coldly. A pause, then, "You know, he wanted to get rid of you, but I asked him to leave you out of it. Wouldn't that have been ironic, after all your hard work?"

The guy's frightened squeak could be heard clearly. "What? What did I ever do to him? I don't even know what he does with the money, or even his *name*, for Christ's sake!"

"It's just how men like him are made. I think he's going to leave you alone, though."

"My God."

"Me? That could be a different story, Will."

A few seconds of silence. "What do you mean?" Will sounded scared, uncertain. "I've done everything you told me to, made sure no two accidents were the same. Nobody can trace them back to any one—"

"You wouldn't do *everything*. I had to hire outside for the last job, he fucked up, and now we'll have a fucking body soon as they finish sifting through the remains of the warehouse."

Tommy's mind whirled. Body? In the warehouse? *The same one I was buried underneath?*

"Tough shit. I won't be a party to cold-blooded murder. No amount is worth that."

"Not even to save your queer ass from AIDS?"

"I have HIV, not AIDS! And no, I won't kill, not even to pay for my meds. I'm through caving to your threats."

Blackmail. Oh, my God, he's blackmailing this Will guy.

To arrange . . . accidents. To destroy those buildings?

"We all have to choose our battles. I'm not keen on murder, either. But if it comes down to me and someone else? I'll pick me, every time."

"Nice, Forrest. You're a real peach."

"You're enjoying the payouts same as me, old friend. Don't forget that."

"How could I?" Will's voice was bitter. "You never let me."

This conversation sounded nearly over. He had to get the hell gone before they came out, and the hallway he'd come down seemed way too long, with no hiding places.

The doorknob turned, and his mouth went dry.

Shit!

Tommy took off, heart in his throat. Praying he didn't get caught listening by a man who, by his own admission, would commit murder.

He rounded the corner as the door opened behind him, and nearly flattened a night security guard.

"Sorry! Gotta run!"

"Hey, come back here! Stop!"

Not a chance, buddy.

He flew right out the front doors, which weren't locked from the inside, fumbled his keys with his good hand, hit the unlock button, jumped in, and fired the baby up.

He was a mile down the road before his breathing started to even out, but then the reality of what he'd overheard set in. Followed by fear. The guard would surely tell Prescott and his companion about a man running away from the direction of his office. If he got a very good description of Tommy . . .

"Fuck me."

Think. What to do. Who to tell.

What did he have, really? Hearsay. Compelling hearsay, but not proof. No real details. Most of the gaps, he'd filled in on his own, the conclusions he'd drawn himself, which the police couldn't use.

He should tell someone, though. Get it on record.

And Shea.

"Oh, God." She'd befriended this crazy fucker. Believed him to be an upstanding guy, had spent time *alone* with him.

With a man who was okay with murder.

And blackmail.

And fraud.

The memory of the kiss Prescott had stolen from her sickened him. Made him want to smash his fist down the bastard's throat. What did Prescott really want from her? Was she to be a trophy of some sort? No, Shea wasn't the type to be happy hanging out with blue-blooded society wives. Prescott wanted something else, and he would find out what.

It was getting late. What was he going to do?

Shea was alone. What if Prescott found out Tommy had been by his office tonight and decided to get to her first?

"No." The word came out feral, deadly.

No man was going to take what was his. Especially not a man like Prescott. He'd been a complete idiot to throw away the best thing that had ever happened to him.

He had one stop to make to throw some clothes in his

gym bag, then had some serious making up to do with the woman he loved.

He just prayed she'd give him another chance.

Joseph was in hell. For two weeks, the agony of indecision weighed on him as he waited for a confession from his grandson that never came. A plea he would've gladly answered.

Will was never going to tell his grandpa what he'd done. The boy was in way too deep, probably felt he had no recourse.

But there always was. Any good soldier knew that.

Joseph picked up the phone, and with trembling fingers, punched a number he hadn't needed to use for a very long time.

"Federal Bureau of Investigations, Special Agent Dominic Westfall speaking."

"Got time to talk to an old codger?"

"I . . . Joseph? Joseph Hensley?" The man sounded incredulous.

"For a while longer, I suppose."

"Damn, I can't believe it! How are you?"

"I've been better, boy. You?"

"Making it. One day at a time," he said quietly. "What can I do for you, Joseph?"

He took a steadying breath, and bit the bullet. "Nicky, I need your help."

Shea twirled her third glass of wine, watching the amber liquid go round and round. "What do you think?" she asked Miss Kitty. "Should I just kill the whole bottle?"

"Meoooow." The big feline kneaded Shea's tummy, turned around, and curled up in a comfortable spot on her lap.

"Well, I'll take that as a yes. In fact, I think I'll just call in sick. Like, for a year."

A knock on her door sent the cat flying under the sofa, and startled her, too. A glance at the clock had her concerned. Eleven at night? Only bad visits happened this late and she immediately thought of her brother.

She lived in fear of an officer coming to tell her Shane had been shot. Or worse.

She plunked down her wine, sloshing some, and hurried to the door. Cautious, she looked out the peephole—and gasped, her heart stuttering. There, in the porch light, stood Tommy.

Without hesitating, she unlocked the door and yanked it open. "What are you doing here?"

"Can I come in?"

"Why? So you can stomp on me some more? You didn't get to kick me on my way out the last time, so you're here to do it in person?"

Wow. She supposed she had a little anger stored along with the hurt. His expression gave her pause, though. His pale blue eyes were bruised. Haunted. He didn't look good, and his scars had nothing to do with it.

"Please, Shea," he said hoarsely. "Hear me out."

She stepped aside and let him in, trailed him into the living room. "You've lost weight. You're not taking care of yourself."

He faced her squarely, wrapped hand hanging at his side. "I am now. I had some stuff to work through in my head."

"And have you?" She crossed her arms over her chest, afraid to hope.

"I have. First of all, I want to apologize for not listening to you in the hospital. You shared a very painful, traumatic experience with me, placed your trust in me, and I didn't listen. You were trying to tell me it's okay to grieve for our losses, but that we get through them. I wasn't thinking of anyone but myself, *my* losses, and I pushed you away."

Do not cry. "You did. You made me fall in love with you

and then you tossed that love back in my face. When the going got tough, you checked out."

At that moment, the ocean between them had never been so vast and empty. She ached with the need to touch him.

"You'll never know how sorry I am."

"What do you want from me?" She wasn't about to make this easy. *Say it.*

"I thought my injuries, losing my looks and the use of my hand, made me not whole anymore, not a man. Not good enough for you. What I didn't know . . ." His voice broke and his breath hitched. "What I didn't understand was that I *was* whole until I lost you."

Her hand went over her mouth and tears streamed down her cheeks.

He took a step toward her. "Baby, forgive me. Please."

With a sob, she launched herself into his arms and was crushed against his chest. His good hand buried itself in her hair and kisses rained on top of her head. Then he pulled back slightly and claimed her mouth like a starving man.

They clung to each other, tasted and explored. Reaffirmed their love, their connection. Couldn't get enough.

"I need skin," she whispered into his mouth.

"God, yes. Missed you so much."

He chuckled as she tore off his clothes, and it hit her how she'd missed his laugh. His smile. His presence in her soul. She yanked off his shorts and underwear and peeled off his shirt. "Sit on the sofa," she ordered.

"Yes, ma'am! Damn, I could get used to this side of you." His eyes glittered as he sat, watched her strip.

"Wait for it. Gets better."

Naked, she pushed his knees apart and crouched on the floor between them. She loved this, him spread for her, waiting to find out what she'd do next.

His cock filled rapidly, happy to get into the action. It

curved toward his stomach, flushed, rising from golden curls. Heavy balls nestled underneath, too tempting to resist.

Lifting them with gentle fingers, she sucked each one, enjoying his earthy male flavor. She wanted to drive him out of his mind, make him beg for her.

"Oh, baby, please." His head fell against the back of the sofa.

That was a good start. She licked and teased each orb, manipulating them, grazing them with her teeth. This drove him mindless, his hips bucking, and so she moved on, running her tongue up the underside of his cock. His groan of pleasure was like music.

Next, she feasted on the plump cap, licking the little drops of precum away. Salty and sweet. Hers. She took him into her mouth, sucking him with increasing pressure, making sure he knew who was in charge this time around.

"Ahh, shit! You're gonna make me go!"

She released him with a pop. "No, you don't."

"I can't hold out much longer."

Straddling his lap, she positioned the head of his cock at her opening. "You'll wait until you're inside me. I want it hard and fast, understand?"

His pupils were blown, and he was almost incoherent with excitement. "C-condom. In my bag on your porch."

Intent, she gazed directly into his eyes. "Not this time."

"Jesus," he whispered, voice thick with desire. "Are you sure?"

"Very. Do me, gorgeous. I want to feel it tomorrow."

She sank onto him and they groaned together, lost in the exquisite feeling of being joined again. Only skin, sliding, sparking the inferno out of control.

As he began to thrust into her, she wound her arms around his neck, hanging on for the ride. He gripped her hip with his left hand, fingers digging into her flesh. They slapped together in noisy rhythm, their coupling feverish in their need to reconnect.

"Shea, baby! Yes, oh . . ."

Her orgasm ripped through her body, taking her by surprise. She cried out, felt herself convulsing around him as he drove into her. One more thrust and he held deep, pumping hot cum, filling her to overflowing. He was so beautiful, expression lost in pleasure, looking at her with such love.

"You turned me inside out," he rasped. "God, that was amazing."

"Had to show you what you've been missing."

Immediately, he was contrite. "I'm so sorry. Believe me, it'll never happen again."

"It better not." Gingerly, she ran a finger along the edge of his scar, following the red line from his temple down his cheek to his throat. What might've happened, had the metal sliced a fraction of an inch deeper and hit his jugular, made her shiver.

He misread her reaction and looked away. "It's ugly. I can't improve it without plastic surgery and even then—"

"You misunderstand. I'm touching it because it's a part of you, and I love *all* of you." To emphasize her point, she leaned in, kissed the scar at his temple, his cheek. "I shuddered because I realize it's a miracle you weren't killed."

"It really doesn't bother you?"

The hope in his voice shredded her. "No. I hate that it bothers *you,* but in time it will fade."

"Maybe, but I don't think I'll ever get used to it."

"You might not. Just don't let it define your life."

"Kind of hard not to, when it's almost a perfect dividing line between my old life and my new."

He had a point. "True. Perhaps you'll come to see it as

one of those hard-won blessings in disguise—you went through a bad period, and something better was waiting on the other side."

He gave her a genuine smile. "You sound like Dad."

"Smart man." As bad as she hated to move, she climbed off his lap. "Want to get cleaned up? Race you to the shower."

"On your mark . . ."

They enjoyed a hot shower, giggling like kids while getting each other soapy and fooling around. A fondle here, a playful pinch there. The water ran cold and they finally got out and dried off, happy, if a little tired.

Tommy, towel wrapped around his hips, quickly retrieved his gym bag from her front porch and returned, donning a pair of clean boxer briefs. Shea put on a pair of panties and a big T-shirt, and they snuggled in her bed, her head on his chest.

Wouldn't you know, the interlude was too peaceful to last.

"Baby, I need to talk to you about something," he said, squeezing her.

"Hmm?"

"I saw you at the diner tonight."

"I saw you, too. Thought you might come over, but I guess I can understand why you didn't." Looking back, she couldn't imagine how seeing her with Forrest must've hurt him. But he *had* pushed her away, so the next move was his to make.

"I should have. That's not what I need to talk about, though." He paused. "The guy in the red ball cap who stopped at your table. Did Prescott introduce him?"

"Briefly. Said his name was Will Hensley and he worked for the city as a building inspector."

Tommy tensed underneath her. "That can't be a coincidence."

"What can't?"

"I'd seen him before. The first time was right before I passed out, after the scaffold collapse. The second was after the gas explosion at the vacant residence. Both times he was among the gawkers across the street."

Shea digested this. "The coincidence is strange, but it doesn't necessarily mean anything. Since he works for the city, especially in inspection, he's around town."

"Normally I'd agree. You didn't see the vibes going on between those two when you weren't looking, though. Prescott was royally pissed to see him there. Even made a gesture at him to get lost. It got me thinking, and I did something I shouldn't have, even though I'm glad I did."

Rising, she propped herself on his chest and looked him in the eye. "Which was?"

"I followed Forrest tonight to see what he was up to. Everywhere he went."

When the full meaning hit, she gaped at him. "You spied on me? Here?"

"Not on you," he assured her quickly. "On Forrest. I left here when he did and tailed him."

"I—I'm not sure what to think about that, Tommy. Why are you 'glad' you followed him?"

"Because Prescott ended up at the city hall in a meeting with Will Hensley, in Prescott's office, at ten in the evening with nobody there but the guard. Your would-be boyfriend was raking Hensley over the coals for speaking to him at the diner in front of you."

"Wait a minute. You sneaked inside the city offices? After dark?"

"They left the side door unlocked, so yeah, I took advantage," he said, starting to appear upset. "Shea, those two are buried up to their necks in all sorts of bad shit. Blackmail, fraud, murder—"

"Whoa. Slow down and explain. Those are some hefty words you're slinging around. I have a hard time picturing Forrest involved in anything illegal."

He aimed a scowl at her. "Plenty of bright and shiny things are poisonous under the surface, like nightshade berries. I know what I heard."

"Sorry," she said, stroking his chest. "Go ahead."

"Like I said, Prescott wasn't thrilled about seeing Will at the diner. He mentioned that some third party—a guy—wanted Will dead, but apparently Prescott convinced him not to follow through."

"Dead? My Lord . . ."

"Yep. They were talking about money and payouts and—look, the fire at the warehouse was arson, according to the investigator I spoke with. Prescott and Hensley talked about the warehouse job and how Hensley wouldn't do what Prescott wanted, but some other man did and now he's dead underneath all the rubble. And, Shea . . . I think *I'm* the job they were talking about."

"What! How?" She stared at him, trying to process everything he was saying.

"I was hit on the head. Twice. And that was before the roof fell. I never saw what hit me."

"Did you hear any movement behind you?"

"No, nothing. But with the noise, how could I? Anyway, Prescott made it clear he's blackmailing Hensley to arrange these 'accidents,' and in return, nobody finds out Hensley is HIV positive, and he has the money to buy his medicine."

Shea was stunned. Forrest? Involved in criminal activity? She couldn't believe it.

"Oh, my God. So why do you think you were the target in the warehouse? What would they have to gain?"

"Not *they*; *Forrest*. He gets me out of the way so I'm no longer competition to be with you."

"Like I'm such a catch that he'd kill for me?—Wait. Oh, no way." Her eyes widened as she recalled her earlier visit with Forrest. "Tonight he asked about buying the property Shane and I inherited from our parents. You don't think . . ."

Tommy was silent for a moment. "It's possible he covets your real estate as a way to pad the income from his other dealings. If he can snag you as well, it's a bonus."

Freaking unreal. "His other dealings being, what?"

"An insurance scam. They buy low, destroy their holdings, and collect the cash."

"Okay. Except, wouldn't the insurance company catch on?"

Tommy shook his head. "Not if they insured with various companies, under different corporate names. Let me ask you something again—how did you and Prescott meet?"

"At a charity event sponsored by the Sugarland Police Department a few months ago. Shane said Forrest insisted on an introduction. I had no idea who he was." Oh, that sounded bad, in light of what Tommy had overheard. And in looking back over her relationship with Forrest, too.

"That's right." After a long moment, Tommy drew the conclusion for them both. "If he courted you and won, he wouldn't have to purchase the property. He'd also inherit if anything happened to you and Shane."

Her stomach lurched. "I can't fathom he'd go that far."

"Baby, I heard Prescott say outright that if it came down to another person and himself, he'd choose himself. He does not have a problem with killing."

She thought she might be sick.

Tommy continued. "We need a plan. Are you off tomorrow?"

"I'm supposed to work, but I haven't called in sick in ages. I could do that."

"Good. Let's talk to your brother first thing and tell him

all of this. See whether he has any ideas about what to do next."

"And the rest of the day?"

He rolled her underneath him and ground his revived erection between her thighs.

"Answer your question?"

17

Tommy's cell phone rang and he stretched, letting out a groan. Whoever was calling was darned persistent. Second call in ten minutes.

"Mmm, you going to answer that?"

"Let's see—warm woman or phone? Let me think."

She giggled. "Could be important."

"Better be." He answered, unprepared for the voice on the other end.

"Son, where have you been?"

"Hey, Mom. I—"

"Your dad and I are so worried about you! You don't call, you hardly answer your phone." Boy, she was upset, not that he could blame her. "It's not right for you to keep yourself holed up in that apartment all alone. I'm coming over to get you, and you're going to come home and let me make you some breakfast."

"Mom—" He glanced at Shea to see her stifling a laugh, and stuck his tongue out at her.

"You're going to get out of there and stop moping. I mean it, Thomas Wayne! I'll be there in ten."

"Wait, Mom! I'm not at home."

"Oh." A pause, then, "Well, where are you?"

His face heated. "Mom, there are some things a guy does not want to discuss with his mother."

"What! You mean you're already running around with another woman right after you broke up with that beautiful girl?" She sounded indignant. "How could you?"

Lord have mercy. "I'm not running around on Shea. We got back together." He held the phone away from his ear slightly, to soften the piercing squeal of joy.

"Oh! Honey, that's wonderful! Bring her over, son. We'll have brunch and mimosas."

"When? Now?"

"Of course now. What else do you have to do?"

"Well, we . . ." *Have to see Shea's brother because the city manager is a fraudulent asshole and wants me dead.*

Um, maybe not.

"Well?"

He held the phone to his chest and whispered to Shea, "Brunch at my parents' house?"

She kissed his cheek. "Sure, sounds nice."

"Okay, we'll be there. What time?"

"Around ten thirty. Bring your appetite!"

"You bet. Love you."

"Love you, too, sweetheart."

He hung up to see Shea smiling at him. "You don't mind? Once she found out I wasn't cheating on you and that we were back together, there was no stopping her."

"I think it's great. I'd love to get to know your folks better."

"Well, you're going to get your chance. She wants us there around ten thirty, so that gives us about an hour to get ready."

"No nooky?"

"Who said that? Let's don't be hasty."

"Ooh, shower nooky?"

She looked so cute sitting there naked with her curly brown hair wild around her face, talking about nooky, he had to laugh.

"I think that can be arranged."

In the bathroom, Tommy turned on the water and they let it heat up, while raising the temperature in other places. He pulled her back to his front and nibbled her neck, reached around her to tweak her nipples.

"Damn, this is hard to do one-handed," he complained.

"I don't know, you're doing a pretty good job." She wiggled her bottom against his groin.

His semihard erection came fully awake, ready to play. "Why don't we continue this under the nice, hot spray?"

After helping him unwrap his hand, she led him into the stall and closed the door behind him. He leered at her, just over a hundred pounds of wet, willing woman. All his.

"I want to soap you up." He grabbed a bottle of shower gel from a hanging rack and thumbed it open.

Since it was easiest, he dribbled the fruity gel all over her back and his front, making certain he could get them nice and slick. She didn't offer to help, which he appreciated. It might be stupid to be concerned about such a small task, but he wanted to feel like he could do things without assistance.

He could damned sure make love to his lady.

Replacing the gel on the rack, he began to soap her back, admiring the glide of the bubbles over her skin. She had such a pretty back, slender, dipping down to flared hips. She had two little dimples over her butt, and he grinned.

His soapy hand wandered over her bottom, slid into the cleft between her ass cheeks. He liked the way she spread her legs, poked her rear out for him with a soft moan. A lot.

Reaching farther, he soaped her folds, making sure to graze the tiny clit. Rubbed until she silently begged, body open for him.

"Brace your hands on the tile, baby."

She did, and he slid into her from behind. Sank his cock into her sweet channel, slow and easy, all the way to the hilt.

"Love you," he whispered. "Never giving you up again."

"I love you, too."

He fucked her with easy strokes, setting off the sparks one by one. Kindling them to flames that consumed them both, and before he knew it, he was thrusting faster, deeper.

"Oh, yes," he hissed. "That's it."

Her little cries tipped him over the edge, and her convulsing around him was like nothing he'd ever felt with any woman. Heaven, pure and simple.

With a hoarse shout, he erupted, spasming as she milked every drop from his body. They remained connected for a moment, coming down, totally blissed out.

"Damn, girl, what you do to me."

"I can say the same to you, stud."

The endearment made him blush and pleased him at the same time. What guy didn't like to be his woman's stud?

With regret, he pulled out and they finished their shower, hurrying since they'd spent longer in there than they'd intended. Even though it was so darned much fun.

They dressed casually in shorts and T-shirts, and he thought it was funny that Shea was so concerned with her appearance.

"Relax. Mom and Dad already adore you. I think they just want to see me happy, that's all."

"I can certainly understand that. I'm assuming you're invoking the Dome of Silence rule on the whole Prescott situation?"

"God, yes. I don't even want to think about how badly they'd wig out if they knew."

"You got it. But you'll have to tell them sooner or later."

"I know. I'm hoping for later. Much later."

Shea had to admit she was a bit nervous about officially meeting Tommy's parents. The hospital didn't really count as an ideal place to socialize, and they'd all been sick with worry over Tommy at the time.

She was feeling just the teensiest bit guilty, too, about what they'd done by his parents' pool. Best not to dwell on that too much.

Tommy led the way to the front door and rang the bell, giving her an encouraging smile. "You're safe. They've never buried a single one of my dates in the basement. Yet."

"I'll keep that in mind."

Bethany Skyler flung open the door, and Shea was immediately crushed in the woman's enthusiastic embrace.

"Shea, it's so good to see you again, and under much better circumstances!"

"You, too, Mrs. Skyler."

"Beth, please." The pretty older woman turned her happiness on her son and gave him just as strong a hug. "And you! Sneaky devil, not even telling us you two had reconciled."

"I haven't had a chance, because it just happened."

"Well, in that case I'll give you a break. Come in. Your father is in the kitchen pretending to help when he's really just snacking on everything."

Tommy laughed. "Sounds like Dad."

They found Don in the kitchen, popping a strawberry into his mouth, and Beth fussed at him to stay out of the food until it was served.

"What?" he said innocently around a mouthful of berry. "Someone's got to make sure it tastes okay. Hi, Shea, good to see you. Son."

They greeted him with hugs and then Beth waved them to the breakfast nook. "I was going to set up outside, but it's already too blasted hot. I hope inside is okay."

Shea exchanged a look with Tommy and saw him struggling not to laugh. The last thing either of them wanted to do was brunch with his parents right on top of the scene of the crime, for God's sake. It was kind of funny, and she almost giggled, too.

They took a seat at the table situated in an alcove, surrounded by plants. "Your home is lovely, Beth. Thank you for having me here."

"Oh, thank *you*. Our house has needed a beautiful young lady to brighten it up for some time. Would you like a mimosa, dear? It's champagne and orange juice, perfect for brunch."

"I'd love one."

Beth fetched the drinks while Don brought in a fruit tray. After setting it on the table, he went back into the kitchen.

"I hope they didn't go to all this trouble for me," she told Tommy. "This is so nice."

"No, my mom enjoys this kind of stuff. She used to entertain more, but hasn't done it in a while."

She figured she knew why, but didn't bring it up. It was hard not knowing how careful she needed to be around his parents regarding the subject of his older brother.

Beth brought the drinks and his dad made two trips, bringing plates and silverware, and a quiche that looked and smelled wonderful.

"Might as well dig in," Don said jovially. "She made enough to feed us and the neighbors."

"I invited them to join us, but they couldn't come. Didn't say why, either." Beth shrugged. "More for us."

Tommy tried to hide his laugh with a cough. "Yeah, their loss."

"Are you keeping up with your physical therapy, son?" Don sounded concerned, as though he worried Tommy might blow it off.

"I wasn't, but I am now."

His dad nodded. "Good. How often?"

"I'll start going three times a week and they'll have me doing exercises, for all the good it'll do."

This prompted a frown from Don. "Why do you say that?"

"Are you kidding? I can't even perform the simplest task with the damned thing. Might as well have lost it."

"Tommy!" his mother scolded, taken aback. "Don't say things like that."

"Sorry," he muttered. "It's just that it feels really useless right now. Why drag around a part of me that won't work the way it's supposed to?"

"At least you have your hand. So many others have nothing."

Tommy gave his mother a sharp look. "I know, Mom. You don't have to tell me that."

Tension hung in the air, what Beth *didn't* say coming through so loud even Shea could hear it—*your brother is gone and you're still alive, so be grateful.* Thankfully, his mother dropped the subject. Tommy wasn't yet in the place where he wanted to hear how grateful he should be, and Shea understood that.

Shea sipped her mimosa and took a bite of her quiche, which was filled with ham and cheese, just the way she liked it. "This is fantastic. Do you cook often?"

"Oh, I used to do a lot of catering, but not so much anymore."

"If you enjoy doing that, you should get back into it," she said. "No sense wasting such a God-given talent."

Don laid his hand on top of Beth's. "That's what I've been telling her, too. We've all been stuck in a holding pattern for the past three years."

An uncomfortable silence ensued, and Shea scrambled to fill it. "What do you do, Don?"

"I'm a PI—private investigator. I used to be a cop in Nashville, but the stress was too much for my family. Gave it up to take pictures of old goats cheating on their wives."

Beth and Tommy chuckled and Shea smiled. Nobody would ever come close to calling Don an old goat, nor could she see him cheating on Beth. A very handsome man still in his forties, Don was clearly devoted to his wife and remaining son.

"Sounds interesting. Does it ever get dangerous?"

Don shook his head. "I've been fortunate. The worst I've ever had happen is I got caught by a cheating husband when I was snapping pictures of him checking into a hotel with his sweet young thing."

"Oh, no."

"He threatened to sue me, but changed his tune when I pointed out that paying two sets of legal fees—suing me and paying out the nose for his divorce—wasn't a good plan when he was sure to lose both cases, therefore costing him more money."

"You must enjoy being your own boss," she put in.

"Definitely. I set my own hours, and there's nobody riding my butt if I don't feel like opening up shop tomorrow."

"Except the bill collectors, dear," Beth said fondly.

"Well, there's that."

They finished eating, making small talk. Shea noted that Tommy seemed a bit subdued, even though he interjected in all the right places. She knew he still had some trouble managing his fork with his left hand, but she didn't think that was the problem. Or not the whole problem, anyway.

Once they'd finished, Shea offered to help clean up, but Beth ordered her to sit while she and Don took care of the dishes.

"There's not much. Just enjoy yourselves. Sit out in the living room if you'd like."

"Come on," Tommy said, reaching for her hand.

Taking his mother's suggestion, he led her into the living room, but didn't sit. Instead, he wandered slowly over to the fireplace mantel, where several framed snapshots rested. He stared at one of them, a photo of Tommy and another young man wrestling in the grass, a football lying nearby. The pair wore huge smiles for the camera, and the love radiating from the picture took her breath away.

Tommy's finger traced the frame. "She doesn't see me," he said sadly.

"Your mom?"

"Yeah. It's like . . . because Donny's gone, I ought to be thankful for every breath I take, every opportunity that comes my way. And I am, but not because he's gone, because he lived. Does that make sense?"

"Yes, I think so." It made her heart hurt for him.

"She rubs him in my face at every turn. I should be this because Donny can't, I should feel this way because Donny can't. Not in so many words, but it's there, all the time. She doesn't see *me*." His voice was rife with pain.

"Oh, honey." She laid her hand on his arm, trying to think of what to say, but was spared from replying.

"I had no idea you felt that way."

Beth stood just inside the room, face white. She was wringing her hands, eyes filled with tears, appearing torn between fleeing the room and running to her son.

Taking a deep breath, Tommy turned to face his mother. "I can't help the way I feel, but I do. I'm not Donny, and I could never hope to be. I'm my own person, so stop measuring me against the man he was."

Beth walked right up to her son and cupped his face in her hands. "Are you so sure it's *me* who's been doing that?"

Tommy's blue eyes were moist. "I . . . you never understand me."

"I understand more than you think, baby boy," she whispered. "I see *you*. Never think I don't. I've never measured you against your brother, and I never will. But I think you've done a number on yourself in that regard."

He swallowed hard. "You don't believe I had help? I gave up my dreams of playing for the NFL because that wasn't good enough. Wasn't heroic enough for you and Dad."

"Why would you think that?" she asked, agonized. "I would've been proud to have my son play for the NFL. I'd be just as proud if you had decided to become an accountant or a construction worker. I don't understand where this is coming from."

He gave a bitter laughed. "You really don't, do you? After I came home, even after we buried him, all I heard was how brave Donny was, how heroic to die serving his country. What a wonderful person he was. And he was, but what about *me*?"

His plaintive cry echoed in the room, and his mother gaped at him, hand going to her throat.

"I don't . . ."

"No, you don't! That's the whole point! I waited for you to tell me that you loved me just as much, that you were proud of me for who I am. Dad told me, but you never did," he said, voice breaking. "I started to question my life, my purpose, and I *needed* you. And when I mentioned I might not go back to school, do you remember what you said?"

"No," she admitted. "Not exactly."

"You said, 'Stay in school, play your game. Don't try to be a hero like your brother.' As though a football player can't be a hero. My pursuit was safe, and somehow less. How do you think that made me feel?"

"I—I didn't mean to belittle your chosen career. I was half-crazed with grief, Tommy."

"I know you were," he said softly. "But so were me and Dad. All I could think was that I'd failed somehow. That I should be more. I lost the heart to play ball, lost myself."

She shook her head. "You didn't fail us; you made your own decisions."

"I needed guidance."

She gave him a sad, tremulous smile. "And you'll never know how sorry I am that I didn't do a better job of giving it. We were grieving, but your father and I should have made more time for you back then, really talked to you about what you wanted to do. You want to blame me for everything that's gone wrong for you since Donny's death? Fine, I accept all of it."

Tommy and Beth stared at each other in obvious misery. Each one mired in uncertainty, longing to breach the gulf. Tommy was silent for so long, Shea wondered if he'd answer.

"Funny, that's what I've wanted to hear, but now I realize it's not completely true," he said, hanging his head. "It still hurts that you pushed me aside, even though you didn't know you were doing it. But I have to own my choices. I became a firefighter for all the wrong reasons, and that's not your fault. I'm so sorry."

She laid a palm on his cheek and he lifted his head. "So am I. You'll never know how much."

"When does it stop hurting, Mom?"

"It doesn't. But it becomes less, and we learn to appreciate the time we have. That's all I want for you, all I've ever wanted. Just for you to find your place where you're happy, being who *you* want to be, with no regrets."

"I'm happy with Shea," he said, giving his mom a watery smile.

"I can see that, and I'm so glad. The rest will work itself out. You'll figure out what you want to do careerwise, and your father and I will be here to help if you need us. Now, I'm going to tell you a secret, something I never would have said while your brother was still alive." Beth took both of his hands, careful with his injured one.

Tommy blinked at her, waiting.

"First, I love you *and* Donny, always will. You know that. But *you*." A tear streaked down one porcelain cheek. "You were my shining star from the moment you drew your first breath and looked at me. You were such a mischievous scamp, always into everything, and I let you get away with it just to see you smile. It used to drive your brother crazy."

"Really?" he asked in wonder. "You never told me."

"There are a lot of things I never told you. A mother should never mention when one child in particular is her bright, shining light. That secret a mother takes to her grave, unless her shining light is aching inside and needs to hear the truth."

"Mom," he said hoarsely, gazing at her with new eyes. Amazement was etched on his face. And hope.

"You are a special man, Thomas Wayne Skyler. I always knew that, but I worried that you never did. I loved your brother with all my soul and always will, but believe me, I see *you*."

"God, Mom, I'm sorry." He wrapped his arms around his mother, crushed her to him. They held on tight for several moments, clinging to each other until his mom finally pulled back. They both had to wipe their faces.

"Like I said, don't be sorry," Beth said, giving her son a kiss. "We've had a lot of stuff brewing for a while now and I let it go too long. That's my fault."

"No, it isn't. I should've talked to you, told you how I felt instead of bottling it up."

"Can we promise not to do that anymore?"

He hugged his mom's slim shoulders. "I promise."

"Jesus, is it safe to come in?" Don stood nearby, his sheepish expression making it clear he'd been hiding out in the kitchen waiting for the storm to pass.

"All's clear," Tommy said. "We're okay."

"Good. Now maybe your mother will stop moping so much."

"I do not." She sighed. "Okay, maybe I have, a little."

Don waved at the sofa and chairs. "Why don't we all sit down? More mimosas?"

The atmosphere was much more relaxed, even happy, as they finished their visit. Shea was glad to see Tommy and his mother at peace, enjoying their morning together.

As the conversation wound down, Tommy stood. "I guess we'll be going. We've got some things to do. Thanks for the brunch, Mom. It was great."

"You're welcome, sweetheart. Bring Shea back over for dinner one day soon," she said, giving her son another huge hug.

"I will. Dad, talk to you soon."

"You bet." Rather than trying to shake his hand, his dad gave him a hug, too.

Shea got the same warm good-bye and they left, heading for his truck. Tommy didn't say anything until they got in and he started it, fumbling some with his left hand.

"That was . . . wow."

She studied him with concern. "Are you all right?"

"You know, I am. It's like this boulder has been lifted off my chest."

"I'm sure your mom feels the same way."

"Yeah. I regret not talking to her sooner. *Really* talking, not just saying what we all wanted to hear."

"At least you did, and now things can get better between you."

He pulled out of the driveway and headed for the edge of town. "I don't feel like being cooped up anymore. What do you say we go for a drive?"

"Sounds perfect to me. Where to?"

"First, we get reinforcements."

"Oh? Of what kind?"

"You'll see."

His quest for "reinforcements" took them to a beer and wine store on the outskirts of town. Inside, he asked her opinion in choosing a rather large bottle of white wine, already chilled. A package of cheap plastic glasses and a travel-sized corkscrew completed the ensemble, and they paid and were on their way in minutes.

"Now where to?"

He gestured vaguely at the scenery, which grew increasingly wooded and pretty on the way out of town. "Not sure. Somewhere that we can spread out the quilt I've got behind the seat, open that bottle, and while away the day together."

"We're going to drink that whole bottle? It's barely after noon!"

"That, cutie, is my new outlook on the joy of living. To do something just because you want to, because it feels good. Right now, I want to savor a bottle of wine someplace quiet and pretty with the woman I love. Got a problem with that?" He sent her a sizzling smile.

God, just looking at him made her skin tingle. "Not a one. I even have a suggestion of where we can go."

"Well, let's hear it."

"How about the land on the river that belongs to me and Shane? It's private property, so we can't get into trouble for enjoying our wine there."

"You're brilliant! That's exactly what we'll do."

"The land is scruffy, needs clearing and landscaping to make it into a couple of attractive home sites, but it's fine for a picnic. The grass isn't as tall closer to the river, and there's a path you can take with your truck to get there so we don't get chiggers walking through the weeds."

"You said a couple of home sites. You're dividing it equally with Shane? Not to be nosy. I'm just curious."

"You're not being nosy." She smiled at him. "Shane and I have our tracts picked out. We decided a long time ago they were ours to do with as we please independent of each other, but I doubt we'll ever sell. We'd both like to build someday."

"You don't think being neighbors with your brother will be weird?"

"Not to me. We're very close. He does tend to get into my business and that aggravates me sometimes, but he's just being protective." She thought about it for a few seconds before she continued.

"No, I think it would be cool for us both to get married and have families, have our kids grow up together. I can imagine how fun it would be for the cousins to be close, how special the holidays would be. And I've always wanted a sister, so I'd hope his wife would fill that role."

The idea made her sigh with happiness. Someday, it could be like that for her and Shane.

"I like your dream, baby," he said, giving her a sideways glance. "It sounds terrific."

He drove until Shea directed him to a turnoff that was little more than a rutted path through the undergrowth.

"Told you it needs some TLC." She grimaced as his truck hit every bump.

"It'll get some one of these days." As the trees broke and the river came into view, he whistled. "Damn, look at this. You've got quite a diamond in the rough here. Trees, the land sitting up on a gentle rise, and your house will sit high enough to be out of danger should the river rise. This is gorgeous, honey."

"Thank you." A flush of pleasure warmed her to her toes. "I've never shared this with anyone else. Park over there," she said, gesturing.

As he pulled to a stop and turned off the truck, he faced her. "You've never brought anyone here? Not even a group of friends for a wild beer party? It's the perfect location for one."

She snorted. "A keg party with an overprotective cop for a brother? Dream on."

"You've got a point. Though he wasn't always a cop, in the beginning." She knew he meant after their parents were killed, and nodded. "True, but he was always mean enough to scare away any unsavory influences on my life. Especially after . . ."

"After you were raped," he finished softly.

"Yes, most certainly after that. Want to pick our spot?"

After a moment, he reached for the door handle. "Sure."

Tommy hefted the sack with their wine and cups, and Shea retrieved the quilt from behind the seat. She led them through the grass closer to the river, to a nice spot she'd visited more than once.

"I used to come here all the time," she said, spreading out the quilt. "Alone, to get my head together. Perhaps not the smartest thing to be out here, away from help, but I always thought the risk was worth the reward. There's such peace here."

"I agree." He sat down with her and fished the wine bottle and opener out of the sack. "Would you do the honors? The cork is more than I can manage with my lefty."

"Absolutely."

While he tore open the plastic bag and removed two cups, she freed the cork with a pop. He steadied each glass as she poured, and then set the bottle on the quilt beside them, scrunching it down so it hopefully wouldn't fall over.

"A toast, to us." He held up his glass, blue eyes shining with pleasure. Love.

"To whatever the future brings, and may it be fantastic."

They bumped glasses and laughed, took a sip. He leaned in for a long, lingering kiss. A simple brush of lips, a little tongue. The contact was so sweet, it nearly brought tears to her eyes. His next words succeeded.

"If you'd like to tell me about what happened to you, I want to listen. The way I should have before, and didn't."

"Oh, I don't know. What's there to tell? It was so long ago, and he didn't get away with it. He paid."

"So did you, baby. I'm so sorry I reminded you of him at first." His tone wasn't accusing, but understanding.

"The problem was never with you, it was me. I want you to know that. And not with sex, but with my ability to trust. To put myself out there, put my feelings on the line for another man to take advantage of, for him to destroy me."

"But he didn't destroy you."

"No. But when you're eighteen, it's hard to see the light at the end of the tunnel. Especially when you've had those things happen to you. Have you ever been violated? Had your choices taken away? In any way, I mean, not just rape."

"I had my stereo stolen out of my truck once, though that's not a good parallel."

"Why not? Someone broke into the sanctity of your private space, took something that belonged to you, without your permission. I'm sure you felt angry and frustrated, helpless to do anything about it."

"Yes, I did," he allowed. "But you weren't helpless at all. You did something about the guy who hurt you."

"With Shane's and my parents' support, that's true. That night, when the guy brought me home and practically booted me out the car door, he sneered that nobody would believe me. My word against his. He said I was asking for it by going parking with him, and not to even bother telling anyone."

"But you did tell."

"I was hysterical by the time I got inside the house, my blouse torn. I was—I was bleeding. The rest of the night is still a blur, but my family called the police, rushed me to the hospital to have the rape kit done. It was a nightmare."

"God, I can't imagine what you went through."

"That was only the beginning. The wait to find out whether I was pregnant was excruciating, and when the test came back positive, the fight that resulted was something my parents and I never had the chance to reconcile before they were killed."

"Why would they fight with you? It wasn't your fault."

"I wanted to keep my baby, and they were devastated. They didn't want any part of a grandchild that had come from such a terrible event. They didn't want me to throw away my youth, as they put it. But I couldn't end a tiny life that had no say. She was my baby, no matter what."

She swallowed hard and blinked back the tears. Tommy put his cup aside and pulled her close.

"Yes, she was, and nobody can ever take that from you. It was your decision, the right one for you. I choose to believe your parents knew that, deep down, because they'd have to if they were anywhere near as wonderful as their daughter."

"Tommy."

He took her in his arms, held her close. So close she couldn't breathe, but that was more than okay, because he was here, keeping her safe. "I get it, baby, I really do. Thank you for sharing this with me, for trusting me with your heart."

"Thank you for listening," she whispered, clinging to him. "For not giving me useless words about how it all worked out for the best, or how I'll have more children. You hear me, like nobody else ever has."

"I'll always listen, and be here for you. You have my promise. I love you so much." He pulled back, kissed her with rising hunger. Stared into her eyes. "Do you think we could put off that meeting with your brother until tomorrow? I just want today to be about us, and to hell with the rest of the world."

"I've never heard a better suggestion."

With that, he flashed his heartbreaking smile and lowered her to the blanket.

And spent the rest of the afternoon making the world go away.

18

Tommy sat with Shea snuggled against his side on the couch and watched her brother swipe a hand down his face.

"You realize this isn't my area of expertise," Shane said, frustrated. "I can't do anything official."

"But you're in homicide!" Shea protested. "Two construction workers were killed in the scaffold collapse, and Tommy was almost murdered."

"I've got nothing to go on that hints his being trapped in the warehouse wasn't just an accident. Notice I said 'official.' I can do some snooping into Prescott's holdings, see if any red flags pop up." Shane's cell phone rang and he snatched it from the holder on his belt. "Ford."

After a pause, Shane hissed an exclamation and demanded to know the particulars of whatever his caller had to say. In a few moments, he hung up and pinned Tommy with a hard stare.

"Seems you might be onto something. There was a man's body found in the remains of the warehouse."

A chill chased down his spine. "Jesus. That's what Prescott bitched to Hensley about—that the authorities would find a body belonging to the man who'd fucked up and didn't do the job right."

"That job being to kill you." Shane still sounded skeptical

about that part, although he was inclined to believe him about the building insurance scam.

"You're the cop, you tell me. All I know is I was hit over the head twice before the building fell, and I nearly got my ass toasted."

Shea spoke up in his defense. "Add that fact with all the others and it makes a pretty damning picture. Especially since they didn't report him trespassing at city hall last night."

"I can't argue with that." Shane rose, readying to leave. "I promise I'll see what I can find out, though it might not be much. The deeper this goes, the more resources it'll take to uncover it."

"Whatever you can do," Tommy said. "I just wanted to go on record with all of this. In case."

In case I'm right, and Prescott succeeds in killing me. Or worse, hurting Shea.

No, he wouldn't think like that. Prescott would get what was coming to him, and Tommy would laugh when that day came. He owed the bastard, big-time.

He and Shea spent a few hours together, hanging out. They watched TV, made love, and ate. In between lovemaking sessions they didn't even bother to get dressed. When the clock starting nudging toward the afternoon, however, he reluctantly got dressed despite Shea's cute pouting.

"You can take a shower here."

"Yes, but then I'll have to put on dirty clothes. I'm just going to dash home, take care of that, and pack a few more clothes. Then I'm going to run a couple of errands and when I'm done, I'll pick you up and we'll get a bite to eat. Work for you?"

"Except for the errands. Tell me you're not going to snoop and get yourself into more trouble."

"I'm not going to snoop and get into trouble. I'm only going to have a look around the warehouse."

"I'm *not* reassured."

"I'll be back soon, baby, don't worry. Okay?"

Finally, she relented, rolled on top of him and gave him a kiss. "Don't be gone long or I'll hunt you down."

"Sounds like fun. Maybe I'll let you catch me." He waggled his tongue lewdly.

She slapped his shoulder. "Idiot."

Laughing, he dressed. He had the love of his life and his world was back on its axis. After promising to hurry, he left before he was tempted to spread her on her back again.

He whistled all the way to his apartment, wondering if it was too early to discuss moving in together. After all, what sense did it make for both of them to keep driving back and forth? Consolidating was a lot more economical nowadays, and damned convenient for his overactive libido. Of course, he had a feeling he'd have to make his suggestion sound a tad more romantic than that. Women were sensitive about that shit.

But with Shea? Yeah, he could do romantic.

He was almost ready to go when a knock sounded on his door. Wary, he placed his gym bag on the floor by the couch, half expecting Prescott to be waiting on the other side. When he peered out the peephole, however, his brow furrowed. An elderly neighbor? He'd never seen this man before, but he appeared harmless enough.

With a mental shrug, he opened the door to see what the man wanted. "Hello," he said with a friendly smile. "Can I help you?"

The old man's shoulders were stooped, and his face was a road map of tough battles fought and won. His height equaled Tommy's and he might've been a big man, once. But his worn button-down plaid shirt, tucked neatly into a pair of khaki pants, hung from his slender frame. He shook, his hands constantly in motion. Parkinson's, Tommy thought.

His rheumy eyes looked Tommy up and down.

"No, young man. But I believe I might be able to help you. May I come in?"

"Uh, sure." He stepped aside and gestured for the man to come in. He stood by, ready in case the old dude stumbled or needed assistance, but he made it under his own steam and turned to look at Tommy.

"I'd shake your hand, but . . ." He held up his wrapped extremity.

The old man nodded, solemn. "Quite all right."

"Would you like to sit down?"

"No, I won't be here long enough to get comfortable. If I do, I might not get back up. So I'd best get to the point. My name is Joseph Hensley."

"Tommy Skyler."

"I know."

At first, the name meant nothing. But as he considered his visitor, the man's last name flipped a switch. "Hensley. Are you a relative of Will Hensley's?"

"Yep, though I can't say as I'm too proud of that fact at the moment." He gave a deep, weary sigh. "Let me just cut through the bull and tell you that I've had my eye on my grandson for a bit, and I know he's gotten himself mixed up with some bad folks. I know you're that firefighter on the news who got hurt in that warehouse, and my Will is at least partially responsible."

Tommy gaped at him, incredulous. "You know? How?"

"That ain't important," Hensley said gruffly. "Obviously you've put together some facts of your own, since you ain't too surprised. The point is, Will's gonna make this right because his grandpa don't plan on giving him a choice. Just maybe, everybody can come out of this with their hides intact. 'Cept for Forrest Prescott. I don't give a rat's hairy ass what happens to that bastard."

Unbelievable. "How are you going to make Will cooperate? Whatever he and Prescott have going on, your grandson is in way too deep to pull himself out. The people he's dealing with are dangerous."

He didn't care to tell Hensley what he'd overheard. First, he wasn't quite sure he could trust the man. Second, something about the old guy tugged at his heartstrings. He didn't want to hurt this man.

"He'll do what's right. I made a phone call to the son of an old friend, and he's coming here to look into things, all official. Might be talkin' to you, too. Name's Nick Westfall, and he's a special agent with the FBI."

"Jesus, you don't screw around, do you?"

"Not when my only family is in trouble, boy. Maybe you can understand that."

Tommy thought about Donny, lost to their family for three years now. If only there had been a Joseph Hensley to call in reinforcements for his brother back then, someone who knew how to work the hostage situation from the inside, Donny might still be alive. He cleared his throat. "Yeah, I sure can."

Hensley straightened proudly. "I survived World War II, got myself out of more scrapes than you or my grandson could ever think of gettin' into for the rest of your lives. Will might be a disaster right now, but he's my disaster and I'll be damned if I go to my eternal reward before he's set to rights."

"He's lucky to have you, Mr. Hensley."

"Joseph." The man studied Tommy's scarred face, and then gestured to his wrapped hand. "That going to be okay?"

"I'm not going to lose it, but . . . there's some things that can't ever be 'set to rights,' Joseph. A man who's survived what you have knows better."

The old man suddenly looked ancient, and he nodded sadly. "Damned straight. Well, I'd best be on my way." He shuffled toward the door, stepped outside as Tommy opened it for him, and faced him once more.

"I don't know if you can forgive my grandson for his part in what happened to you, but I can tell you that boy will pay for his bad choices for the rest of his life. Sometimes that's enough of a price for any man."

"Sometimes it is, Joseph," he agreed around the knot in his throat.

In that moment, any lingering resentment he'd harbored about his newfound disability vanished. No matter how tough life became, there were always those who had it worse.

The old man nodded and made his way down the sidewalk to a waiting taxi Tommy hadn't noticed before. As it pulled away from the curb, he pondered Joseph's parting words and wondered what sort of price the old man might've paid for *his* choices.

He supposed he'd never know.

Shea fidgeted, impatient for Tommy to get back. He hadn't been gone all that long, but she wanted him here, at her side. So what if she was shamelessly addicted to the man? Who wouldn't be?

She puttered for a while, fed Miss Kitty early to stop her howling, and settled on the end of the sofa in her favorite spot to read a good John Sandford thriller. She'd just managed to get into hunky Lucas Davenport's latest scrape with a nasty killer when the phone rang.

Getting up, she hurried to the bar and answered without checking the caller ID, hoping it was Tommy. "Hello?"

"Hey, Sis. Been trying to reach your better half and he must have his cell phone turned off."

"Oh? What's up?"

"Got some interesting developments in the matter we've been discussing, to put it mildly. Can't talk here, though. I've got a dinner break coming to me in about ten minutes. Can you meet me somewhere?"

"Sure." She fretted, knowing if Shane wanted to meet right away, and wouldn't discuss it on a work phone, it was important. "Tommy's supposed to be back soon, but I'm not sure when."

"Tell you what. I'll call and leave a message for him to meet us. How about that Chinese place over by Wal-Mart? It's quiet this time of day."

So nobody would be around to overhear. Her anxiety ramped up a notch. "Okay. Twenty minutes?"

"See you then."

Quickly, she retrieved a pad and pen from the bar and wrote Tommy a note, just in case he didn't think to check his voice mail. Either way, he'd catch up with them.

Slipping on a pair of flip-flops, she grabbed her purse and keys and headed out. All the way to the restaurant, the possibilities of what Shane might have learned ran through her head. Wasn't much good obsessing over it, though, until they heard it from him.

Inside, Shane was already waiting in a corner booth at the back of the restaurant. As usual, he was seated facing the dining room rather than with his back to it. Cops were a cautious bunch, and often with good reason.

Flashing her a smile, he got up and gave her a brief but fierce hug, and kissed her on the cheek. "Thanks for meeting me on such short notice. Hope I didn't interrupt anything."

"Nope. An hour earlier, however . . ." She let the statement hang, unable to resist needling her twin.

He made a face. "Oh, God. Don't make me lose my appetite. There are certain things a man does *not* want to envision about his sister."

As she laughed, a waitress came to take their drink orders and ask if they just wanted the buffet. They both ordered soda and said yes to the buffet, but that they were waiting on one more person. When the waitress left, she studied her brother.

"Okay, what did you learn that you couldn't tell me over the phone?"

"Sorry, but there were too many ears there." He glanced around, then pinned her with his gray eyes. "I had an enlightening visit in my office a short while ago. An FBI agent named Nick Westfall showed up with some intriguing information about Prescott."

Her brows lifted. "How on earth did the FBI get involved so fast?"

"Seems Agent Westfall received a tip about what's going on from an unnamed source, or more likely, he just didn't choose to tell me who it was. Anyway, the agent was actually there to speak with the chief and a buddy of mine who happens to be assistant chief about what he's learned. All of this insurance scam stuff isn't my department unless a homicide occurs."

"So why did he come to see you?"

"During the course of the conversation, my buddy became concerned. Told the agent that one of their detectives had a sister who was at least friends with Prescott and that I ought to be in the loop. The agent agreed to stop by and talk to me, as much to pump me for information about your involvement with Prescott as from any real concern for your welfare."

"He doesn't honestly think I've got anything to do with what Forrest is up to, does he?" The idea was alarming. She wasn't overjoyed to be on the FBI's radar, innocent or not.

"By the time we finished talking, no. I don't think he believes you're guilty of anything but ignorance."

She scowled at her brother. "Gee, thanks."

"I didn't mean it like that." He sighed. "The point is, he

gave me some information even though he was certainly under no obligation to share. Seems Prescott's got a nice racket going."

"Was it what we suspected?"

"Looks that way so far. The FBI hasn't been able to dig up proof of every single property he owns—that will take time. But of the ones they've found so far, each one is listed as being owned by a different dummy corporation. Westfall said the paper trail could pave a road to Mars. The properties are insured by different companies to avoid suspicion when one of them has a claim made against it for damages."

"This means they've traced some of these recent building disasters back to him?"

"Yeah, and not just around here. There are several properties in other states, too. Two of them have been destroyed and received a payout. If it was just a simple scam for Prescott to get rich, though, that would be too easy."

"What do you mean?"

"Prescott doesn't have nearly enough money in his bank accounts—at least the ones the FBI has found—to account for the massive fortune they estimate has been scammed. And Will Hensley's obviously just a lackey. He has a mere fraction of the amount."

"Perhaps Forrest is diverting the money to a numbered account, planning for the day he skips the country?"

"No, it's much more sinister than greed, I'm afraid. This is where it gets scary. They've found evidence to suggest that the lion's share is being funneled to a known antigovernment terrorist group being operated right here in the good old U.S.A. We're talking dangerous Timothy McVeigh types, but more organized."

"Holy shit."

"Exactly. And it gets worse. This group was already on the FBI's and the ATF's radar, but now the path has finally intersected with tangible evidence of how they're getting at least some of their funding. The fact that these ties connect to our city did not thrill the shit out of the chief."

Shea stared at her soda as the waitress set them down and hurried away. "Good God. And I thought this man was my friend. I even tried to convince myself he'd make a good boyfriend, before Tommy and I worked things out. I thought he was safe and boring! How could I have been so blind?"

"He's a smooth operator, good at feeding people what he wants them to swallow. Needless to say, I want you to stay far, far away from Prescott until they can nail him."

"As if that'll be a problem." She glanced at her watch. "I should try Tommy again. He should've called back by now, and this is going to blow his mind."

Digging her cell phone out of her purse, she checked her messages, but there were no missed calls. She dialed Tommy's number again, and was exasperated when it immediately went to his voice mail again.

"Hey, Shane and I are at the Chinese place. Come on over when you get this. Love you." She flipped the phone closed.

"He'll be here soon. Don't worry."

"I know. We'll just hang out for a while longer, if you won't get in trouble at work."

"Hey, I'm a homicide cop. My middle name is *Trouble*," he said, teasing.

She laughed, but her heart wasn't in it. What was taking Tommy so long?

As soon as he got here, she'd rest easier.

After Joseph left, Tommy took a drive out to the site of the burned warehouse.

He was drawn here as though by a magnet. He held no real illusion that he could find any clues here, not without training as an arson investigator, but that was okay.

Putting his truck in park, he got out and walked toward the charred mess, getting his first good look at the aftermath. He'd lived through this? Fucking insane.

Nobody crushed underneath this tangle of wood and metal should have made it out alive. The other guy sure hadn't. Tommy hadn't realized how truly lucky he'd been. Not in that oh-fuck-I-should-be-dead way.

Until now.

Clenching his good hand into a fist, he recalled the hazy memory of the debris coming down. Being pinned, almost unable to breathe. Of fading to unconsciousness, certain that was to be his last view of the world.

So weird to stand here, safe and sound. Who was the man who'd died in there? *Did he truly intend to kill me?*

He didn't know how long he stood there when he remembered Shea. Crap, he'd said he wouldn't be gone long, and it had been over an hour. On top of that, his phone had been off. Turning it on, he checked his messages and winced to find three. One from Shane and two from Shea. Shane had information and wanted to meet, and they'd decided on going for Chinese.

He dialed Shea's number and she picked up on the second ring.

"Tommy! Where are you?"

"At the warehouse site. Sorry, baby. I had an unexpected visitor at my place, and then I lost track of time. I'll tell you all about it when I get there. You guys still at the restaurant?"

"Yes, and we haven't eaten yet. We wanted to wait for you."

He felt bad about that. "I'll leave now, okay? Shouldn't be more than ten, fifteen minutes."

"All right. See you soon."

"I love you, cutie."

"Love you, too. Bye."

Damn. He needed to get going. The phone went into the pocket of his loose shorts.

The noise of a car's engine caught his attention and he turned to see a dark Escalade approaching, tires crunching on the vacant lot. A familiar man with sandy hair was at the wheel, and Tommy braced himself for an unpleasant little chat.

Shifting on his feet, he didn't take his eyes off Prescott as the man stepped from his SUV and approached. Despite the heat of the day and the hour, he wore a crisp suit. He moved with confidence, almost a cocky swagger, and Tommy wanted to rip his lungs out just as he had the urge to do on the day of Zack's wedding.

"Skyler." The man's expression was impassive.

"Prescott. Nice afternoon for a drive."

"Isn't it?"

"Yep. Thought I'd come here and take a look around, remind myself how lucky I am."

"You are that, Skyler," he said thoughtfully. "You are definitely one lucky bastard."

Something nasty in the depths of Prescott's gaze made his heart race. "Quite a coincidence, you showing up here. Guess you're just really dedicated, being city manager and all."

"Oh, I'm dedicated all right, but I think we both know that's not why I'm here." He chuckled softly. "Every lucky streak has to come to an end, wouldn't you say?"

Tommy concentrated on remaining calm, on bluffing his way out of this. "Not necessarily, and I have no idea why you're here, unless it's to harass me for winning Shea. She chose me, so get over it. Have a nice day, Prescott."

Prescott's hand disappeared into his suit jacket. A gun suddenly leveled at Tommy's chest halted his steps.

Oh, fuck.

"What the hell are you doing? Put the gun away," he said, surprised at how calm and steady he sounded.

"No, I like it just like this." Prescott shook his head, appearing almost sympathetic. "Poor kid. You just had to get in the middle of business that doesn't concern you, and now I'm forced to make sure you understand the error of your ways."

Tommy swallowed hard. Time to pull out all the stops. "I told the police what I heard, and the FBI knows everything, too. Killing me will gain you nothing. If you grab your cash and head out of the country, you can still live like a king. Someplace where nobody knows you, with a new identity."

Prescott's smile was cold. "What a marvelous idea! I might just do that, too, after I take care of you for being such a pest. Then again, no one can pin anything on me. Maybe I'll just stay here and comfort sweet Shea after you're found dead of an apparent suicide. Everyone will believe the horrible scar and your disability was just too much for you."

"My friends know I'd never kill myself for such a superficial reason. They know I'm too resilient for that."

"What they believe won't matter much in face of the evidence. Get in your truck, behind the wheel. We're going for a drive."

A glimpse of red in the trees caught Tommy's attention. A man ducked behind a tree trunk . . . a man wearing a red ball cap.

Shit. "Where are we going?"

"Just get in," Prescott snapped, waving the gun.

As he complied, Tommy felt Fear Central in his brain sort of . . . shut down. Was this what Donny felt like when he'd been led away to be tortured and eventually executed? Just numb, the scene surreal, as though he was on the outside watching it happen to someone else?

Tommy liked to think so. Maybe the human brain, unable to accept the inevitability of its own demise, simply departed for greener pastures. Or maybe your thoughts became clearer, the world around you sharper, as you became utterly calm. Waited for an opportunity to strike back. Anything except going blindly to your fate like a calf to slaughter.

Yes, this last was how he felt. Calm, waiting. He would not accept that some asshole was going to take him away from Shea after all they'd been through. It wasn't going to happen.

"Take a right out of the parking lot, away from town. We're going to a more secluded place, where you'll decide to end your life."

Tommy started the truck and followed Prescott's directions. Had Will Hensley followed, or called for help? He hoped so. The winding road took them to a higher elevation, twisting and turning, with sheer rock on one side, a long, treacherous slide down into a wooded hollow on the other.

In that moment, Tommy knew what had to be done. He couldn't allow Prescott to get him to their destination, which was sure to be far away from any witnesses. He had two choices, and both of them might sign his death warrant.

But the choice he made would be *his*.

He hoped it was worth the price.

Hitting his brakes, he swerved toward the narrow shoulder of the road.

And drove right off into thin air.

19

Shea checked her watch for the tenth time. "He's not coming, Shane. Something's wrong."

"He was fine when he called. I'm sure he got held up again."

"No. It's been thirty minutes. He was only ten minutes from here. I'm telling you, I have a bad feeling."

"Well, call him. He must have his phone on now, right?"

So reasonable, her brother. "Right. I'll try him."

She called, listened to it ring. And ring. This time his voice mail didn't pick up right away, and that increased her anxiety.

"Thomas Wayne, where the hell are you? Either get your ass here or call me!" She hung up and frowned at her brother's half smile.

"Wow, what motivation. A man knows he's in deep doo-doo when his lady calls him by both names."

"And you came by this tidbit, how?"

"Never mind. How much longer do you want to wait before we go looking?"

"I'm ready now. I can't stand this."

"No problem, we'll go." Shane stood, threw a couple of bills on the table to pay for their sodas, and gave the hostess an apologetic look. "Sorry, family emergency."

As they walked outside, Shea latched on to what he'd said. "If all goes well, he will be family."

"I'm glad, Sis," he said, hugging her shoulders. "I'll drive."

"You probably think I'm being silly."

"Nope. A good cop *never* disregards his gut feeling. And you're my sister, so it's in your genes."

"That may be, but I don't want to be right."

"Hey, maybe you won't be. We might run into him coming from the opposite direction, on his way to meet us. In fact, I'd bet on it."

He would've lost. They must've passed five trucks that resembled Tommy's, but none of them were his. As they approached the site of the warehouse fire, Shea's dread grew. When the parking lot came into view, she gasped.

"That Escalade belongs to Forrest! What is he doing here?"

Shane frowned. "I don't know."

He pulled close and circled around the vehicle. It became obvious right away that no one else was around.

"Where is Tommy's truck? Where is he?" A sense of desperation blossomed in her breast. The beginnings of real fear.

Her eyes met her brother's, and the message was conveyed without words. There was one reason that made perfect sense as to why Tommy hadn't arrived at the restaurant, why his truck was not here, but Forrest's SUV was.

"Shane." She gripped her brother's arm. "He's got Tommy."

"All right. Let's stay calm. Where would Forrest take him?"

"I don't know! Not—not back into town."

"Well, there's only two ways to go from here, into town and away from town. Let me make a quick phone call, tell dispatch to have the patrol units keep an eye out for his truck."

After he'd done that, he took a right out of the parking lot and headed into the hills.

Shane gripped the armrest and tried to push down her panic.

They'd find him, and when they did, he would be all right.

Forrest was going to pay for everything he'd done.

Tommy groaned, the steamy hiss and *tick, tick, tick* of the engine block penetrating the fog. He struggled to remember what had happened and automatically brought his right hand to his face.

"Dammit!" He'd forgotten about his injury.

Immediately, two facts were made clear—his right wrist hurt worse than ever, and so did his head.

Opening his eyes, he stared at the bandages. Blood. Whether from the wrist or his head, he didn't know. From the relentless throbbing, it could be either. Lowering his arm, he directed his gaze forward and tried to make sense out of what he was seeing. The trees were upside down.

No, wait. *He* was upside down. Looking out his shattered front windshield. "Christ . . ."

Everything came back in a rush and he turned his head, seeking his captor. Prescott hung beside him, and any hope that the bastard was dead vanished when he moaned and began to stir.

Time to go.

Tommy wrestled with getting his seat belt unlatched, no easy task under the circumstances. The button was stuck and didn't want to release, and he had to work on it for several minutes. Hurt like a son of a bitch because he had to use his injured hand. The left one wouldn't reach that far over on his right side.

Finally, it popped open and he was dumped on his head. "Ow!" He supposed he ought to be grateful since the blinding pain all over meant he was alive.

Wiggling, he inched forward through the opening, aware

of being cut to hell on his arms and belly by the jagged glass. But he'd walk over boiling oil to get away from the man now moving around in earnest behind him, cursing a blue streak.

"Where do you think you're going to go, Skyler? You can't get away from me!"

Wanna bet?

He wriggled onto the carpet of dirt and weeds and pushed to his knees, fighting off a wave of sickness. Looking over his shoulder, he winced to see his truck lying on its roof in a crumpled, smoking heap. He'd rolled the thing down an embankment a good fifty feet. Fuckin' A, his insurance rate was going to skyrocket.

Pretty ironic, considering.

Prescott's head appeared, the man hot on his heels, and Tommy cursed, staggering to his feet. His left ankle complained and he swayed, took a couple of tentative steps. A twinge shot through it, but the pain wasn't too bad. Other places hurt worse.

Which way? He sure couldn't make it up the steep incline, so he might have to—

A gunshot popped, the bullet whizzing close enough to his head that he felt the heat cause his scalp to tingle.

"Fuck!"

Every ounce of pain vanished in the flood of adrenaline that rushed to his limbs. It didn't matter which way he ran—forward suited him fine at the moment.

And so he ran like a quarterback on the twenty-yard line with no open receivers in the last three seconds of the Super Bowl. Balls to the wall.

He plunged through the brush, using his arm to block branches, protecting his face. His breath was harsh in his own ears, legs pumping. The fear that had eluded him before owned him now, pure self-preservation. Because while a soft man like Prescott couldn't hope to beat Tommy in a foot race, his gun had no such problem.

A couple of bullets pelted the brush and a tree trunk next to him as he bolted past, leaping a fallen log. Hope flared as he realized he was running toward the river. If he could get there, he might be able to get help. Prescott would be forced to abandon his chase if he could reach a populated area.

The trees ahead began to thin out and Tommy could see blue sky. The river was close. So close.

He burst from his cover and ran full speed for the river-bank. That must be it, right there . . .

His eyes widened and he skidded, almost stopped too late. Almost went straight over the sheer one-hundred-foot drop to the river below.

Rocks skittered over the edge, kicked up by his tennis shoes. Chest heaving from exertion, he stared down from the dizzying height, from side to side, frantic to find another escape route.

"Told you," Prescott said, panting from behind him. "You're not going anywhere but to hell."

The bottom dropped out of his stomach as he turned to face the man he hated.

He was absolutely, totally screwed.

Shea hoped and prayed. They had to find him.

As they rounded a bend in the curvy road, a plume of smoke could be seen rising from a gulley some fifty feet below. Even more curious, a Sugarland city truck was parked off to the side of the road. Shane slowed down, pulled to the shoulder behind it. "Let's see what this is about."

He got out and she followed him to the side, and looked down at the twisted wreckage of a dark truck.

"Oh, my God! That's Tommy's truck!" A sob welled in her chest as she scanned for a quick way down.

"Hang tight. I'm going to call for backup."

"What about an ambulance?"

"Let's see if we have any injuries first." He flipped open his phone and called the station, requesting more officers. "And someone call the chief and that FBI agent who came to see him, Nick Westfall. Let them both know what's going on."

After he hung up, she yanked on his arm. "Let's go!"

"You're staying here. I'll check Tommy's truck."

"No, I'm not. Don't waste time arguing with me because it won't help. Let's move!"

Shane shot her a foul look, but when it didn't work, he took her by the hand and led her down the road a ways, to a spot where the incline wasn't so steep. Before they'd gotten far, the unmistakable crack of a gunshot split the air.

"Oh, God! Where did it come from?"

"I don't know. Sounds out here echo all over the place. Come on."

They had to hike back to the truck, and halfway there, two more shots sounded, farther away. By the time they got to the wrecked truck, they were running. At a glance, it was easy to see the cab was no longer occupied.

The front windshield was shattered. Shards of the glass stabbed inward like broken teeth, some of them bloody. A scrap of cloth dangled from one sharp finger.

"He got out," she whispered. "He got out and he's hurt and Forrest is chasing him."

Shane clasped her hands. "Please, stay here and wait for my backup. I don't need you hurt as well."

"I can't—you know that. I'll just follow you, so you might as well take me with you. Let's hurry."

"Dammit." The tenseness of his body, the grim set of his mouth, revealed his frustration. "You stay behind me, understand?"

"Got it."

Palming his gun, he started away from the road, deeper into the brush. As they walked, she asked, "How do you know we're going the right way?"

"Blood on the underbrush," he said quietly.

"Oh." She wished she hadn't asked.

"And this. Hello," he said, bending to pick up something. He held up a black cell phone. "Must be either Prescott's or Tommy's."

"Tommy's," she said, lungs constricting in anxiety. "Forrest's is silver."

Shane pocketed the phone. "I'll hold on to it for him."

Like everything was normal and they were simply going for a little nature hike. He'd just give it back to Tommy, and they'd all smile and go home, crack open a bottle of wine.

Somehow she doubted today would end on such a pleasant note, even if Tommy was fine. There would be police, endless questions, and they'd all be exhausted.

When they found Tommy and put Forrest in prison to share a cell with a lonely inmate in need of a bitch.

Tommy took a couple of steps away from the ledge.

"Stop right there," Prescott snarled, jabbing the muzzle of the gun in his direction. "You're going to go over the edge, Skyler. This is a great place for you to commit suicide. I appreciate you choosing so well."

"Fuck you, asshole. I'm not jumping. If I'm going to die, it's going to be murder, and here's a news flash—once you shoot me, you'd better take my advice and skip out of the country, fast. The FBI is already onto you." He laughed to cover his nerves. "Dude, you can't even go home by now. They're probably crawling all over that nice house—"

"Shut up."

"—and they've probably seized your phone records, your computer—"

"Shut up!" he yelled, advancing. The black hole in the end of the muzzle wavered as his body shook in rage.

Tommy swallowed hard. That hole was centered on his heart, held there by a lunatic. He shouldn't have pushed so hard, done such a good job convincing his nemesis of his imminent downfall, even if it was true.

"You can still get away," he said, coaxing. "But not if you waste time here with me. My death gains you nothing now, nothing but trouble. And I heard you say yourself that you don't prefer to resort to murder."

A maniacal light shone in Prescott's eyes. "You also heard me say if it's you or me, I'm saving myself."

Tommy raised his hands, palms out. "Hey, I can't do a thing to you, so it's not a 'me or you' situation. Think. You haven't actually killed anyone yet except by accident, right? Once you cross that line, there's no going back. You've got a shitload of money. Take it and go."

For a few seconds, the gun began to lower, and he had hope that his words were taking root. But Prescott quickly raised it again, the hatred overshadowing all else.

"What money? I scammed him too, kept some of his cut and now there's nowhere to hide. I might've been okay, played it cool, if it hadn't been for you, but you had to have Shea for yourself!"

He pushed down his anger. *Focus.* If he could give the FBI a name, they'd cream their Jockeys.

"Who did you scam? Maybe we can figure a way out of this, then you can go."

"You're the reason I have to go! You! She belonged to me, her and that gold mine in scraggly riverfront property that she and her brother don't even realize is worth a fortune. Everything fell apart when you interfered, and now you're going to die."

Tommy sucked in a breath as Prescott shoved the gun out and his finger tightened on the trigger.

Oh, God.

"Don't do it!"

Tommy barely had time to register the shout from behind Prescott, had just a split second to throw himself to the dirt before the gunshots erupted.

Shane moved faster through the brush and Shea hurried to keep the pace, driven by desperation.

Hurry, hurry.

He's in trouble.

Shane broke through the trees and she looked past him, saw the clearing. The edge of an overlook.

And the tableau before them filled her with horror.

Forrest had Tommy backed up to the edge, a gun trained on his chest. He was screaming, shaking the weapon, losing it. As he stiffened his arm, a man in a red ball cap stepped from the trees, raised a rifle toward the pair.

Will Hensley!

"Don't do it!" Will yelled.

Shane was already running, raising his own gun, shouting, "Police, freeze!"

Forrest whirled and fired at the nearest threat, which was Will. The younger man flew backward, hit the ground, rifle knocked from his grasp. Shane closed the distance but didn't fire as Prescott swung the weapon his way.

"Freeze, goddammit!"

Shea saw why—her brother couldn't fire at Prescott for fear of hitting Tommy, who right at that moment tackled the older man from behind.

Prescott's gun went off and Shea screamed as Shane jerked, fell. Tommy and Prescott rolled in the dirt, struggling for control over the gun.

Shea ran to her brother and fell to her knees, crying out when she saw the blood seeping through the shirt on his side. "Oh, God! Shane!"

"Jesus fuck," he gasped, pressing one hand against his side. He scrambled to his feet, listing a bit. "Shit, they're going to kill each other."

Torn, she followed his gaze to where Tommy fought with Forrest, doing his best to hold off the man with one arm, landing a few blows with his good hand. He was holding his own surprisingly well given his disadvantage, but she was terrified by how close to the ledge they were.

Shane took off, ignoring his own wound to get to Tommy. On the way, he paused to check on Will. The man was sitting up now, one hand clamped over a gushing bullet wound in his shoulder. When Shane bent and would've reached for him, Will flinched and scooted backward.

"No! Don't touch me," he said, gasping. "I'm HIV positive. I'll be fine until help comes."

Shane nodded and straightened, kicking the rifle out of easy reach. "Shea, call for a couple of ambulances."

Her brother half jogged toward the pair of men bent on destroying each other, yelling for Prescott to give up. Prescott had Tommy pinned on his back and Shea froze, phone in hand, as he angled the muzzle under Tommy's chin.

Tommy got his legs underneath Forrest, and with one powerful shove, flipped the man over his head.

And over the ledge.

But Forrest still had a solid hold on Tommy's good arm, and his momentum nearly pulled Tommy off the edge with him.

Tommy's yell of pain echoed over the river. "Ahhh! Fuck!"

He flipped onto his stomach, trying to crawl backward, his entire arm hanging over the edge. "Shane!"

He was losing ground, slipping.

Shea tossed her phone at Will. "You make the call," she said over her shoulder, and sprinted after Shane.

Her brother threw himself across Tommy's legs just in time to halt his sliding. Shea knelt next to him and clutched a fistful of his shirt, peering over the edge to where Forrest dangled over open space.

Incredibly, his face was full of hatred, and he seemed focused only on directing that rage at Tommy, no matter the cost to himself.

"I can't . . . hold you . . . much longer," Tommy rasped. "Drop the gun . . . and grab on."

"Do as he says," Shane barked. "Drop it and hold on with both hands. We'll pull you up."

Forrest sneered. "I don't think so. I'm taking you with me to hell."

With that, he swung up the hand with the gun and pointed it at Tommy's head.

I'm taking you with me to hell.

Those words burned into Tommy's brain, along with the sudden, grim reality of being pinned with a gun aimed between his eyes.

Shea screamed.

Without even thinking, he released his hold on the other man. Shook his arm, trying to dislodge a parasite that would take his life.

Suddenly he was jerked backward with violent force so hard that the weight was ripped from his arm. He flipped onto his back and heard the hair-raising scream, down, down.

Until it abruptly ended.

And just as abruptly, he found his arms full of near-hysterical woman. A soft, pretty, curvy woman with big, tear-filled brown eyes who needed major comforting. He could so do that.

"Oh, God, I thought he was going to kill you," she sobbed. Kisses rained all over his face. And more kisses.

"Had it under control, baby. Solid gold."

That earned him a little whimper and some tongue, sneaking in there for that life-reaffirming thing that blindsided people after near disaster.

He could do that, too.

A snort came from nearby. Shane. "Under control? You look like something Miss Kitty barfed on Shea's rug."

"Dude, whatever." He eyed Shane's side, soaked in blood. "You're the one who went and got yourself shot, charging from the trees like fuckin' Rambo or some shit."

"At least I didn't get nearly yanked off a cliff."

Shea interrupted. "Will, did you call for the paramedics?"

Jesus, he'd forgotten about Hensley.

"Yes, ma'am." The guy hung his head, sort of slumped. Whether in shame or from pain, Tommy couldn't tell.

"Hey, Hensley?"

He looked up, expression haunted. "Yes?"

"You made the right choice. Your grandpa will be proud."

That seemed to brighten him some. "You think so?"

"I know so." He did, too. After the Feds got done with Will, he might end up getting his act together after all. "And thank you."

Face pale, Shane gave Tommy a tired half smile. "You did good, too, kid. Real good."

"Not a kid," Tommy said. But he smiled. For some reason, it didn't really bother him anymore.

"I can see that." Shane's gray eyes closed. "Good enough for my sister, good enough for me."

And that made Tommy one lucky boy.

20

Shane was in real trouble.

Even if she weren't a nurse, Shea would have known her brother needed help, fast. His wisecracking with Tommy had stopped and he was silent. His skin was clammy and he was going into shock.

"Give me your shirt," she demanded, holding her hand out to Tommy. Quickly, he stripped off the tattered garment and held it out. She balled it up and pressed it into Shane's side, causing him to groan.

"*Fuck*, Shea."

"I'm sorry, Bro. Have to keep the pressure on." He didn't answer. "God, where are the paramedics?"

"They'll have to hike in here the same way we came," Tommy said, voice laced with concern. "There's no road."

Shea grew light-headed, her gaze snapping to his. They both knew that might take too long. "I can't lose him."

"You won't." Scooting close, he rubbed her back. "He's not going anywhere."

Tears coursed down her face. "He'd better not. He's got decades to be nosy and try to run my life. I won't be cheated out of a one of them."

Soon, they heard voices. Lots of them. Paramedics jogged from the trees carrying their equipment, and hot on their heels were the police. One of them was Tommy's friend

Daisy Callahan. Shea hadn't spared a thought for her since the wedding.

Shea also didn't miss how the woman dropped to her knees by Shane's side, face anguished, and touched his hair before she realized what she was doing. She snatched her hand away and nodded to Shea.

"He'll be fine. He has to be."

Shea filed that away for future reference. Right now, all that mattered was getting help.

The paramedics nudged them all aside and began to work on Shane. She couldn't hear everything they said, but she heard enough to know the bullet that struck his side hadn't hit anything vital, but he'd lost too much blood and his pressure was taking a nosedive.

They ran an IV, placed a pressure bandage on his abdomen, and moved him to a backboard. She watched the process in a daze, the thought running through her head that, after all of this, she could lose him. Shane could die.

The paramedics bore him away and when she and Tommy would have followed, the police waylaid them with endless questions about what was going on. Evidently, these guys weren't in the loop, so the explanation took a while. The fact that she was Shane's sister, however, smoothed the way some.

Shea caught sight of an impressive-looking man in a suit. He had two other equally important-looking men with him who spoke to the police, and Will Hensley was immediately borne away by another pair of paramedics, the men in suits following them.

One of the uniformed men approached her and Tommy. "Miss Ford, Mr. Skyler, you two are free to go. Mr. Skyler might want to get checked out at the hospital as well."

"He will. We're going there now, as soon as we get back to my brother's car."

"I hope Shane's okay," the cop said. "He's a stand-up guy."

"Thank you."

"Come on, baby. I'll drive."

She shook her head as they began the trek back through the woods. "You're scratched up, and you were in an accident. I don't want you passing out behind the wheel."

"Um, it wasn't an accident, really. I drove into the gulley on purpose."

Her mouth fell open. "You idiot. You could have killed yourself."

"Would've been better than whatever Prescott had planned, honey."

"Jesus." She couldn't think anymore. And they still had a long night ahead.

At the hospital, Tommy didn't have to wait long to be seen by a doctor—one good perk about being a nurse there and most everyone knowing her.

He sat on a gurney in one of the exam rooms, enduring the checking of his vitals and reflexes, all of the poking and prodding, without a complaint. And what was there to fuss about, really? He was alive.

She was so very grateful he was essentially unharmed, but fear for Shane wouldn't let her rest. When Tommy was dismissed, they sat huddled in the ER's waiting area, anxious for word. They'd taken Shane to surgery right off, so it should be anytime now. What was taking so long?

When the surgeon came out the doors wearing his scrubs and a tired smile, her knees went weak. She hadn't even realized she'd bolted to her feet and was squeezing Tommy's hand as though it were a life preserver.

"You're Shane Ford's sister?"

"Y-yes. How is he?"

"Your brother is going to be fine."

"Oh." Tommy had to help her into a chair. "Oh, thank God."

Her worst fear had not come to pass. Her brother was going to be okay.

"We had to give him two units of blood, and he gave us a bit of a scare at one point, but he came through like a champ. He'll need plenty of rest, but I'd say he'll be up and around, going home in a week or so. Back at work in two, if he behaves."

"We'll make sure he does—count on it." She sent the doc a watery smile.

"Good to know he's got such a great sister on his side," he said kindly. "He'll be taken to the recovery room in a few minutes. You can stay for about five minutes, just to reassure yourself he's okay, but he won't know you're there. Go home after that, get some rest, and come back tomorrow. He's not going anywhere."

"Thank you, Doctor."

As he walked away, Tommy hugged her. "He's fine, baby."

"I know." But there was a horrible, tight bubble in her chest. A pressure that needed to be eased.

Seeing Shane in recovery didn't help. If anything, the pressure got worse, which didn't make sense. His vitals were strong, and he was resting. She stroked his sable hair for a few minutes, kissed his cheek.

"I'll be back tomorrow. I love you."

When they left, Shea was surprised to find that it was almost one in the morning. Hospitals seemed to create some sort of weird time warp when you were there for an emergency, on pins and needles for endless hours. Then it's as if the clock got wound forward when nobody was looking.

When she let them in her apartment, they were met by Miss Kitty, screeching unhappily about her missed dinner.

"Poor sweetie." She fed the cat and washed her hands, then held her arms out to Tommy. "Take me to bed."

"With pleasure."

She would've thought they'd be too exhausted to make love, but that was the funny thing about near-death encounters. They made a person want to feel more alive, to be held and touched. Or so she'd heard.

Seems they were right.

Neither said a word, just undressed. He simply pressed her down, covered her like a warm blanket. Slid his tongue into her mouth and his cock into her sheath, and she accepted their joining for a beautiful gift. They were here, together, and nothing would ever part them again.

It was so big. More than sexual.

This was what love between a man and a woman should be.

She sobbed as their climax shattered together, cried as she held him to her breast.

The horrible bubble in her chest was gone.

Shea sat next to her brother's hospital bed, Tommy standing behind her kneading one shoulder. Since yesterday's nightmare—which, admittedly, could have turned out much worse—he touched her constantly.

"Shouldn't he be awake?" She chewed her lip, anxious. "He never sleeps like this."

"He's never been shot before and had surgery, either, right? He'll be fine, baby."

"I hope so. He's my only family."

"I'm your family, too. Or I'd like to be," he said softly.

Reaching up, she curled her fingers around his. Was that a hint? She was holding out for a real proposal. "Of course you are. You know what I mean."

"I do, cutie."

Shane's lashes fluttered, and his eyes opened. "Hey, you guys."

"Shane! I thought you'd never wake up." Bending, she

kissed his cheek and cupped his shadowed jaw. Relief washed over her like a tide.

"Woke up earlier for a bit. You weren't here. Been trying to wake up again for a while now, but I feel like I'm wrapped in cotton."

"Are you hurting anywhere?"

"My side is complaining some," he admitted. Which must mean it was killing him, because Shane never said a word, even when he was sick with a fever.

"This button here will give you a shot of pain medicine through your IV every few hours," Tommy said, holding it up. "Want a hit?"

"Please." He smiled as Tommy did the deed. "Thanks."

"No problem. Anything for the guy who saved my ass."

"Ho, now. *Anything* is a big word. Make sure you're that grateful before throwing it around."

"Okay, almost anything. For example, if you wanted me to give you a sponge bath? I'd have to take a pass."

Shane chuckled and then hissed in a sharp breath. "Don't make me laugh. And I've got a couple of sweet nurses here to take care of my person, thanks."

"Good to know. So do I—just one, though."

Shea craned her neck to look up at Tommy and he waggled his brows suggestively. "Boys are all alike," she said, facing her brother again. "Always thinking with the little head."

Shane sent her a droll stare. "There's more to life and someone didn't send me the memo?"

"Apparently not, brother dear." She knew he was teasing. The man worked way too hard and didn't take enough time for himself. Maybe this would force him to slow down some, enjoy a couple of weeks off, at least.

"Excuse me," a deep, masculine voice said. "I hope I'm not interrupting."

All of them looked toward the door, Shea in surprise because she hadn't heard anyone come in.

Holy cow! She was totally in love with her man, but she wasn't dead. The big man standing there was dressed in an expensive suit that clung to broad, powerful shoulders. His jet-black hair was styled in layers, just covering his ears, and his eyes were a startling blue that missed nothing. He looked like he'd just stepped off the pages of *GQ*, but for all that, he struck her as no pretty boy.

"Dangerous" was the word that came to mind.

Shane tried to sit up some and winced. "Nick, come in. Guys, this is Special Agent Dominic Westfall. Sis, he's the agent I was telling you about."

"Oh! It's nice to meet you," she said, extending her hand. "I'm Shea Ford. I saw you at the scene last night, but in the chaos and with getting my two men here to the ER, we didn't get to speak."

"Nice to meet you, Shea." His gaze roamed her face in appreciation, but when his attention turned to Tommy, he dropped her hand. "You, too . . ."

"Tommy Skyler, Agent Westfall." His tone was polite, but a little stiff.

"Just Nick." They shared an awkward left-handed grip and Nick smiled. A beautiful smile indeed. He turned the conversation back to Shane. "Came to check on you, give you an update before I head back to Virginia. I know you're not yet involved in an official capacity, but I knew you'd be curious about the outcome."

"I appreciate that." Shane's brows drew together. "What do you mean *yet*?"

"I told you, this insurance scam had deep roots. The money was being funneled to an antigovernment group. Real bunch of nut jobs, but they're organized and that makes them even more dangerous. We've been watching them for a while, put an agent in undercover, and they killed him. We know for a fact that Prescott wasn't their only source. The question is, what are they accumulating such massive funding for? Their tie to Sugarland is disturbing, and if they plan to come here—" He broke off and shook his head, pursing his lips as though he'd said too much.

"Why does that part bother you? What on earth would they want with a nice community like ours? We're close to Nashville, which is the state capital, but we're not exactly a teeming metropolis." Shane appeared perplexed.

Nick's laugh was ominous. "If I told you what they might want, I'd have to kill you."

Shea blinked at the agent. He hadn't really sounded like he was kidding.

"Suffice it to say, the FBI is sticking to them. We want every possible witness who has any tie to this group kept safe and under wraps."

"Including Will Hensley?" Tommy asked.

"Yeah, that's why I came by. Will and Joseph Hensley have been taken into protective custody, and Will is being treated for the gunshot wound to his shoulder. Eventually, for Will's cooperation and hopefully his testimony, they'll be given new identities and a fresh start."

"I guess it worked out for the best, then," Shea said. Still, she felt strangely melancholy on Will's account. She'd barely met the man. Maybe it was knowing what Forrest put him through, and then seeing him make a stand, trying to save Tommy's life.

Yes, that was it. She'd never gotten to thank Will Hensley for creating that split-second diversion when Forrest would have shot Tommy. Now she'd never have the opportunity.

"Damn, I wish I could've spoken to Joseph before they left," Tommy said wistfully. "That old man is pretty cool."

"Yes, he is. I've known Joseph for a long time. One more thing." Nick reached into his suit jacket and pulled out a small manila envelope. "I want all of you to study this picture. Memorize it."

The pic was handed around, everybody doing as he asked. When the photo was handed to Shea, she saw it was a close-up of a man striding down a street. He was tall, built hard, all lean muscle. His hair was dirty blond, shoulder-length, tied back with something to reveal a sharp, angular face. He had a rose tattoo on his neck.

"Keep it," Nick said. "I've got plenty of copies, and so does your police chief. If you see this man, or anyone you *think* could be this man, call me. No matter what time it is, day or night, no matter what you're doing. Here's my card, too, in case you need another one."

Shane took both the picture and the business card, and looked at the photo again. "Who is he?"

"That's the devil in the flesh. His name is Jesse Rose and he's the late Forrest Prescott's contact. Rose is the leader of the group we're after, and a more evil man never drew a breath. He likes keeping his finger on the pulse of things, so to speak. He's a hands-on leader, so if you see him, something is going to go down."

Shea suppressed a shudder and wondered what would bring such a terrible man here. For now, they'd just have to keep an eye open since Nick wasn't saying.

Nick stood, signaling the conclusion of his visit. "I've got to catch a flight. Detective, glad you're on the mend. Shea, Tommy, good to meet you both."

"You, too," Shea said, echoing her two men.

"Just pray you never have to meet me again." With a wink, he turned and walked out.

After the agent left, Shea looked at her brother. "Well, that answers some questions."

"And opens up a whole new batch," he muttered. "What the hell would a terrorist group want with Sugarland?"

"With any luck," Tommy said, "we'll never know."

Shane yawned and his eyes drifted closed. "Sorry. I can't stay awake."

"Sleep. Everything is fine now," she said, patting his arm affectionately. "We'll be back tonight or in the morning."

She watched until his breathing evened out in slumber, and finally stood.

"Take you home?"

She leaned over to whisper in his ear, "And ravish me, if you're . . . *up* to it."

His lips curved up. "Getting there, fast."

The drive to her apartment seemed endless, though it was only a few minutes. Tommy kept shooting her sultry glances from the driver's seat of her car, sending her libido into hyperspace. When they arrived, he hurried her inside, dragged her to the bedroom, and shut the door in the cat's face.

"Poor Miss Kitty," she crooned.

He pulled off his shirt, went for the button on his shorts. "That cat is *not* going to watch me make love to my future wife."

She yanked off her shirt and the rest of her clothing as well. "If that was a proposal, it gets a five out of ten for sucky delivery."

"Hmm, let's go for a better score." He finished stripping, giving her an awesome view of his beautiful body.

The scratches and bruises stood out in stark contrast on his golden skin, made her shiver. But he was okay, and he was hers.

Angling his body, he leaned in to her, easing her back onto the bedspread. Following her down, he lay half on top of her, their legs entwined. Burying a hand in the tangle of her hair, he brought a curly strand to his nose. Inhaled.

His crystal blue eyes captured hers.

"Marry me," he said, voice full of emotion. "Be my soul mate, my friend, and my lover, as long as we both live. Make babies with me that have curly hair and big brown eyes. Grow old with me, and we'll watch the sun set together in the evenings. And when I leave this world I'll be happy, knowing I was the best man I could be for having loved you."

"Oh, Tommy," she breathed. Tears spilled from the corners of her eyes, streaked into her hair. She clutched at him, needing to crawl inside him. "Yes, yes!"

The wattage in his smile could power a small nation. She relished his weight on top of her. Solid, strong. She could feel his heart thumping in his chest, hard and fast.

"Love looks good on you, Thomas Wayne."

"*You* look good on me. Underneath me, too."

He kissed her. Not gentle, but hot. Hungry. Deeper, his mouth ravaging, tongue thrusting. She wrapped her arms tighter around him, hands splayed across his back, urging him closer, if that was possible. Loved the play of lean muscles under her fingertips.

How had she ever survived without him? What could have happened to him didn't bear thinking about.

She drank him eagerly, his lithe, naked body sinking between her thighs. Heat unfurled, became aching desire. She lifted her hips, seeking. With a groan, he eased his cock between the lips of her sex and pushed inside, shooting spirals of pleasure through her limbs. He swiveled his hips in pure, animal rhythm, setting them both afire.

Elbows braced on either side of her head, he quickened the pace. Thrust deep, balls slapping her bottom. Again and again, withdraw and thrust, faster, harder. She came undone with a cry, held him tight, her orgasm shattering her senses.

Through a languorous haze, she watched as he threw his head back and stiffened. Blond hair fell around his face. His eyes were closed, dusky lashes feathered on his cheeks. Lost in ecstasy. The muscles of his biceps and chest corded, and his body shuddered until he was spent.

"You're the most gorgeous man I've ever seen. The only one I want," she said, stroking his face. Tracing his scar.

He smiled. "I'm glad, because as far as I'm concerned, I look like a beat-up alley cat these days."

"You're *my* alley cat."

"I love you."

"I love you more."

"Impossible."

"What do you say we have a contest to prove the winner?"

"I'd say I adore your idea of friendly competition, baby." He grinned at her.

"Let the games begin."

EPILOGUE

The second weekend in October turned out clear and warm, with none of the stifling heat of several weeks ago. Tommy's tennis shoes scuffed through the leaves that were just beginning to fall from trees splashed with oranges, reds, and golds. He had Shea's hand as they walked along her property—it was still hard to think of it as his, too—and admired the stunning view of the Cumberland.

"This is it!" she squealed, hugging him. "Our house goes right here!"

"And you're sure that Shane doesn't want this tract as his half?"

"Nope. He's fine with the other one. Come on, what's wrong?"

He tried a smile, not wanting to bring her down. "I just want to be able to provide for us, cutie. Do my share, at least. I wish they'd give me some word."

"Don't worry, they will. I have faith."

Personnel should have called by now. After resigning as an FRS—fire rescue specialist, better known as a firefighter—and enduring long subsequent weeks of physical therapy on his hand, he'd applied for a job in Fire Prevention. Mark McAllister had met with Tommy, toured him around and introduced him to the staff over there, including the AI guys and the fire marshall.

"What if they don't want me? I'll never have full use of my hand." He flexed his fingers, doubting he'd ever get used to its limited function.

"Honey, your hand has nothing to do with your ability to teach classes or investigate arson. You're going to get certified as an investigator soon, and you're a damned fine, smart man. They'd be dumb not to hire you."

"Always my cheerleader," he murmured, giving her a kiss.

"You bet."

Just then, his cell phone sang a tune. He dug in his shirt pocket and brought it out, checked the caller ID. Eyes wide, he looked at Shea. "I think it's them."

"Answer it!" She jumped up and down, even more nervous than he was.

Taking a deep breath, he flipped it open. "Hello?"

"Yes, is this Thomas Skyler?"

"It is," he said, his tone friendly.

"Mr. Skyler, this is Gretchen Strauss in personnel, over at Fire Prevention. I have an offer for you to come on board as one of our Certified Arson Investigators, contingent on you finishing your state certification, of course. Are you still interested?"

"Um, yes!" He grinned at Shea and pumped his fist in the air. "I am. Thank you, Ms. Strauss. When do I start?"

"Come in Monday and we'll get you oriented. Sound good?"

"Absolutely! I'll be there first thing."

"See you Monday morning at eight, Mr. Skyler. Congratulations."

He hung up and grabbed Shea, spun her around. "Yes! Woo-hoo! I can't believe it!"

"Well, you'd better, because you did it!" She kissed him soundly.

After a long, luscious minute, he pulled back. "It didn't

hurt that Bentley and my friends at the station put in a good word for me."

"Don't you do that, buster. You got this job on your own, and it's time to celebrate. Shall we?"

"Wouldn't want to be late for my own party."

She linked her arm through his and he smiled, at peace with the world. He had his lady, and his friends were throwing him a good-bye cookout at Kat and Six-Pack's house, even though it wasn't really good-bye. He'd see them around, and they'd still get together whenever they could. Now he just had more good news to add to the occasion.

They were a tad late, but no one seemed to mind. The celebration was in full swing, the Paxtons' backyard brimming with their friends and significant others. He and Shea were quickly swept into the fun.

Tommy found himself surrounded by his old crew, all of them savoring a cold beer, except for Six-Pack, who didn't drink. Tommy relished being able to hold the bottle in his right hand, a simple thing he hadn't been sure would ever happen.

"So when's the wedding?" Julian asked.

"I don't know. We haven't set a date. No rush, I guess. I've got the girl, so what does it matter?" They all laughed, and Tommy shrugged. "Seriously, she's talking about New Year's Eve, but I'm not sure if she's decided."

"Remember my motto," Six-Pack said. "Happy wife, happy life. Just do what she wants."

"You got that right," Zack muttered, taking a big swig of his beer.

Tommy grinned at him. "Trouble in paradise already, Romeo?"

"Are all pregnant women hormonal?" he blurted.

"I heard that!" Cori, his blushing bride, yelled from across the yard, hand on her swollen belly.

Zack moaned. "Kill me now."

Six-Pack slung an arm over his shoulders. "I'm in the same boat, my friend. Nine weeks to go until D-day, and I'm in hell. She cries if I raise my voice above a whisper."

Tommy snickered. "We want kids, but I think we'll wait a while for the drama."

"Right," Julian said, arching a brow. "I seem to recall *someone* saying he'd never fall in love, either."

"Well, that's different."

"Sure it is."

Just then, Clay Montana joined the group, and gave Tommy a hesitant smile. The former B-shift FAO clapped him on the arm. "Man, it's good to see you. Looking great, too."

"Thanks. These bozos treating you okay?" Tommy had no idea why the confident cowboy seemed so sheepish about taking his vacated spot on A-shift. Hell, he'd had to accept a lowering of his rank to do it, so he must've wanted to work with A-shift team awfully bad.

"Most of the time. You know how it is."

"Yeah, I do. I'm going to miss their bullshit, but . . . I'm looking forward to my new career as a Certified Arson Investigator!"

"Whoa!"

"No way!"

"Shit, congratulations!"

Tommy soaked up the kudos, and he didn't miss how this news seemed to greatly relieve Clay. Maybe the guy thought he'd taken Tommy's job, but nothing could be further from the truth.

"Well," he amended, "I've got to finish my certification first, but they're going to work with me."

"When did you get the news?" Six-Pack asked.

"Just a short while ago. Thank you, all of you, for putting in a good word for me."

"Not me," Jules said, a gleam in his dark eyes. "I told them you were a punk-ass kid, but obviously they didn't listen."

Everybody cheered and gave a toast. Tommy was so happy he felt light-headed. He floated on beer and laughs until Six-Pack took him aside a couple of hours later and spoke to him in private near the back gate.

"Listen, there's somebody here to see you and it's really important that he get to say his piece," the lieutenant said, serious. "Promise me you'll hear him out."

"You mean . . ."

"Yeah. Just go through the gate. He's waiting out front."

Suddenly nervous, Tommy nodded and slipped away from the party, and walked around to the front yard. Sean was standing on the sidewalk, expression unreadable. But something had changed about the man, softened. As Tommy came to a halt in front of him, he thought Sean appeared younger. Less volatile, more approachable.

"Sean," he said, offering his correct hand. The injured one. "It's damned good to see you."

Sean swallowed and gazed at his hand before taking it. "It's good to see you, too, kid. You're looking great."

"So are you, and I mean that."

Sean's mouth curved into a soft, sad smile. "It's amazing what a few weeks in rehab will do. No haze, no manufactured anger to hide behind. Just me, hanging out here, twisting in the wind."

Tommy sensed he had more to say, and waited.

"I'm going to speak to the others soon, but I wanted to talk to you now, since you're leaving." He took a deep breath. "Tommy, I'm an alcoholic. I used booze as an anesthetic to deaden the pain of losing my wife and children, and in the process, I hurt a lot of people. You're foremost among those I hurt, because I came to work hungover the day of the warehouse fire. I didn't give the order for you and Eve to pull out in time, and your career as a firefighter ended. Because of me."

"But Forrest Prescott had someone inside, and the bastard hit me over the head—"

"As far as my part goes, it doesn't matter. I hesitated. If I hadn't, the man never would've had a shot at you. I don't expect you to forgive me, but I hope you will."

Tommy knew what Sean needed. And the words were so easy, because he meant them. "I do forgive you. Move on, Sean."

The man pulled him into a crushing embrace, a shocking move because Sean had never been a very demonstrative man. Tommy patted his back and they parted, Sean's green eyes suspiciously wet.

"Nothing will bring back Blair and the kids, but I'm trying so hard. I'm doing okay, except for my baby girl." He hung his head, looked down at the sidewalk. "The witnesses said she died screaming for me to put out the fire. If I'd gotten there sooner, I might have been able to save her. Did you know that?"

Oh, my God. They'd never spoken about the accident, and it was unfathomable. He couldn't imagine the horror this man carried inside him every day. "Yes, I'd heard. I'm so very sorry."

Sean nodded. "That's the part that still gets me, makes me want to slide back. To just let go and die. But I won't." He lifted his chin, looked Tommy in the eye. "I want to change, because Mia wouldn't recognize what her daddy has become. She wouldn't know me. I want to be someone she would've been proud of."

"You will, Sean. You're on the way. I totally believe that."

"Thank you. Hearing you say so means the world to me."

He stared at Sean. *This is the man I wish had been my captain for the last couple of years.*

But that thought would never cross his lips.

"When are you going back to work?"

"In just a couple of weeks. I have to be cleared by the department shrinks and the brass, and then I'm gold. No problem." Sean smiled at his own joke.

Tommy grinned back, and gestured toward the backyard. "Come and join the fun."

"I don't know . . ."

"Unless you'll be too tempted to take a drink. There's beer all over the place. Even some hard stuff."

Sean cocked his head. "No, I'm not tempted. Not tonight. I've worked too hard to slide, and you know, I'm tired of my own company. I'll take you up on the offer."

"Great! Let's go. Just be prepared for quite a reunion."

Tommy walked with Sean into the backyard, and his prediction proved correct. Everyone was truly overjoyed to see him. Eve thrust a can of soda into his hand, and he took it in stride, the smile he gave her genuine. His gaze lingering.

The *look* a man gives a woman.

He was still watching the interplay between the captain and Eve when he felt an arm slide around his waist.

"Sean looks like a different man. A huge change from the first time I met him," Shea said.

"Lots of things have changed for the better." He pulled her around to face him, hugged her close, settled her between his spread legs. "Would it be rude of me to cut out early from my own party?"

"I think they'll forgive you."

"Want to hold another competition? I predict I'll win this time," he whispered seductively, kissing her lips.

"You're on, gorgeous. Make our apologies."

"Mmm. Happy wife, happy life."

"What?"

"Nothing, baby." He gave her a mischievous grin. "Just something a wise man told me. A very wise man."

Two weeks later . . .

Deep in the Smoky Mountains, Jesse Rose slid behind the wheel of his Range Rover and fired it up, aiming it in the direction of Nashville. Dark excitement coursed through his veins, better than meth. Better than anything.

He didn't need drugs to get him high. All he needed was the culmination of years of shady deals, the correct contacts, backbreaking work.

All he needed was the promise of revenge and glory, his name in the history books. Both within his reach.

The media would say many things about Jesse Rose, but they would have to admit he was a man who kept his word. Once he set his boots upon a path, he never wavered from his goal. He would move mountains to see the task complete, even if it took a lifetime.

The smell of fruit assailed his nostrils and he glanced in the back. Laughed. One of his lieutenants had said he was crazy. The fucker had died with those words on his lips. Jesse had no patience for negativity.

The crates rode smooth as you please, innocuous. Fruit for his grandma to sell at her stand, should he be pulled over.

He wouldn't be. Jesse was a conscientious driver.

Though he'd pay a fortune to see the expressions on the cops' faces should they get a gander at what lay underneath.

That would be worth the price of admission.

Business on his mind now, as the miles sped by. Phase two of his revenge first. Glory later.

Palming his stolen cell phone, he dialed the number he planned to call more than once. Waited for the man to answer, anticipation almost making him hard.

"Hello?"

He'd waited forever for this moment. A fucking lifetime.

Jesse purred his greeting into the phone.

"Did you ever ask yourself . . . what if it wasn't an accident?"

Ending the call, he flipped the phone closed, wiped off the prints with his T-shirt, and tossed it out the window.

Laughing, he hit the accelerator.

Miles to go before I sleep.

Turn the page for a special preview
of the next book in the
Firefighters of Station Five series,

RIDE THE FIRE

Coming from Signet Eclipse in December 2010

On the night the world ended, Blair Tanner told her husband to go to hell.

The argument was stupid. Just one of many they'd had lately, going at each other like scalded cats in a sack. Sean leaned his back against the grille of Engine 171, arms crossed over his chest, and stared out the open door of the fire station's bay, watching brown leaves drift from the trees to litter the ground outside.

Everyone assumed he and Blair were blissfully happy, the quintessential Barbie and Ken couple with their two gorgeous children, lavish home—thanks to Blair's fancy job—and a pair of nice vehicles.

His teenage son and six-year-old daughter were perfect. Even more than the job he loved so much, he breathed for his children. Not, however, according to his pissed-off wife when they'd had it out over the phone earlier.

Your son is going to be so let down. How can you do this to him, Sean?

Bobby understands. I can't leave my men in a bind—

Oh, save it! Always with the excuses, and they're getting old. You know, if you can't appreciate what you have here, someone else might.

What the fuck is that supposed to mean? Blair?

"Hey, Cap. What's with the long face? In the doghouse again?"

Sean turned to see Clay Montana swagger toward him, grinning like a fool. "Is my name Sean Tanner?" He couldn't help but smile back at their resident cowboy.

"Ouch." Clay grimaced in sympathy. "That's what happens when you break the first rule of bachelorhood."

"What's that?"

"Never sleep with the same woman twice. Unless a man wants to end up like you—pussy-whupped and with a couple of rug rats biting at your ankles."

Sean laughed, shaking his head at the cowboy's earnest expression. The guy wasn't joking. "Yeah? At least I know where my woman's been, and I happen to like my rug rats just fine, thanks."

Clay shrugged. "Whatever, it's your blood pressure, not mine. So, what happened?"

"Blair ripped me a new one for working overtime tonight instead of going with her and Mia to watch Bobby's football game. He's the starting quarterback again, and he's doing really well since he took over for the first-string kid who got injured. He's even been approached by a couple of college scouts." His chest puffed out with pride at that.

"Hey, that's great! For Bobby, anyhow. We can probably swing it if you want to take off and catch the last half. If nothing else, we can try to call in the lieutenant to cover."

For a long moment, Sean was tempted. "Nah, that's okay. I already asked Six-Pack, but he couldn't make it in, and I don't want to leave you short a man. Besides, there're a couple of games left in the regular season, and I promised Bobby I'd make those."

"Sucks being the boss, huh?"

"Only when I have to disappoint my kids to come ride

roughshod over you bozos," he said, shooting the other man a grin. "Someday you'll understand."

Clay shuddered. "Not me, man. No freaking way will you see me stick my head through the golden noose."

Sean snickered as Clay strode back inside. His friend protested too much. Firefighters were family people, nurturers at heart. They all fell eventually, and he'd bet Clay would be no different.

The evening crawled at a snail's pace with only a couple of minor calls, and Sean began to think he'd given up his day off for nothing. But if he hadn't come in, the station would've gotten called to some real disaster, and he would've ended up here all the same. Murphy's Law.

It was almost a relief when dispatch sent them out to an accident—except this one was major with two possible fatalities and a third person, a screaming child, trapped in the burning car. In the front passenger's seat of the quint, Sean stared intently down the highway, knowing time wasn't on their side. They weren't going to make it before the fire consumed the vehicle, and he hoped the police or bystanders were able to free the child and anyone else involved.

Behind the wheel, Clay gestured to the blaze in the distance, growing closer. "Is that what I think it is?"

"Sure as hell is," John "Val" Valentine said grimly from the back. "We've got a car bred to an eighteen-wheeler, folks."

The police hadn't yet arrived. The eighteen-wheeler was parked on the shoulder, as though it had some sort of engine trouble. The car that had hit the rig from behind was fully involved with flames, the blaze beginning to engulf the back end of the big semi. Clay pulled the quint as close as they dared, the ambulance on their tail, and they all jumped out. Clay and the others scrambled to grab hoses while Sean and Val went to assess the situation, check on survivors and their injuries. Other cars had pulled onto the shoulder, and shocked witnesses stared at the spectacle, a couple of women sobbing.

One older woman grabbed the sleeve of Val's heavy coat. "They c-couldn't get the little g-girl out! The older boy who was driving the car, a-and the woman, they were dead. But the little one was screaming for her daddy to put out the fire and—and . . ." The woman clapped a hand over her mouth, overcome by recounting the horrifying events.

Sweet Jesus. Her words made Sean's blood run cold. "Ma'am, are there any other survivors you know of?"

"The driver of the big truck says he's fine. He's over there," she said in a wobbly voice, and pointed. Sean followed the gesture to a distraught man sitting on the shoulder of the highway, face in his hands, and doubted the man was fine at all.

"Val, check on the driver while I go talk to the witnesses."

"Got it, Cap."

Pushing his fire hat back on his head, Sean turned and began to walk toward the inferno and the agitated witnesses. Three men were pacing too close to the fire, hopeless expressions on their faces. There was nothing they could have done, and Sean felt sorry for the poor bastards. Nobody should have to encounter something as sad as this.

He opened his mouth to yell at the three men to move back—

And that was when he saw the license plate on the back end of the car, curling and blackening from the intense heat. Saw the letters and numbers rapidly being consumed by the flames.

Blair's car.

An older boy and a woman.

A little girl screaming for Daddy to put out the fire.

"No." He stopped, rooted in place, his mind resisting the truth. Unwilling to make the final connection, to make it real.

Because if it was real, he had nothing. *Was* nothing.

"Oh, God . . ."

His knees buckled, hit the asphalt. He struggled to draw in a breath, to scream, but his lungs were frozen.

"Cap! Cap, what's wrong? Talk to me!" Someone crouched beside him and a gloved hand grabbed his arm.

"That car," he whispered. "That's my wife's car. My family . . ."

"What? No, no, I'm sure you're mistaken. Sean?"

The truth swept in, as black and bitter as the stench of gasoline and burning bodies, and he couldn't stop the images.

Blair. Bobby. Mia, his sweet baby.

Blair was right to damn him to hell. He'd put work above his family, and they'd paid the ultimate price. He hadn't deserved them, and now . . . *No, please, God. Please.*

He slumped sideways, falling into darkness.

"Sean? Oh, Jesus. Somebody help me over here!"

But there was no help for him.

Not ever again.

Sean Tanner leaned against the porch railing and wrapped his hands around his coffee mug, relishing the warmth. The fall morning was crisp and cool, sporting enough of a bite to justify the light jacket he wore over his navy fire department polo shirt. As he watched the horses graze, his thoughts tumbled one after another, a lengthy, confusing list of things to do.

Amends to make.

Emotions assailed him, a cacophony of trepidation, anxiety . . . and hope.

Hope, because as terrifying as the tasks before him, the miles left to travel, all of these intimidating thoughts and emotions had one important thing in common.

They were those of a sober man.

But for how long? Would he screw up tomorrow, next week? Even now his hands trembled as he clutched the mug, longing to skip the much-anticipated reunion with his team. To jump into the Tahoe and make tracks to the liquor store outside of town, grab a bottle of bourbon to add some kick to his coffee. Replace the raw pain of reality with the comforting haze of oblivion.

Closing his eyes, he clamped down hard on the temptation and beat it into submission. If he went down that road again, he might as well be dead. *No.* When he finally joined his family on the other side, he'd go to them as a man they could be proud of, not the mean, drunken wretch of the past two years. The man who became so sloppy and inattentive at work, he'd cost Tommy Skyler his firefighting career and nearly his life.

That man isn't me. Never again.

Heading inside, he rinsed out the mug and placed it in the dishwasher. Turned off the coffeepot. Wiped down the counter. Watered the ivy on the windowsill. Anything to keep him busy and his mind off another drink, not to mention his dubious reception in—he glanced at the kitchen wall clock—forty minutes.

A deep sigh escaped his lips. No sense in putting off the inevitable. Even if he'd rather get caught in a back draft with no hope of escape than face five of the people he'd let down time and again.

"Jesus, grow a pair and get going, Tanner." End of pep talk.

Before he could change his mind and do something truly idiotic, like call in sick, Sean snatched his keys off the counter and headed out the door.

The drive into Sugarland had never seemed so long, and singing country music along with the radio didn't provide much of a distraction. Then suddenly he was at the station, parked in his usual spot around back, sort of frozen in place by the difficulty of taking the next few steps.

If they'd strung up banners and shit, he was going straight home.

He slid out of the Tahoe, locked up and pocketed his keys. Walking around the side of the building, he steeled himself for whatever was to come. Awkwardness? Or, worse, sympathy?

Taking a deep breath, he stepped into the bay and found . . . complete normalcy.

Zack Knight, their FAO—fire apparatus operator—had his back to Sean and was busy buffing the quint to a candy-apple shine. A couple of guys just getting off C-shift were standing around bullshitting with Julian Salvatore and Howard "Six-Pack" Paxton. Clay Montana, who'd moved to A-shift and taken Tommy Skyler's vacated spot, was fishing around in the back of the ambulance. Sean scanned the group for Eve Marshall, Station Five's only female firefighter, but didn't see her, and figured she was inside, maybe manning breakfast. A day just like any other.

Thank fuck.

Sean cleared his throat. "Is that all you lazy boneheads have to do, stand around and jaw like a bunch of old fishermen?"

A bead of sweat rolled down his temple, the only outward sign of the knot in his stomach. Conversation halted and all eyes swung his way, wary and uncertain—until he gave them a tentative smile.

"Hey, Cap!"

"How's it hangin'?"

"Damn, you look good! Don't he look good?"

The general explosion of heartfelt well-wishes wrapped around him like a blanket, eased a sore place in his gut as the guys migrated toward him. No cheesy banners, but he had to admit the backslapping and manly hugs that ensued were all right because it meant his boys still gave a fuck about him. This was their way, he realized, of making sure he knew they respected him—or at least were willing to forgive. Even after the crap he'd put them through.

And, yeah, he must have gotten some dirt in his eyes, making them sting.

Dammit.

"Let the man breathe," Six-Pack boomed, pushing the others aside and promptly ignoring his own dictate. He scooped Sean into a bone-crunching bear hug that lifted him off his feet with no effort whatsoever, which was saying a lot since Sean wasn't a small guy.

Sean laughed, the sound strange and rough to his own ears. "Put me down, you big ox!"

Six-Pack did, and Sean had to look up at him, standing this close. His best friend was six feet, six inches and two hundred fifty pounds of solid, intimidating muscle. Sean was no shrimp but he was much leaner in build. Hell, everyone was smaller next to the lieutenant.

Six-Pack grinned at him, brown eyes dancing. "Man, it's great to have you back. Trying to keep these guys in line is like trying to herd baby ducklings." This prompted a round of good-natured protests.

The lieutenant waved a hand. "Come on, slackers, get to work and let Sean get his bearings."

The two men from C-shift said their good-byes and left. Zack went back to buffing the quint, Clay to whatever he was doing in the ambulance, probably stocking the meds. Yep, a normal day. Except for one thing.

"Where's Eve?" he asked Six-Pack. He'd be damned if he'd admit how much it stung that she hadn't come out to say hello.

"Inside, making your favorite breakfast, though you're not supposed to know. Act surprised."

"Oh." Pancakes and bacon? Especially for him. Well, that sure went a long way toward soothing his remaining unease. In fact, it caused a weird little bubble of something in his chest that he couldn't define. Something different from how relieved the guys' greeting made him feel. "Damn, that's really thoughtful of her."

"Ain't it? Why don't you go inside and say hey. I'm gonna go call Wendy Burgess back about the charity thing."

"What charity thing?"

"You know, the auction and calendar deal."

"No, I don't." A sneaking suspicion crept over him that he wasn't going to like this.

"Jeez, I didn't tell you when you came to the barbecue? Could've sworn I did. The City of Sugarland is holding a fireman's auction in about three weeks, and also choosing twelve of our guys to do a calendar shoot, all for charity. Wendy and some of the other department brass are taking care of the details."

Sean eyed him warily. "That doesn't sound too bad. What are we auctioning?"

His friend smiled, his expression a bit too mischievous. "Ourselves."

He snorted. "Get outta here! No way."

"Yep. Us in front of a bunch of squealing ladies, wearing nothing but our fire pants and red suspenders."

"Hold on. Us? There is no *us* in the equation," he said firmly. "Have fun living your Chippendales fantasy."

"Oh, we will, all of us. I already signed you up, my friend." Six-Pack clapped him on the shoulder.

"Well, you can just scratch my name off the list, *friend*. There's absolutely no way in hell I'm going to stand around half-naked in front of a bunch of screeching women."

The other man arched a dark brow. "Even when I tell you the event will benefit the families of fallen firefighters?"

Sean groaned. "Don't do this to me."

"Even if your participation could add hundreds or even thousands of dollars that will go to a grieving widow and her children? Even if you could single-handedly ease someone's burden long enough to let them get back on their feet?" Six-Pack speared him with a pointed look.

"You suck," Sean declared in defeat.

"I knew we could count on you! Think how much better about yourself you'll feel, doing a good thing for someone less fortunate." His friend beamed as they started inside together. "Besides, it'll be a blast. You'll see."

"Yeah, yeah. I'm a regular Mother Teresa and party animal, all rolled into one." Christ, he was forty-three years old, his brown hair turning silver at the temples. He was too old for this shit.

The issue was put on hold as they walked into the kitchen and were greeted by the smoky aroma of frying bacon. Sean's stomach rumbled in approval. He marveled, not for the first time in the past few weeks, how good it felt to be hungry without alcohol killing his appetite.

"God, it smells good in here," he said. At his declaration, Eve turned from the stove to face him, and his stomach did a funny lurch that had nothing to do with hunger pains.

"Well, if it isn't our fearless leader."

A broad, dazzling smile transformed her angular face, bright against her smooth coffee-with-cream skin. The smile reached all the way to her big blue eyes, warm and welcoming. Dark hair shot with reddish highlights fell in gentle curls to her shoulders.

Holy shit, she's beautiful. Why haven't I noticed before?

Or perhaps he had sometime in the past few months . . .

but he didn't want to dwell on those fuzzy memories at the moment. He didn't have time to, because Eve was striding toward him while he stared like a witless fool.

She wrapped him in a fierce hug, and he found himself noting how wonderful her taut, sleek body felt pressed against his. How well she fit in his arms, her chin resting on his shoulder, soft curly hair tickling his nose. Her fresh scent, not floral but clean and herbal.

"It's so good to have you back." She drew away some to hold his gaze. "I mean *really* back."

"Thanks," he said quietly. "I've got a ways to go, but I'm right where I belong. Just don't give up on me." Hell, that last part just slipped out. God, could he sound more needy?

An odd flash of emotion crossed her expression, there and gone. "Are you kidding? We haven't, and we won't. You're going to be fine." Releasing him, she went back to tending breakfast.

The way she said that, he almost believed her. Immediately, he missed her heat pressed to his body, the soft words just for him. *Why? What's wrong with me? I'm her captain, for God's sake. Hopefully her friend. To entertain anything more is highly inappropriate.*

He'd tested the department's goodwill and stretched it to a microscopic filament. Fooling around with a female firefighter under his watch after they'd all stuck out their necks to save him and his career? That would be the end.

The others drifted in from the bay, saving him from getting too maudlin. Leaning against the counter, he watched them horse around like a litter of goofy puppies, razzing one another and cracking jokes. Julian attempted to steal a piece of bacon from the platter only to get his hand smacked by Eve.

Sean spent a few private moments thanking God he hadn't

lost this, his second family, in the wake of trying to drown his grief. All along, he should've been seeking the comfort and strength his friends had to offer, not pushing them away. Time and counseling were finally getting that through his head.

"Let's eat!"

Eve's announcement was met with hearty approval, and they all settled around the table, digging in. Sean took a bite of fluffy pancakes and listened to the chatter around him, content to soak in the scene. Okay, so this was good but a little weird. Like he was a guest in his own body, watching everything from a perspective that was suddenly too close up and bright.

And it frightened him, too, the idea of living up to their faith in him. There would be no third chance. If he failed—

"Right, Cap?"

He blinked at the group, caught Eve and Six-Pack exchanging concerned glances. "I'm sorry. What?"

"I said we've decided to wear red G-strings for the auction instead," Clay drawled, grinning. "Across the front they'll say 'Firemen have more hose.'"

"Shut up, moron," Julian said, pelting the cowboy in the face with a balled-up napkin. "Half the women in the county have already seen you in less, so where would be the surprise?"

Clay snorted. "There's still the *other* half to conquer. You could get a piece of the action too, except . . . Wait—you're neutered now."

"I've got your 'neutered' hangin' low, cowboy, and Grace has no complaints. Don't you have an off switch?"

"Jules finally has to put up with someone more annoying than he is," Eve whispered in Sean's ear. "Sweet, huh?"

Sean laughed, the sound not quite as alien as before. "True justice."

No sooner had they finished their breakfast than the intercom emitted three loud tones, and the computerized voice dispatched them to a traffic accident with a major injury out on I-49. Those calls were the worst, the ones that made his blood run cold and threatened his sanity. The victims' faces would haunt him for days, and now he had no buffer to place between himself and the nightmares.

They reached the scene to find a single car in a gulley. The driver's door was buckled inward just enough to prove impossible to open, a long scratch running down the side of the vehicle. An elderly man sat slumped behind the wheel, unconscious and bleeding profusely from a long gash in his head.

The lieutenant and Zack brought out the Jaws of Life and went to work on the door, prying apart the stubborn metal. Moments later, Clay and Eve had the man stretched out on even ground, working feverishly to save him. The man's face, the unmarred half, was parchment white. Slack. Shaking her head, Eve began CPR.

"Sideswiped," an officer told Sean grimly. "Some bastard cut off the old guy. Ran him right off the damn road and didn't stop to help."

"Road rage?"

"Shapin' up that way, according to the witnesses. Helluva way to start the mornin', if ya ask me."

Sean nodded, unsure whether the cop was referring to them or the victim. He crossed his arms over his chest, watching the futile attempt to revive the man. As he did, it occurred to him that there was something vaguely familiar about him, though he couldn't place him. The man was, what? In his eighties? Hard to tell.

Whoever he was, he didn't make it.

Sean and his team stayed out of the way after that, using

their vehicles to block the far-right lane, routing traffic around the police and emergency vehicles so the officers could take photos, make reports. A mound of paperwork always followed a traffic death, particularly one now labeled a possible vehicular homicide.

Welcome back, Tanner.

A knock sounded on Sean's office door a second before Eve popped her head in.

"You got a minute?"

Sean swiveled his chair away from the computer screen and the report he'd been typing, gesturing her inside. "I've got several if it means putting off my paperwork. Come in."

Eve closed the door behind her and sprawled in the chair across from his desk, all sleekly muscled limbs, like a cat. Strong enough to hold her own in a male-dominated profession, yet no less womanly. A combination Sean found intriguing. Sexy.

An observation he had no business making.

"Funny how most stuff is done online nowadays, but it's still called paperwork," she said, giving him a guarded smile. As though he might find an excuse to bark at her like he would've done a few short weeks ago.

He leaned back in his chair, linking his fingers over his flat stomach. "And it's still a pain in the ass, too. How did we ever cope without computers and e-mail?"

A mischievous twinkle lit her blue eyes as she relaxed. "Some of us are too young to remember not having them."

"Ouch! Third-degree burns on my first day back," he joked.

"Just making sure you're reinitiated properly."

"Why do I get the feeling this is only the beginning?"

"Because it is. Don't be fooled by the pancakes—they were merely an evil ploy to lull you into complacency."

"Hmm. I'll consider myself warned. So, what's on your mind?"

Humor fading, she hesitated before getting to the point. "I want to clear the air between us once and for all, and to do that I need to apologize."

He stared at her in surprise. "What for?"

"For not being more supportive these past few months," she said, guilt coloring her voice. She held his gaze, though, unflinching. "I've bucked you at every turn and even been a real bitch, at times in front of the others. For that, I'm deeply sorry."

"You're kidding, right? I was an unbearable, drunken, self-pitying son of a bitch, and you're apologizing?" Pushing out of his chair, he stalked to the small window behind his desk and looked out at the view of the field beyond the parking lot, where the guys sometimes played football. But he didn't appreciate the scenery, as he hadn't appreciated so many good things in his life when he'd had them.

"Yes, I am. You don't kick someone when they're down, especially when they're no longer in control of their own actions, and that's exactly what I did."

He shook his head. "No, you didn't. You had the best interests of this team at heart every single time we butted heads. You and the guys were afraid I'd do something to seriously fuck up, and I did—so badly I can't believe I still have a job, much less that I'm still alive. I understand that, and I'm trying to make peace with what I've done."

The words were horribly familiar, as though the movie reel of his life had rewound twenty years. They left him shaken.

He could never atone for what he'd cost Tommy, any more than he'd been able to atone for his family's deaths, or for that other tragedy so many years ago. But he could try really hard to live a good life for the rest of his days—a life denied to so many he'd loved and lost.

A soft hand gripped his arm, and Eve's sweet voice whispered next to his ear, "Everything is going to be okay, Sean. I believe in you."

Startled, he turned to find her practically in his arms. Right where he wanted her to be, and damn him to hell for feeling this way. They stared into each other's eyes, the moment stretching into a thin wire, supercharged, and he forgot where he was. His responsibilities, his reputation, his position as her captain.

Gone, with the first brush of his lips against hers as his palm slid down her arm. Lost, with the need in her eyes and her beautiful face tilted up to his, her taut body pressed close, warm and safe.

Heaven. *Oh, God, it's been so long. Need this, need you . . .*

The cell phone on his desk shrilled a rude interruption, and they sprang apart as though the fire chief himself had walked in unannounced. Off balance from his lapse in judgment, lips tingling in pleasure, Sean grabbed for the phone.

"Hello?"

A man's voice responded, quiet and amused. "Did you ever ask yourself . . . what if it wasn't an accident?"

Click.

A couple of heartbeats passed before Sean lowered the phone from his ear, his brain scrambling to assimilate the caller's meaning. Weird. What could that possibly . . .

"Sean? Sean, what's wrong?" Eve's voice called to him from miles away.

And the phone slipped unnoticed from his frozen fingers.

ABOUT THE AUTHOR

Jo Davis spent sixteen years in the public school trenches before she left teaching to pursue her dreams of becoming a full-time writer. An active member of Romance Writers of America, she's been a finalist for the Colorado Romance Writers Award of Excellence, has captured the HOLT Medallion Award of Merit, and has one book optioned as a major motion picture. She lives in Texas with her husband and two children. Visit her Web site at www.jodavis.net.